REUNIONS

10/20/16

To Patty,

Stay young & Healthy!

J. CH/D

Richard Chmielewski

ISBN: 978-1-3292-2571-8 (sc)
ISBN: 978-1-4834-4310-2 (e)

Library of Congress Control Number: 2015920298

Because of the dynamic nature of the Internet, any web addresses or links contained in
this book may have changed since publication and may no longer be valid. The views
expressed in this work are solely those of the author and do not necessarily reflect the
views of the publisher, and the publisher hereby disclaims any responsibility for them.

Any people depicted in stock imagery provided by Thinkstock are models,
and such images are being used for illustrative purposes only.
Certain stock imagery © Thinkstock.

Lulu Publishing Services rev. date: 1/13/2016

Contents

CHAPTER 1

Harvey Weinberg

It was a cool, overcast day in the snow-covered hills of Bavaria. Harvey gripped the leather-covered steering wheel with his gloved hands as he maneuvered over the icy, winding roads just outside of the small town of Bischofswiesen, near Berchtesgaden, once a popular resort for the leaders of the Nazi regime. The wheels of his new German built 1954 Lloyd LP 400, with an optional back seat and rear trunk, crunched along over the icy road as he downshifted expertly from third to second gear and rounded one more endless curve. In his rear view mirror he caught a glimpse of Mount Watzman, the third highest mountain in Germany. The cloud cover over its jagged snow-capped peaks reflected an orange violet hue as the sun began its westward descent.

His eyes caught a glimpse in the mirror of his two young sons, leaning one against the other, with eyes closed and their wool caps pulled snugly over their ears with shocks of delicate, blonde hair sticking out like straw bedding under a blanket. Although twins, Fritz wore a larger wool overcoat with upturned collar, which made him appear much bigger, allowing Hans to snuggle deeper into the folds of his brother's generous coat. While they were very comfortable in the cramped rear seat of the coupe, they nevertheless would not have complained if the vehicle's heater couldn't keep up with the freezing weather outside or if they had even less leg room than now. Harvey let that thought slip quickly through him as he felt admiration and pride for his two young boys. Their mother, Nadine, would agree without hesitation that they could endure the harshest of circumstances without complaint and quickly add that they were the best young sons that a mother, or stepmother, could have. When speaking of the boys, Nadine would often catch herself talking and bragging about them and then excuse herself with, "I'm so sorry, I didn't mean to go on so about the children. You must stop me or I would go on for hours about them." And indeed there were a lot of very good things to say about the twins. And none of it was exaggeration or hyperbole. They were excellent students, and such good athletes, with physical prowess that would equal and exceed any skills of speed, strength, and endurance that other children of their age had. At ten years of age, they could match their wits, their intelligence, and their physical abilities with others twice their age. They were top scholars in all of their classes, from kindergarten to now.

This did not go unnoticed. The school administrator contacted his superiors in the Berchtesgaden Department of Education in Bavaria. Two men and a woman, representatives of that department, were sent to their school and over a two day period reviewed the children's' files, the curriculum they were using, and pored over their scholastic and athletic scores. They conducted various aptitude and physical prowess tests of their own. The children cooperated, but seemed somewhat bored in the beginning. However, whereas most children would soon tire and become impatient with all the testing and questions and being away from their classmates, the twins soon became interested in what the researchers were doing and what they were coming up with.

The twins were just as surprised as the group from the Berchtesgaden State Education Department that they were scoring well above average in everything they were tested on. Their proficiency scores in all areas exceeded not only other European children in the genius category, but even went beyond the scores of the few students that the State department had from other prodigal children.

Harvey and his wife were visited one day by a retinue of elderly gentlemen of undoubted financial means and political connections. After the introductions and cordialities were finished, one of them stood before the parents and with a huge smile, offered his hands to each of them, and congratulated them on their wonderful children.

"This is indeed a wonderful family you have here," the man began. "I have been so impressed with how our Germany has raised itself up out of the ruins brought upon us during the war. I have, in my own way, as have my colleagues here, expended so much of my energies and money and influence to get us back on track with the way things could have been before losing to the Kommunisten from the East, and the fierce attacks by the Americans and the English, and their allies, who did not understand what we were doing."

The visitors all nodded their heads in agreement. Some quietly voiced their support of the man's words with various words of affirmation, such as *ja*, *jawohl*, or *richtig*.

The man continued, "We feel that your children are more than just bright children or good students. No, we feel that they have something inherent in their blood, in their genetics, which makes them who they are. They are indeed special. They seem to embody the spirit and character and the skills of true Aryans!"

The men again quickly, now more loudly, voiced their agreement.

"*Jawohl!*"

"*Das ist so!*"

"*Genau!*"

The elder spokesman pressed on. "Harvey Weinberg, you are the proud father of these remarkable children. You were chosen by Himmler's officers to become an SS man yourself before the war. You were a remarkable soldier during the Poland campaign and distinguished yourself in the early days of Operation Barbarossa with Army Group Centre in the Ukraine in 1941.

"As you now know, the Fuhrer, Adolph Hitler, had a four-step plan for domination of the east, giving Germany raw materials and room to spread the new Aryan race, lebensraum. We were to conquer and destroy the Soviets, allowing us free reign over Poland and the Ukraine, and Belarus and Russia. The next step was to starve millions of those untermensch with a Hunger Plan to deny them food during the harsh winter. Thirdly, would come the Final Solution or Endlosung. The Jews of Europe would be eliminated. Lastly, the Master Plan East, or Generalplan Ost, would be put into motion, resulting in the elimination of, deportation of, enslavement of, and eventual depopulation of the peoples of Poland and Belarus, the Ukraine and Russia. It was a wonderful plan of expansion, a cleansing of all the historical wrongs, setting the world right again!

"All of these plans came to an end with the Allies' victory over our beloved Germany. So many of our wonderful young men and women and children were destroyed in their effort to rid the world of the Jews and the Kommunisten. Our hopes of rekindling the Aryan race were dashed with the destruction of the New Order of Europe, the Third Reich, Hitler, and the Nazi government in Berlin."

The man paused for a moment of silence. Some of his colleagues took out handkerchiefs to wipe tears from their eyes or blow their noses. Some wiped the brow of their foreheads and looked down to the floor. Harvey sensed the sadness in the room.

"But now, now we see a new hope. I refer to your beautiful children, your sons. Fritz and Hans," the man resumed. "They are the true embodiment of what we understand to be the best of the Aryan attributes. They have a gift…no, they are a gift from God Almighty to our Nation. We have been monitoring their development for some time now and have been impressed, and now, moved to action.

"My friends and I are offering your sons the best accommodations for learning and honing their physical skills at a university level. We would like also to study them biologically to see how genetically their makeup is different from our average Aryan types here. The field of genetics is making incredible progress in our understanding of what makes us function as human beings. There have been some incredible scientific breakthroughs in Germany, and England, and even in the United States on this.

"I do not pretend to understand it all. Enough that I know that your sons may be the key to the genetic development of a new, superior Aryan race!"

Again the man's friends nodded or muttered their agreement to his statements.

The sun was low in the west as Harvey drove further along the winding roads in southern Bavaria. He thought of the meeting with those gentlemen in his home only a few short weeks ago. He thought of the generous offers made by the group. They offered to pay for the tuition and upkeep of the twins as they pursued their education in a special university designed specifically for extraordinarily gifted and unique children. Harvey and his wife, Nadine, would be very well compensated for their agreement to this arrangement. They would never have to worry about planning for their retirement, let alone having sufficient money for living and vacationing.

Harvey had taken his children out of the Volkschule that morning and was headed home to discuss the final plans for their two children. He and his wife had already had some brief discussions about accepting the generous offer of the elder group. Although she was not the biological mother of the boys, she had helped raise them as best as she could over the last 8 years or so, since they were only about 2 years old. She loved them dearly and wanted only the best for them.

She wondered what had happened to their real mother. Harvey never said too much about it. It was wartime. Relationships and marriages during that dreadful time came and went as quickly as storm clouds and rain would suddenly appear and then fade away. Poetic descriptions with little information. That was how she viewed Harvey's now inconsequential relationship with the birth mother of her stepsons. She accepted the past as just that. No need for questions. Like individual clouds that dissolved as the weather changed, she had no interest in Harvey's relationship with someone else. She was the new woman in Harvey's life, the new mother in the children's. That was enough. That defined her. *Alles klar.*

Nadine had been a secretary to Nazi party officials in Bavaria during the war. After hostilities ended and Germany was divided between the Soviets and the Western Allies she found other administrative work in the civilian government.

She met Harvey Weinberg at a friend's party one evening in the spring of 1946. He was introduced to her as a young former SS officer who had had some very exciting, adventurous moments. He shared some of those memories in the weeks that followed as they got to know one another better. She learned that he was living with a sister just outside of Munich, in Bavaria, and with his two little sons from a previous marriage. Nadine met the twins and saw immediately that they were strong, healthy, beautiful, and exceptional little boys. She had no difficulty in accepting them as her own when Harvey proposed marriage. In that same year, 1946, they had a small wedding and reception in the picturesque town of Kalvarienberg and honeymooned for a few days by the lake and nearby mountains of Schliersee. There had been essentially no destruction here, as the war and the armies seemed to have passed them by.

Ahead Harvey could see a detour sign in the road with an arrow pointing to the left and the writing Umleitung, or detour. He dutifully turned, as directed, onto a small, paved road leading into a lightly wooded area. He drove through some tall pines and down into a gorge. There was a narrow, shallow stream with countless rounded, snow-covered rocks and boulders in the churning waters that bordered the road. He eventually came to a small bridge on his right that went over the little stream and he noticed in the rear view mirror that there was a car not far behind him. It was getting dark enough now in the woods, nearly dusk, so he turned his headlights on.

A short distance further down the road, now away from the stream and surrounded by thicker pines and brush on the roadside, he saw another car ahead of him. It had its headlights on and was slowly coming his way. The road was just wide enough for two cars to pass one another without having to drive off the road into the snow and the softer shoulder.

The car in front came to a stop directly in front of him only a few meters away. Stunned by the suddenness of that action, Harvey adjusted the rear view mirror to check on his children when he noticed that he was blocked from behind by the other car. He felt a chill descend on him as he realized that he was trapped. He had no weapon and no idea what was happening.

Suddenly two men were outside of his car, one on either side. They were carrying German Lugers. His driver side door was ripped open and a voice commanded, *"Aufsteigen!* Get out!"

"OK, OK," Harvey replied in a muffled voice, as if not to wake his two children. "What do you want? Why are you doing this?"

"Please be quiet," the stranger growled. There was a tinge of an accent in his voice. Harvey couldn't place it.

"What are you going to do with us? If it's money you want, I can arrange it, but not here. I need to get home. I can arrange whatever you need. Please!"

"We need to take you to a special location nearby where you will be meeting with some very important people. We need to have you cooperate and calm down."

Harvey thought about the elderly committee that had met with him and Nadine a few weeks ago. Was this what this strange meeting was all about?

"Get in the trunk of the car." The man motioned with the Luger. "We will be going by a checkpoint and my man will drive your car. We can't have you seen as we drive in."

Harvey hesitated, thinking this an odd request. He decided that he had best cooperate, hoping that he and his children would soon be safe. He got into the truck of the car. He did not see that the second man had quietly opened the passenger side rear door and was gently putting the twins to sleep with chloroform soaked gauze pads firmly placed over their faces. They barely had time to wake up from their own slumber or offer much of any protest or resistance.

A third accomplice stepped up from the car behind the Lloyd, slipped behind the wheel and started to drive on, with the other two vehicles following close by. In the cramped trunk of his own car, Harvey could only hear the sound of the motor, the wheels crunching snow and ice and the shifting of his own body in the tiny trunk. He hoped the ride would be short as his legs were starting to cramp from the awkward position into which he had been placed.

He was afraid, very afraid. His mind raced as he thought of what was happening to him and he thought anxiously of his children. He hoped that everything would be all right, that he and the twins were being taken to a secret location to meet someone. Who?

Was it the Berchtesgaden education department? That didn't make sense. They had already visited him and his wife and had set up the transfer for the twins to the new school in Stuttgart.

Harvey had kept up his connections with former officer colleagues in the SS and was told that, at some time in the near future, they would be contacting him as they reestablished their order in the aftermath of the war. Yes, this could possibly be why he was forced to lie, curled up in a ball like a fetus, in the trunk of his car. Of course! Even in the last days of the war, Hitler himself had said that the Third Reich was not about him. It never was. It was always about the German people, about the Aryan race, about the superior beings that would survive the war and continue on for a thousand years! Of course!

The car lurched forward slowly and continued along the icy forest road for what seemed like an hour. Harvey strained to hear any voices in the seating compartment. The twins were quiet, which was not unusual. They were such stoic children, the kind that Himmler would have been proud of. There were no sounds from the two men who had entered the car, one to drive, the other to sit with the children in the rear seat.

The car came to a stop. Now, Harvey thought. They will open up this damn trunk. I can straighten out my clothes and pat down my hair, and get my children and find out what this is all about. He eagerly waited for the latch to open.

For a few minutes, silence. Then he heard footsteps in the snow around both sides of his car.

A voice suddenly spoke. "Herr SS officer. In the trunk. Can you hear me?"

"Yes, yes I can. Now please open up and let me out of here. I'm cold and it's cramped in here. Do you understand? Now open up! And my name is Harvey! Harvey Weinberg. If I'm going to meet someone, I can't exactly do it while still in here, now can I?"

"Very true, Herr Weinberg. Very true," the man answered. "And you will be meeting someone very special right away! This I can promise you."

"*Ja, ja, gut dann.* Open up the trunk!"

As he lay there impatiently locked in the back of his car, Harvey could smell faint fumes of gasoline that got stronger with each inhaled breath. He became very anxious with this development and banged on the lid of the trunk.

"Get me out of here! I smell gasoline! There must be a leak. It's choking me! Get me out of here! Now!" He pounded on the trunk hood again, and kicked with his cramped legs as best he could.

"Ah yes, the fumes. The gasoline," a voice spoke up. It was a stern, measured, strong voice of the first young man who had opened his driver's door and had beckoned him out of the car.

"Smell those glorious fumes, mister SS man from Auschwitz! The acrid chemical fumes of gasoline being poured all over your car, inside and out, and even onto your chloroformed children. Can you feel the fear building inside you….that something's gone wrong….that things are not what you thought they'd be?

"What are you doing? Let me out of here! And don't hurt my children! Do you hear me? I know many people, I'm very well connected. If you want money, I told you, I can get it for you. What do you want?"

The smell of the gasoline was much stronger now and it was starting to suffocate him and make him cough. His eyes welled up with tears from the chemical irritation.

"We want you to feel the fear and the confusion and the nausea and the vomiting as you are overcome with the fumes of the gasoline," the man responded. "But we want you to feel and understand even better what we are doing and why we are doing this.

"We are Zegota, Polish members of the Committee to Help the Jews. We were there when you and your cronies were gassing Jews and beating and shooting and starving fellow Poles in Auschwitz."

Zegota. Harvey knew of this organization. "I was only one of many, a low ranking officer who had nothing to do with everything that went on there. Let me out of here. You are mistaken. You have the wrong man!"

"Oh, mister SS man, we have the right man. You were part of the experiments done at the camp. You and your SS fellows experimented on Polish children, Jews and non-Jews. When you were done with them, they were sent off to the gas chambers."

"I had nothing to do with that. Those were orders from my higher ups. You have the wrong man! Please, I beg of you. Let me and my sons go!"

"Ha! Your sons? And what of the young Polish woman prisoner who you impregnated, as part of the experiments. She bore you these two young boys in the camp who seemed to embody all of the traits that one would want in a true Aryan offspring! A next generation of Nazis!

"As the Russians were closing in on you, you took those two young babies as your own and fled with the rest of the garrison to Germany!"

"I did what I had to do! They were my sons, and yes, they were very, very special. I was ordered by my superior to take the two boys with me. It was an order!"

"And what of the other 40 little children who didn't fit in with the plans of your SS? Instead of leaving them to fend for themselves, you took it upon yourself to go to their building and, with the help of a few other SS men, personally shot each one of them in the head. You call that doing what you had to do?"

"It was war time. We were all afraid, things were happening at a very fast, crazy pace. Let me out! I can explain everything, but not while I'm in here choking on petrol fumes." Again he pounded and kicked at the hood of the trunk.

"No, my friend. You didn't give the people in the gas chambers a chance. And you definitely didn't give those 40 little children a chance when you executed each and every one of them with your own hand!"

"Look, I don't know who you are or why you are doing this. Vengeance against me is one thing. But please, my sons didn't do anything. You must let them go. They are innocent. Please."

"True, they are innocent and should not suffer. They did not ask to be brought into this world. They will not experience terror and pain and the horror of the gas chambers the way you and your buddies murdered the men, women, and children at Auschwitz," the man replied in a seemingly understanding, calming tone. "For that you are going now to meet your Creator. You can answer to him for what you have done. We have heard enough of your excuses.

"We do not make war on children. For that reason we have put your sons into a deep sleep. They will feel no pain. But they must not be allowed to live for they carry somewhere within them some very special traits that will be exploited by your Nazi buddies to reconstitute the power that was the Nazis. We know of their interest in your boys, oh yes, we know only too well about their fiendish plans. We have had enough of that. They cannot be used to spawn a new generation of your dreamed ubermensch, of Nazi 'supermen.' It needs to be put to an end now, as we speak.

"We, members of Zegota now exact revenge on you for what you have done to all of those little children, who could not protect or avenge themselves. And we gladly step across the line of ethics and morality to stop this nonsense of constituting a revitalized German Reich and a new Aryan race."

Harvey pounded and kicked and screamed as the temperature in the truck rose. He soon had great difficulty breathing as the surrounding oxygen was consumed by the fireball that enveloped the car. His clothes started smoking and soon his hair and then entire body was aflame. He could feel the searing, burning pain in his eyeballs as they swelled in their sockets and then burst into a sizzling, burning gel. His lungs burned as he inhaled each breath of fire. Every nerve in his body was signaling danger, fear, and incredible pain. His heart quivered in his chest as his oxygen starved body, wracked with pain and nowhere to go, and no hope for escape, simply shut down. He lost consciousness as the outer skin of his body was developing a charcoal black crust and his inner organs and blood began to boil.

The sun was setting in the west. In the forest it was already dark except for the bright fire and smoke of the Lloyd, burning in a clearing deep in the Bavarian woods. The men from Zegota stood and watched for as long as they dared until they were certain that the entire car had been destroyed beyond recognition and the bodies of the twins and their father, stowed in the trunk, were completely destroyed and turned to ash. The two vehicles that had blocked Harvey now rode off deeper into the forest.

CHAPTER 2

Lisa in Paris

Paris is a beautiful city. Except for the fact that she came here by design rather than choice, she found much about it to like. The art galleries. Ballet at the Opera Gernier. Evening walks along the Seine to Norte Dame as teenagers rode their skateboards, illuminated by the pale orange lights of the famed cathedral. The Ritz Paris Hotel with its bar lavishly furnished with red velvet, golden wall lamps, and a beautiful terrace overlooking a manicured lawn. The little cafés and the below street level bars with a wide assortment of live music. And of course the exquisite tourist attractions of Versailles, the Louvre, and the Jardin de Tuilleries. Lisa had been living here for a year now. She felt much more comfortable than in Albany or New York City. Not that she felt any safer. The thoughts of being exposed or being executed was never far from her.

It wasn't because of fear. No, she had let that emotion die many years ago. She was driven by an insatiable desire for justice, for retribution, for revenge. Most nights now she was able to go to sleep without the recurring memory of gunshots in the night throughout her house back in New York, and the recurring, shameful memory of her hiding in the bathroom. It was over in seconds. It took only those fleeting moments for her whole life to be destroyed. All that she had loved and cherished was taken from her that awful night years ago. What seemed like an eternity had taken a mere handful of ticks of a clock for the whole reason for her being to change.

No. She felt no fear. She did feel loneliness, the aloneness of being someone other than who she really was. Lisa had been a devoted wife and mother, proud of what her husband had done to try to make a better world for her and their children and their families. He had been killed by people who wanted to stop him and send a message to others like him that they were vulnerable. That they should be afraid.

She let her thoughts drift back to a lifetime long ago, to a comfortable, three-bedroom town house on Long Island where she, her husband, and their three wonderful children had lived. Mornings were fairly routine with coffee, eggs, bacon, and toast on the table, to nourish them all as they went to job and school. There was an occasional blueberry pancake morning and weekend breakfasts that might consist of bagels and chopped liver with tea, while the kids ate crepes topped with preserves and whipped crème.

She allowed herself the luxury of remembering such moments, and many others, but only briefly, savoring these memories like the finest wine. She could feel herself come alive at such times, and a smile would often cross her lips. She would remember nursing her infant son, Bobby, holding him in her arms as she rocked him and hummed a lullaby. She could see daughter Melissa standing on a step stool, on tiptoes as she leaned over the sink and brushed her teeth. She had so wanted to be a grownup. Older brother Raymond would be in his room, dismantling an old radio or old computer. This inquisitive eight-year-old was the pride of his father, and many evenings Lisa would see Ron and little Raymond sitting at a table, poring over the mechanical or electrical components of a toaster or a broken vacuum cleaner.

Lisa recalled coming home one evening from a party with Ron and finding her bedroom closet ransacked by little hands. To one side was Melissa wearing one of Lisa's blouses and a short skirt (which reached to the 5-year-old's ankles). The little girl's neck and shoulders were hidden under circles of necklaces and a loosely and stylishly thrown scarf. Her little feet teetered as she balanced herself in a pair of Lisa's high heels. On her head was a tan leather shore man's cap, cocked to one side, adding even more style to this rakish scene. Brother Raymond had gotten into the spirit of this "dress up" moment as well. He had put on one of Ron's dress fedoras and a sports coat three times too big for him. A pair of oversized sunglasses completed the picture. To complete this "family portrait" the children had placed sleeping little Bobby into his stroller and Raymond was proudly pushing him around in circles in the bedroom as Lisa and Ron unexpectedly walked in on this comical scene. Lisa and Ron often shared that priceless moment, and many other similar ones, at dinners and parties with their friends.

In even rarer instances Lisa had allowed herself the luxury of reliving intimate moments with Ron. She didn't dare venture too closely, or too deeply, into that pool of memories. Her intent and purpose were different now.

With Ron it had been for sheer delight, to share loving moments with him and to celebrate their friendship, their love, their commitment, and their bond to each other, to their children, and to life. Ron had been a loving, sensual husband who adored Lisa and everything about her. He reveled in watching her walk naked from the shower, watch her every body part as she bent over to pick up some panties or a bra off the floor after their lovemaking. Lisa was aroused by his attention as well and often would brush her full breasts past his mouth and cheeks or attend to his swelling manhood when she saw that she had "gotten a rise" out of him. She loved to be looked at and touched and fondled and kissed and admired, as much as he loved to adore her.

In her new life as an undercover FBI agent, in her present raison d'etre, she was using her body as a weapon. Before her sexuality was used to experience life at its best, now she was using her womanhood and all her cunningness to bring about death and destruction, and retaliation, for a life that had been stolen from her and her family.

Deep inside she knew and remembered who she was. But when she stroked her skin now or looked into a mirror, she felt separateness, a distance from the reality of now. As she spread lotion across her shoulders and arms, it felt as if she were softening an outer leather garment, not touching herself. Circling her fingers around her breasts and nipples she could only feel the weight of them as she lifted each in a cupped hand. There was no tingling, no pleasure or arousal from her nipples. They were like epaulets on a military coat or little sacks slung over a horse's back.

She smoothed her hands over her sleek belly with the lotion and onto her thighs. Again she perceived herself as a smaller replica within, residing inside of an even larger body that was no longer hers. Over the years, the thickness, the distance, of that skin seemed to grow even larger. Lisa knew that she was psychologically separating her real self from the persona that she had voluntarily put on, like a cloak or costume. She had to live most of her day in this outer shell, in this lie, this ruse, if she ever expected to attain her goal. And the real Lisa would remain sheltered within her, locked away in some tiny recess of the mind where only she could go.

This was her secret hiding place. A place where she could go and rest, relax, to afford herself some element of joy, and to remember who she was. She would do this for survival. Not just physical survival, but for survival of her soul.

If she accepted completely her new role as vamp, sex kitten, whore, confidant to drug lords, lover of the drug cartel kingpin, then her enemies would win. They would have killed her entire family, and in the end have killed the last remnants of Lisa.

She was the keeper of the flame. The last of her nuclear family. She resolved to keep their memory alive, to remember and nurture who she had been, and hoped someday to return to a life of normalcy.

The phone suddenly rang. She picked up the receiver, took a deep breath, and let out a faint sigh. "Hello." She paused then asked, "Who is this?"

There was a sound of heavy breathing on the other end, then silence. Lisa had heard this before. She knew this silence. It was like a silent collar slipped around her neck, forcing her to remain where she was, calm and expectant. She could almost feel the tightening pull of this imaginary short leash. The stillness was maddening. She dare not hang up. Even with no sound, no voice, no greeting, she knew instantly who this was. She could feel the vibration, the tight presence of her controller, like a large hand encircling her throat, ready to crush the air and the life out of her at a moments notice.

Renee Gallois, she thought. In consummating her union with the boss of the entire Northern Hemisphere's largest drug cartel, she would eventually bite his head off, roll it around in her mouth, enjoy the salty taste of blood, and spit it out. Only then would she be vindicated.

After a long pause a voice on the phone spoke. "Good afternoon, my lovely lady. I wish to see you. I will be in Paris this evening and will have you dine with me. I will have my man pick you up at seven. Be ready. And don't wear anything…restricting."

Silence, and then the sound of air being exhaled. Lisa knew he was blowing smoke out of his nostrils, a favorite habit of his. Then suddenly it was over, a click and a dial tone, and the call was over.

Lisa peered into the mirror while she methodically dressed for the evening, as if putting on a uniform. What would my mother say, she found herself wondering in silence. Lisa had grown up in a small midwestern town in Iowa. She was an orphan and had been adopted by an elderly couple who hadn't been able to have children. She grew up in Des Moines, Iowa and attended the local schools. There was a time when she had considered going into nursing, but she soon realized that it was not for her. She quit the nursing program after a couple of years of college and instead went to work for a finance and loan company. Being somewhat adventuresome, she decided to visit a relative in New Jersey.

Lisa had found work there in the East and decided to stay. She met her future husband, Ron, fell in love and they soon were married. Those were the happiest years of her life.

Her mind shifted in nanoseconds now back to her home on Long Island and to the previous life when she had a loving husband and three beautiful children. She relived the sounds of gunfire, the pop-pop and loud bang of machine guns and shot guns as her family were murdered in their beds while they slept. Momentarily frozen in fear, hearing the screams of her husband as he yelled, "Run away! We're being killed. Run away." She knew instinctively that he was right and she obeyed him. She was at the back of the house in the bathroom. A window had been left partially open to let the cool summer breezes in. Fighting the desire to run back to them, unarmed, while her husband screamed for her to save herself, she crouched in the bathtub behind a shower curtain waiting for the shots to stop. In a very short time the shots did stop. All was quiet. She waited for some sounds, some footsteps. She especially waited for the voice of her husband. When she didn't hear his voice or any movement, she crawled through the window and quietly circled around the one side of the house.

They had been through such scenarios before. As he was getting ready to testify in the upcoming trial of a very well connected drug lord in the New York and New Jersey area, he occasionally reminded her of the dangers facing him and, as a consequence, their family. He knew that he might be targeted for assassination and that the family might be dragged in to this. He had wanted her and the children to move in with friends in Utica, in Upstate New York, while he was testifying. She wouldn't hear of it. She couldn't know how long the trials would last. There would be great disruption as she pulled the children out of school. Their friends all lived nearby and she knew no one in Upstate New York. She couldn't understand how that would offer her any greater protection. Couldn't the FBI just post some police outside their home in an unmarked car for surveillance and protection? She was not going to leave her husband at a stressful time.

He had told her that if there ever was an "incident" or a dangerous situation, that she had to listen to him, that she had to do everything he said, and quickly, without questioning or hesitation, because it could mean the difference between life and death, for him, for her, and for their children. He asked her to trust in him, and to promise him that she would do exactly as he said, in the event that an emergency situation or predicament arose.

And this she did. And in the end, he and their children were dead. And she was alive. She suffered from a survivor's guilt, that only made her present sacrifices seem too trivial for the atonement that she knew had to come in order for her to continue living. Had she rushed back through the kitchen and the dining room to the other end of the house and the bedrooms, she would surely have been killed. She had no weapon. She knew that her husband slept with a small machine gun, and had heard its loud bursts a few times as he yelled to her to run and hide. And then the short bursts, the popping sounds and the loud piercing sounds of shotguns stopped. It was over in a matter of seconds, yet it had seemed like an hour to Lisa.

She would not, and could not, now allow herself to justify this present situation here in Paris through any rationalization, that she had volunteered to go deep undercover and to be here now. To do so would invite choice, the idea that she could either continue with her deep involvement in this most dangerous, despicable, horrendous criminal element in the eastern American continent or just walk away. To invite that element of choice would also allow weakness to enter into her persona, making her more vulnerable to discovery.

No. This was beyond choice. Beyond any "call to duty", and even beyond revenge. This was a necessary, surgical operation to rid her universe of a malignancy, a cancer that had struck once, and continued to threaten the existence of anything and all that she held dear.

To be discovered, "outed", would mean certain death to her and all of the valuable contacts she had made over the last two years. It would also mean that her sacrifice would be lost and that her husband and her little children would have died in vain. It was unimaginable to her that she could turn her back on all she had done, to reclaim her own sanity and to return to a civilized life. No, she had told herself many times before when doubt and uncertainty had seeped into her mind's eye, "There is no choice." She had only to finish what she had set out to do. She was the mole, a vamp, a predator, the penultimate sexual goddess.

CHAPTER 3

Lisa and Rene Gallois
at the Hotel Ritz

Lisa was attending a business meeting in at the Hotel Ritz de Paris. She was escort to Renee Gallois. Long tables lavishly covered with the famous Hotel Ritz buffet were set up on one side of the spacious meeting room where she now stood. She held a glass of champagne. She had lost her appetite earlier in the evening as she looked through some photo albums that one of the clients had opened on the conference desk. She had found, to her inner shock and amazement, a faded, grainy, black and white photo of human legs floating in a watery solution in an open railroad boxcar. There were dozens of these legs, like sardines in oil, packed in and floating, having been neatly severed from their owner with the head of the thigh bone smooth and shiny.

There were other photos as well in the large album. Black and white pictures of emaciated people in ragged, stripped uniforms. Hair as twisted and gnarled as their faces. Men and women, old and young. She immediately identified these as being from Nazi concentration camps during World War II. What a stark contrast to the opulence that surrounded her now. Here were clutches of people, mostly men and a few women, all very well dressed, coiffed, bejeweled, and well fed…some obviously more well fed than others.

There were a couple of dozen people standing about the large room, broken up into small clutches of three and four. Hostesses in short dark skirts, white blouses, and black fishnet hose scurried about offering hors d'oeuvres and champagne to the guests. Lisa knew some of them, having been at other gatherings put on for the organization, as they liked to call it. In one corner stood Rene Gallois.

He will tall, thin, almost effeminate in his build. His shoulders were small and sloped downward. He had grayish-white hair with streaks of black tied into a ponytail behind him. He had a long sharp nose that angled slightly downward and ended just above his thin, pale lips, which never seemed to open for a smile. He wore a well-fitted black tuxedo with shiny lapels. He had large, garish diamond, ruby, and emerald studded rings on most of his fingers.

Lisa turned her gaze away from him, hoping not to attract his attention. She was having enough of a problem at this moment trying to absorb the stark contrast between this gathering and the photos on the table before her.

Lisa had become very upset but tried not to show her true reaction or the sickly feeling that was welling up inside of her. To make matters worse, this catered affair offered sumptuous, deliciously prepared and artistically presented, pastries, sushi, and a carving station with an open bar off to one side.

"Looks awful, doesn't it?" asked a man to her left.

She looked at him with a blank stare, trying to control her outward reactions as best she could. She was known in this inner circle as a hardened woman, a player who would just as easily kill someone as offer them a cup of coffee. She had played the part many times over the last couple of years. In so doing she gained the confidence and respect of many of the leaders of the drug cartels.

Now was not the time to look weak or sensitive or ethical. She was swimming in a sea of sharks, a gathering of sociopaths who probably would even have preferred to see the actual dissecting of the legs off their previous owners, whether still alive or freshly dead. She quickly conjured up the memories and the motivation for why she was now standing here amidst these misfits, these predators on society.

She casually looked around at the meeting room, the long conference table, and the gruesome photos in an album, and eventually at the forty –something long-nosed face of a thin man who stared at her, as if patiently waiting for a reaction to his question. She stared back at him. "No different than when I debone chicken for supper."

He smiled, sighed, and shrugged his shoulders. "Ah, yes. Like deboned chicken!" He nudged a portly male companion next to him and they both laughed. The large grey haired friend accompanying the long nose wore a well fitting dark suit and a large opal ring on his right ring finger. In his left hand was a wooden skewer with tahini marinated chicken pieces from the catering table. He took a bite of the meat, smiling as he chewed. He repeated, "Like a deboned chicken!" They all laughed. Chicken grease dribbled down one side of the man's mouth as he chewed and laughed and nodded his head in support of the joke. Lisa nodded in recognition and also laughed. She laughed the loudest, giving her ownership of the joke.

"You see," long nose said as he pointed to the photo in the album, "you see the surgical expertise of the German wartime surgeons. The skin around the hip joint is cut clean and the muscles are finely dissected so that one can see the tendons that were gently stripped from their anchor points on the pelvic bones."

"Why did they do that?" Lisa asked in a half interested tone.

The man put out his hand and introduced himself. "I am Conrad Dorfmann. I have a great interest in history," he paused momentarily, as if to intentionally add mystery to his introduction. "And an even greater interest in how it affects and influences us now in the present."

He paused again.

"And how we can profit from the actions of the past." he added.

"And where is the profit in looking over photos like these of what the Nazis did to people?" Lisa asked, hoping not to sound too interested or affected by the horror.

Mr. Dorfmann continued, "Oh, there is no profit in looking at these photos, except from a personal vantage point. Knowing what was accomplished through the efforts of those valiant German surgeons would make one who has the facts feel great pride. These photos are just a documentation of what was done by those surgeons under great stress and hardship, with poor equipment and none of the marvelous medications that we take for granted today."

He took a sip of wine from a large glass he was holding, and exhaled a sigh of satisfaction. "The German army had suffered a major defeat at

Stalingrad in an attempt to push through Russia and on to the Middle East and to the oil fields there that would fuel the machinery of the Third Reich. While many thousands of soldiers were killed or taken prisoner, there were many, many terribly wounded young men. There was the specter of a repeat of World War One wherein an entire generation of German youth would walk around with crutches or in wheelchairs as a result of having an arm or leg blown off or amputated."

His friend went back to the buffet to refresh his dinner plate. Apparently all this talk of amputations and having limbs blown off fueled his appetite. He returned with a full plate of meatballs in a crème sauce as Mr. Dorfmann continued.

"The German surgeons were very well trained and were known for their speed as well as their dexterity. In their schooling in the Wermacht, or through the SS schools, there was no shortage of dissection materials. The konzentrationslagern or concentration camps were filled with material that could be used for training. Many of the prisoners were to be killed anyway or worked until they were no longer useful. So, why not use them for the benefit of the Reich anyway? Why waste!"

His friend nodded in agreement as Conrad made his point. Lisa could hear a hint of an accent. Possibly German? Or French? Now he spoke.

"What you say is true, Conrad. Why waste such a great opportunity to further the scientific knowledge, for dissection and for surgery, and to help so many soldiers who had suffered so much and had given so much! Why? Many prisoners from Auschwitz had their bodies dissected so that Dr. Sobota could draw one of the most accurate anatomy books of the 20th century, produced since Vesalius published his woodcuts in the 16th century."

"Yes, Josef. Why waste when you have the materials, and you have the need. Don't you think, Miss…..." Dorfmann's voice trailed off as indirectly asked for Lisa's name.

Lisa was surprised at how easily she was able to control her revulsion over the entire topic and with the ease that which these two men would refer to human beings as material, and dissections and killings as an instrument to prevent "waste".

"I guess I've never given it too much thought. I know that the Germans did experiments on people in the concentration camps but my understanding is that nothing ever came of it. I thought that people weren't allowed to use any of the information because it was done poorly or couldn't be reproduced."

"Ach, Josef. You see. People don't know what really happened during that time."

"Maybe it is as it should be, or things might be much more difficult to develop, offered Josef.

"Maybe in a time before, but now, Josef, times have changed. We can be more open with what we discuss."

Now Josef became serious and stopped chewing the last of his meatballs. "Some things are always better left in the dark or unsaid."

"Maybe," replied Conrad. "But our beautiful young lady…"

"Lisa," she said and offered her hand.

"Yes, Lisa." Conrad kissed her hand in the European fashion and smiled under uplifted eyebrows as he bowed. "Lisa, you are here with whom?"

She turned and motioned with her head towards Rene Gallois. "He is my benefactor. My friend." Conrad smiled and nodded in agreement. He understood benefactor.

"Well, let me continue then. Those brilliant surgeons of the SS and the German army became very adept in taking off the limb of one man and attaching it to the hip joint or shoulder joint of another prisoner. Their performance was superb."

Lisa shuddered inwardly at the thought, but maintained her composure. "But how could that be? I'm not a scientist or a physician but I've read some things where one body would reject the skin or organs from somebody else."

"This is true," Dorfmann acknowledged. "First the doctors practiced their surgical skills on dead prisoners, mostly so that they wouldn't move. Later they used others that they had medicated, again, so that they wouldn't move. As the war dragged on and supplies dwindled and the surgeons' skills improved, there was no need to sedate or anesthetize the donor."

Lisa breathed in and slowly exhaled, trying to steady her nerves and stomach. "So sometimes they would amputate a good arm or leg without using any pain killers or stuff to numb the areas they cut into."

"Absolutely! In fact, the idea was to quickly dissect off the arm or leg of a prisoner and then sew it on to the waiting cavity of the host prisoner."

"By cavity, you mean that the doctors had already cut off an arm or a leg from a second prisoner so that they could then sew on another arm or leg from the first one?"

"Exactly," Conrad said as he proudly beamed and raised his wine glass. The two men continued, excitedly added comments as they proceeded with their discussions, obviously hoping to impress Lisa.

"At that time they didn't understand tissue rejection. Oh, they knew that you couldn't just take some blood or some piece of tissue and stick it into somebody else's body. That was well known to the entire scientific and medical community," Conrad said as he took another sip of wine and bit into a small square of cheese. "They didn't know how to block that rejection. Drugs like steroids and cyclosporine, that we take so much for granted now to block rejection of transplanted tissue, why, those weren't even developed until the 1950's and 1970's!"

Dorfmann nodded his head in agreement. He mumbled a weak "*Jawohl*" as he chewed on a chicken wing and washed it down with some red wine.

Conrad continued. "Leave it up to the English and the Americans to show the way to a new method for altering our biology." He chuckled. "James Watson and Francis Crick deciphered the structure of the DNA molecule that carries the blueprint for all human beings."

"And they stole the ideas of how the DNA looked from that girl working on x-rays of the stuff, Rosalind Franklin," added Dorfmann. He licked grease off his fingers and added, "And a Jewess at that!"

Conrad became more animated as he continued, apparently relishing in his own grasp of past events and modern developments in science. "The thought back then, during the war, was to repair the injured and broken bodies of our warriors so that they could return to the battlefield, or whatever was needed, to maintain our military strength. But, such things take time and money and resources. Something that had become more difficult as the war dragged on. Then it was over before it started!"

Dorfmann took out a handkerchief and wiped his eyes. "Yes, a tragedy. To think, we could have gone on for a thousand years. But it was not to be with Hitler dead and the Russians and the Americans each taking the best of our people back to their countries. Our scientists, our doctors, our intelligence people, our analysts, and our officers. The crème of the crop, as they say.

But things have changed, and I would say changed for the better. Now, we have a much brighter future ahead for our people and our organization."

Lisa perked up when she hear Dorfmann mention "our organization". Carefully she skirted his remarks, not wanting to show an obvious interest. "Yes, the drug trade is certainly lucrative. A lot of us are making a lot of money."

Dorfmann quickly swallowed another bite of chicken teriyaki on a stick. "Ah yes, but I meant the larger entity, The International Alliance. Of course control and sale of our products all over North America bring in a steady income, but that is only one part of the revenue streams that flow together into the coffers that make the Alliance so strong. The money brought in from all of the operations all over the world is what will sustain the Alliance and allow us to go to the next step."

Lisa needed to say something to avoid alerting the two men to her ignorance on what they were talking about. She had heard snippets of conversation at various times about "the Alliance". Renee Gallois had spoken of it on a couple of occasions while on the phone in her suite at the hotel or at other times at his mansion just outside of Paris. "And with all the food that you two seem to be enjoying, it appears that the Alliance has been quite profitable."

The two men laughed.

"Very good, very good. It is so wonderful to be able to talk with so witty, and may I add, so lovely a woman as you!" Conrad gently took Lisa's hand and with a quick, light click of his heels, kissed her hand.

Dorfmann continued, "Ah, yes. Indeed. Money flows into the coffers of the Alliance like water streaming over those famous Venezuelan waterfalls. And all for the good. All for the good!"

"For the good," Josef piped in. There was a slight slur in his speech as he toasted his friend in agreement and nodded his head.

"Those early experiments were done during a different time, like in a different world," Conrad added. He gestured towards the nearby table with the old photos that they had been commenting on earlier.

"Things are so different now. We know so much more now. All knowledge comes at a price. Some of it is in dollars, and sometimes the currency is in the form of pain and suffering.

"Why look at World War One. All of the head injuries and burns and blindness and lung problems from all the gunshots and poison gas attacks. Surgery, especially plastic or reconstructive surgery, made tremendous advances because of all of the suffering that went on at the battlefields.

"We have now entered a new world in our understanding of the genetic code. We have isolated so many of the genes that are responsible for many of the physical attributes and the behaviors and predilections or addictions that people have. Why soon our scientists will be able to manipulate our human genetic code and produce whatever type of being we want…. made to order!"

"Made to order," Josef echoed again.

"But haven't there been some spectacular failures in trying to manipulate the genetic code in humans, "Lisa interjected." I had read that some people died when scientists tried to manipulate the test subjects' genes. And in trying to grow a test tube baby with specific desired traits or characteristics, that also hasn't panned out yet, to my understanding."

Dorfmann raised his hand politely. "Yes, you are right, for now. That is true. But just like your Wright brothers who flew their flimsy little planes again and again, one has to keep on trying. Success in science is built upon a mountain of failures. It was Sir Isaac Newton, the English mathematician and philosopher who said, 'If I see beyond, it is because I stand on the shoulders of giants who went before me.' He paid great tribute to the scholars and scientists who, in earlier times, asked the difficult questions about Life and the World and went about their lives, thinking and experimenting until they found some little nugget of truth."

Josef cleared his throat, obviously to gain Lisa's attention. "You see, *liebchen*, we are standing at a new threshold in the evolution of Mankind. A new future for the world, something that our predecessors could only have imagined. Over the years and in the shadows, so to speak, our movement, The Movement, has been making contacts and networks and friends all over the globe. In the process, billions and billions of dollars have been accumulated, and spent, to push the research necessary to further our goal of creating a New Order. This New Order must be populated by a superior type of human being, as envisioned by Our Furher, Herr Hitler. We have funded thousands of projects, perfecting the manipulation of the human genetic code. As you rightly pointed out, many people have died in these experiments. Some were publicized, especially when the research was carried out in famous institutions such as Johns Hopkins University or the Cleveland Clinics. Many other times however, the failures went unreported or unrecorded. The subjects were not all volunteers."

Lisa shuddered at the meaning of his last words, "not all volunteers". She tried again not to show her inner revulsion.

"And of course, your friend Mr. Gallois has made incredible contributions to this long process. He has been of invaluable service. He and many others like him all over the world have used their business and political contacts to bring in large amounts of money and special favors. We are all forever indebted to him for his work."

"I must admit that Monsieur Gallois has been a loyal, very productive supporter to the Alliance, over the years. And he, of course, is not alone. He is one major fish in our grand endeavor to reshape the genotype and phenotype of human beings, and the destiny of Mankind. He is not however the driving force, the hauptman or fuehrer, if I may, of our International Alliance"

Jozef nodded his agreement. *"Ja, doch. Sehr klar."*

"That distinction goes to our Board, and especially to the expert helmsmanship of Bruno Metzger. With his youthful energy and belief in the mission, he brought together the diverse elements of the old guard of the tattered Third Reich and the various elements of government representatives, intelligence operatives, scientists, and the heads of the world's largest drug cartels. It was a superb feat of diplomacy and business!"

"That is so! Well said Dorfmann, well said!" added Jozef. "But in one sense our ultimate goal still evades us. While we have some general ideas of how to construct the next generation of humans, the steps taken so far have only led to failure and some deaths, as our charming guest has mentioned. There is an elusive template if you will, of the direction in which we would like to go. There was a wonderful model that the Fuehrer had alluded to, from which the best elements of our proud Teutonic heritage had sprung. This was the Aryan race, which Hitler had alluded to repeatedly."

"It is not well known that Himmler had sent an expedition to Tibet and Nepal in the late 1930's to study the people there in hopes of identifying some persons who might be the last surviving carriers of the genetic code of the Aryan race. In fact, it has only recently come to our realization that there may actually be a listing of these people, the original Aryans, in some of the monasteries in Tibet and Nepal. And also that there may be a carrier of these genes, as well, somewhere in Europe!"

"Why that's incredible," Lisa found herself exclaiming. "You wouldn't have to rely on all of those 'volunteers' to try and get it right, now would you?"

"*Doch*," exclaimed Dorfmann. "It would be more efficient and cheaper."

"And truly get us to where we wanted to go," added Jozef. "We would, in essence, be applying the gold standard. Why settle for second best when you would have the original? The very best."

CHAPTER 4

The Petrie Family Reunion

"And so they went, walking in loose military formation into the ravine, on their way to save their fellow patriots from the guns of the British and the tomahawks of the Indians." William Petrie looked around at the throng seated before him as he spoke. Some were sinking their teeth into butter-slathered corn-on-the-cob, while others were playing with their mashed potatoes and gravy and turkey slices. Mr. Petrie, patriarch of the Petrie clan, and now approaching 80 years of age, relished in his yearly recounting of the Battle of Oriskany at the Annual Petrie Family Reunion.

Some relatives wore brightly colored t-shirts specifically silk-screened for the occasion. There was a picture of the old Fort Stanwix on the back with the caption "Annual Petrie Family Reunion" with the dates and locations of previous celebrations. As the Petrie's had been in America since at least the 1700's, and had been prodigiously fecund, offspring of the ancestral tree had spread far and wide not only in America, but around the world. Reunions had been held in numerous locations over the last 100 years including Utica and Herkimer, New York; San Diego, California; L'Aigle in Normandy, France; in Sidney, Australia; Katowice, Poland; and Washington, D.C. Early on, rather than have the relatives always travel to the same location, it was decided, even in the last century, to encourage people to open up their homes to their relatives in the very successful enterprise of building a network of cousins and nieces, aunts and uncles, and grandparents, as well as those peoples' friends and co-workers. Many business deals and partnerships and philanthropic ventures had resulted from that strategy.

William Petrie had been attending these yearly reunions since he was a baby. Other than a few years as a child, when he had either the measles or whooping cough or, one year, was in the hospital with a fractured hip, as an adult he had not missed a single family reunion.

Now he stood, arms outstretched, and continued with his story. It was a story he relished telling and retelling year after year, reunion after reunion. He never told the story the same way twice. In some years he focused on the tragic ambush of General Herkimer's relief column as it hurried during the hot August 1777 summer to save Fort Stanwix from a British siege. In other years he would talk about the men of Herkimer's militia who gallantly fought and died, and of those who ran away at the first sound of shots. And always he would somehow segue into the story of his namesake and great-great-great-great grandfather, William Petrie, that is, Dr. William Petrie, personal physician and surgeon to General Herkimer during the Battle of Oriskany. The doctor had tied a tourniquet around where a ball had shattered the general's leg about 6 inches below the left knee. The ball continued into his horse and killed the animal. Herkimer survived the battle. Petrie himself was severely wounded during the battle, was himself bandaged and taken home and was not able to later care for his general. That duty fell to an inexperienced apprentice surgeon, Robert Johnson. About ten days after the battle, at Herkimer's home in Little Falls, it seemed that there was no option but to amputate the gangrenous leg. Apparently the operation was done poorly and sutures to the major arteries unraveled. Dr. Johnson was not able to stop the flow of blood from the stump of the amputated leg. General Herkimer slowly bled to death, surrounded by his family and friends, smoking his pipe and reading Bible psalms.

The present day William Petrie continued, "You see, New York was called the Keystone State because, like the keystone that holds up a stone archway, it was the connection for travel and commerce, and troops between New England and states south of New York. And the whole Mohawk Valley west of Albany up to Utica and beyond was where George Washington and the American army got most of its food. And the British…well, they were ruthless. They wanted to send Gentleman General Johnny Burgoyne from Montreal, and Lieutenant Colonel St. Leger from Ontario, and the fat old, lazy General Howe from New York City. Like a pincer the plan was to come at us from three directions, from the North, from the West and from the South, and to meet in Albany." As he had done so often in the past while recounting this part of the history, William put his hands on his hips and with a smirk on his face and a repeated nod, he gazed out at the interested little gathering.

Sam Petrie sat at a nearby picnic table, munching on a piece of grilled chicken as he listened to his father recount today's version of the Oriskany battle. He had just gotten off his day shift in the emergency department at St. Clare's Hospital where he had been involved in his own battles, to save lives and repair the damage from domestic strife, car accidents, gun shot wounds, and heart attacks. As father William described how the Tryon County militia patriots were rushing from tree to tree, reloading and firing at the surrounding enemy, Sam thought of the ambulances rushing into his ER, dropping off their patients, of nurses scurrying from stretcher to stretcher, starting IVs and injecting medications into plastic tubing. Oriskany had been a surprise, an unorganized melee that eventually was turned into an effective response to an ambush by the Indians and their Tory loyalist forces.

As he listened, Sam remembered that his morning had started out quietly but the department was soon inundated with the sick, the dying, and the dead. His staff had risen to the occasion, as they always did. Unlike the American patriots on that hot August day in a ravine near the Indian village of Oriska, Sam's "troops" were well trained and expected the daily incoming gush of patients. Yet even knowing that they would be busy, no one could ever confidently predict what their "routine day in the ER" would look like. Sam remembered a sign that he had posted on the inside of the door to his office when he was a medical student in Iowa during his first clinical rotations: "I never know what will come through that door". He put that up to remind himself to try and be as prepared as he possibly could, yet knowing that he could not predict, nor prepare for, every contingency.

He thought that this was possibly why he had such a fascination with emergency medicine. In teaching CPR classes he would explain to a sometimes-bored classroom where his excitement for teaching these basic resuscitation classes came from. In the four links of the "chain of survival" the second and third links were "early cardiopulmonary resuscitation" and "early defibrillation". If the CPR was poor, and there was no defibrillator available, then the chances of a successful resuscitation would drop from a high of sixty to ninety percent down to zero or maybe five percent, depending on the scenario. A dead patient was a dead patient. No amount of money poured into a multimillion-dollar medical center would help that dead patient. Sam felt strongly that it was of vital importance to focus on the weakest link, the link between CPR and defibrillation, in order to allow the patient a second chance. If the patient survived their initial shock and sudden cardiac arrest, only then would the medicines and advanced techniques like coronary bypass intervention or even heart transplants be of any value. A dead patient was still a dead patient.

William Petrie could be heard above the casual conversations of family members drinking beer and juice and biting into hamburgers and potato salad. "By now General Herkimer was wounded in the leg. His men wanted him moved to the rear, and to safety. He would have none of that!" The elder peered into the eyes of many of the younger audience seated on the grass in front of him. Some of the children had stopped chewing on their hotdogs or their potato chips. Others munched with even greater speed and stuffed more chips into their mouths.

"The general said 'No, I will face my enemy!' And with that, and with bullets whizzing around in all directions, smashing into nearby tree trunks and snipping off branches and leaves, he had his soldiers set him up on the saddle taken from his dead horse and leaned him up against a beech tree. With all that confusion and smoke and shouting, the general started yelling out commands to his troops. 'Leave the wounded where they are, they're safer there on the ground.' Herkimer also noticed that when a militiaman fired his rifle, an Indian would come out of hiding and try to club and kill the soldier. Herkimer told his men to double up. One man fired while the other behind was loaded and ready for the onrush. This tactic worked so well that the Indians couldn't keep rushing on 'em."

Sam again thought of his own ER. How often had he been inundated with more patients than the staff could handle? Sam had to hurry from room to room and triage the patients, just as Herkimer did at his battle. Leave the wounded where they are, they're safer there. In an analogous fashion, those patients less wounded or not as ill would lie on stretchers and wait, while the meager staff of St. Clare's ER would attend to the life threatening injuries of others. One team of two nurses or assistants would stay with a patient while Petrie went from patient to patient, intubated one here, gave orders for medications there, sent others off to CT scan, or secured a cervical collar on another patient. As always, just like in the ambush at Oriskany in 1777, Petrie's job was to establish order out of unexpected chaos. Teamwork was essential to success. Those who were stable would "lie on the ground where they were" so to speak, while the more seriously ill and injured were tended to immediately. This was triage. As Herkimer had triaged his troops by the little ravine in Oriskany, so Sam had triaged his team at St. Clare's.

Sam looked beyond his plate to the steps leading from the rear of his parent's home. There sat Carl Thurston. His eyes were crossed and his tongue hung out and off to one side as he wore a plastic gold crown. A small circle of children, gathered around this large man, were giggling at his antics.

At times he would look serious, as if scolding his subjects. Then he would break out into an ear-to-ear grin and contort his face into unimaginable shapes. A roar of laughter and clapping would follow. Carl took out three green tennis balls and expertly juggled them in front of the amazed children. As the youngsters watched, spellbound by his dexterity, Carl let one tennis ball "accidentally" hit him on his head. He let out a comical groan and fell backward onto the steps. The children laughed and clapped as they saw this gentle giant sprawled on the deck steps. A few rushed up and landed on him and he playfully wrestled with them as he too laughed loudly.

Thurston loved children. He truly was a "gentle giant". As a policeman, he could be as tough as nails, ready to respond to threats of violence, to angry people, or criminals shooting at him. He had nerves of steel, or so it seemed on the outside. He also had a softer, gentler side. Inside.

At almost six foot and 250 pounds, he was a trained machine of muscle and sinew. Carl trained regularly at the Police Academy gym. Over the years he had watched too many of his fellow officers let themselves go, preferring to sit in their squad car or at a local coffee bar and munch on their favorite police food group, donuts. Carl was devoted to physical training ever mindful that at any moment his body might be called upon to perform, to react, and ultimately to survive any ordeal that "the bad guys" might subject him to. In the aftermath of the Quinterra drug cartel debacle, he quickly learned that speed, strength, agility, and cunning all needed to be sharpened to a razor's edge. Leonardsville, and rescuing Sam Petrie from the clutches of the murderous drug lord and his minions, seemed like only yesterday even though it had happened more than three years ago.

Lying on the steps of the deck, wrestling little children, and putting on funny faces and juggling tennis balls belied a deeper persona that resided in Carl. He was an expert marksman and was trained in all of the various weaponry that the Utica Police Department had at its disposal. Rifles, pistols, smoke grenades, riot gear, rappelling equipment, and machine guns. Upon his return from Montana and the killing of Justin Taylor, Carl had been offered a position with the city's SWAT team. He accepted this readily, knowing it would allow him the opportunity to advance his learning of the skills necessary to subdue and, if required, to kill his assailants.

The promotion was not without resistance. Thurston had already been investigated by a combined police and citizen's commission after his killing of a Hispanic criminal. His gun had been taken away then while the commission met in closed doors to weigh the options of dismissal from the police force, rehabilitation, counseling, or reinstatement and exoneration. Carl had taken this all in stride, at least externally. He knew that any cop who killed someone, even in the line of duty, was required by law to have his actions and the situation scrutinized by a combined government and citizenry panel. What bothered him however during the proceedings was that he was accused by the very people that he had sworn to protect, the area's Hispanic community, of being a racist.

Thurston could trace his ancestry to the Anglo-Saxons and the early days of Britain. His great-grandparents emigrated from the small town of Thurston in the county of Suffolk in eastern England in the early 16th century. They had settled first in New York City and, later, Albany, along the Hudson River which at that time was at the edge of the wilderness. As more and more immigrants came into New England and southern New York, some Thurstons ventured further west into the wilds of Upstate New York. Carl at one time had traced some of his relatives to Johnstown where they worked for Sir William Johnson, the representative of the English

Crown for Indian Affairs. Other Thurstons lived in Canajoharie, Little Falls, and German Flats.

One relative in particular, Seth Thurston, was a member of the Tryon County militia. He had served under the command of Nicholas Herkimer, the general who was called upon to rescue Fort Stanwix when it had come under attack by the British and their Indian allies. The militia's forced march from Little Falls, German Flats, and along the Mohawk River to reinforce the small American garrison at the fort resulted in the ambush and battle at Oriskany.

In one sense, Carl felt a strong, kindred relationship with the Petrie family as he listened to the elder William Petrie recount the Battle of Oriskany. Some of his own flesh and blood had been there as well alongside theirs. In another sense however, he felt a distance, a longing, an envy of sorts, whenever he attended a Petrie family reunion.

Carl Thurston had been brought up around an infamously violent area of Brooklyn near Flatbush Avenue where everyone struggled for work, food, and even survival. These were tough neighborhoods. Carl learned to be diplomatic when he could, and forged alliances with other kids for protection. He and his two younger brothers, Tommy and Matt, were often picked on by local street toughs. Carl eventually learned to use his two fists and to wrestle his opponents to the ground after having been beaten and robbed and humiliated too many times before he was even ten years old.

Brother Tommy seemed to have a penchant for opening his mouth at the wrong moment and angering or insulting a gang tough when he should have just let matters rest. He was skinny and short and had a half-smile or perpetual smirk on his face that some of the other older kids didn't like. It often seemed to them that he was mocking them. Bloody noses and bruised ribs or a concussion seemed to be regular weekend events for him.

Tommy often came home after school, hungry and bruised because his lunch money or bagged lunch had been absconded by some ruffian at noontime. Carl grew up finishing fights that Tommy had inadvertently started by word or foolish action. While the older brother was angered by Tommy's lack of insight into his own behavior or timidity, he always protected him or bailed him out of a dangerous situation. It was the unspoken pact of brothers: "If you pick on my brother, you are picking on me. And when you pick on me, you better be sure that you can match your words with action." Put in the more correct vernacular of Flatbush Avenue at that time: "You fuck with him, you're fuckin' with me!"

Matt was the intellectual of the family and their mother often said that he would be the first one in the family to get an education, go to college and be a success. He loved to read and thoroughly enjoyed school. He did engage in sports as a kid, loved putting model cars and airplanes together with his older brother Carl. He also had a passion for reading and learning. One week he would dream of being an archeologist, even though he couldn't spell it. He fantasized digging up relics in Egypt or crawling through narrow passages in the Pyramids. Another time he would want to be like Dr. Doolittle, talking with the animals and flying on a giant moth to the moon to talk with King Bopo up there.

All of their trials and tribulations and dreams came to a screeching halt one day when their parents were gunned down in broad daylight outside of a grocery store by a street gang. A crowd of teenagers had wanted their mother to hand over the bag of groceries she was carrying and told their father to hand over his wallet. When the two refused, they were attacked from all sides as if by a pack of wolves. The gang members were merciless, kicking and punching both parents, and taking them to the ground. At one point, when Carl's father had the upper hand and was on top of one of the boys and started punching him, a shot was heard. His father jerked suddenly and rolled to his side. Blood poured from his head. As his mother screamed, another shot rang out and she too was silenced.

There was a police investigation, but no one was ever charged or brought to trial for the murders. Carl, Tommy, and Matt found themselves alone in the world. They had no close relatives living in or around Brooklyn. They were moved to an orphanage on Long Island until relatives were found in Utica. Raymond and Concetta Thurston were awarded custody of the three brothers. Their lives now started anew in Upstate New York.

The years went by and the boys grew under the loving care and watchful eye of their Aunt and Uncle. Concetta made sure that the brothers had clean clothes, did their homework, developed good manners, had a respect for the law, and honored family. Raymond and Concetta had never had children of their own. When they died, Carl, Tommy, and Matt were left with no immediate family other than each other.

When he was of age, Carl enlisted in the U.S. Army. He was sent for training as an M.P, something that he relished and excelled at. While serving in Germany, he got notice that Tommy had died. He had become ill with a fever, rash, and a stiff neck. He was diagnosed with spinal meningitis. He was dead within a few days.

Matt Thurston had finished high school, but instead of enlisting in the Army, fearing that he might be drafted for Vietnam, he moved to Canada. No one ever heard from him or about him again. When Carl returned home to Utica he was all alone. There was no Aunt Concetta or Uncle Raymond, no brother Tommy and no word about Matt.

Carl decided to stay in Utica. He applied to the Police Academy and, because of his military experience, was readily accepted. It seemed so natural for him to be a policeman. He was very sociable, diplomatic, and good-natured, but also athletic and as quick on his feet as he was with his hands, and later, with a gun. After his stint as a rookie he was embraced by the brotherhood of police. He made many friends in the community in and out of the police force, including one Samuel Petrie, emergency physician at St. Clare's Hospital.

They had met in the E.R. on many occasions, whenever Carl came in to get information about a motor vehicle accident, a gunshot wound, or an assault. Eventually the policeman and the doctor would meet for a beer or coffee after their shifts were over. Over the years they had became steadfast friends. They hunted and fished together, celebrated birthdays, the births of Sam's two children, Elaine and Nathan, and many, many holidays together.

Carl felt that emptiness, a longing, to have relatives, a family of his own, as Sam had. He looked around the reunion and smiled as Helen flitted about from table to table, making small talk with all of the relatives. Even though approaching sixty, she had made sure to take care of herself with regular exercise, a very healthy diet, and judicious use of makeup. She was very attractive with her slim body, long brown hair, and her large, open smile that made anyone feel warm, happy, and welcome.

Carl looked at the tee shirts that many of the Petrie clan, young and old, were wearing, with the Petrie family crest on the back. Below it were the names and dates where previous reunions had been held; Syracuse, San Diego, Phoenix, Montreal, Montauk Point, Long Island, Paris, and even

Sidney, Australia. The Petrie family had indeed branched out over the last century or so that they had been having these gatherings of the clan.

Carl did maintain a flame of hope deep in the recesses of his heart and wondered if he too might some day start a family that would grow and prosper as Sam's had, that he too would someday have a reunion. That flame was Lisa, the woman who he had loved as he had never loved anyone before. He had learned another, darker side of her after the Leonardsville rescue of Sam, that she was an active mole for the FBI. He had made a commitment to her as well as himself after it was explained to him that she was part of a long sting operation involving the biggest drug cartel in the Northeast.

He would wait for her, until she retuned to him, accepting that she was to stay undercover for a long time, perhaps three years or more. He had braced himself for and accepted that she would be damaged goods. Nevertheless he would wait for her, as he had said then, "For however long it takes."

CHAPTER 5

Dr. Gottwald and Mitochondrial DNA

Dr. Gottwald finished drawing a sausage-like shape on the chalkboard before him, with his campus-acclaimed technique of using both arms whenever drawing symmetrical portions of a form, picture, or diagram. With colored chalk in each hand, he drew undulating waves starting from the center of the shape outward, waving his arms up and down like a conductor leading an orchestra. The class followed his artistic flourishes with subdued awe.

"There!" he said triumphantly. "There you have it. This is the energy powerhouse of the cell. This is where all foodstuffs and anything connected to nutrition end up, in the mitochondria. It is here that, through a cascade of enzymes, electrons stream across the surfaces of these separations or baffle-like structures like water flowing across flat shale rocks, that adenosine triphosphate is made. ATP.

"This ATP is the storage currency of all living cells. When the body demands energy for any activity, be it to make proteins, or to retain potassium in the body, or contract a muscle, or conduct a signal across a nerve fiber, there has to be payment. That payment is made by the body's common currency...ATP."

He turned to his audience, physicians, nurse practitioners and professors, who were attending a scientific update conference hosted by the Mohawk Valley College of Osteopathic Medicine. Sam Petrie sat in the front row taking notes. He had been to a few other lectures earlier in the day and he thoroughly enjoyed each one. Genetics however, and Dr. Gottwald's approach to it, fascinated him.

"Now, we have been talking about the inheritance of traits in the classical Mendelian sense, that all of our attributes come from the chromosomes in the nucleus of our parent's cells, and most specifically the germ cells, as they are called. The sperm from someone's father has one half of the set of chromosomes, that is 23 of them, and the egg of the mother also has a 23 chromosomes. When the sperm fertilizes the egg, as you all know, magical things happen. The chromosomes from the father line up with the half-chromosomes from the mother and, voila! There you have it...a complete set of 46 chromosomes. And all of the genetic characteristics that make us who we are: hair color, eye color, our intelligence, predisposition to many diseases such as breast cancer, heart disease, drug addiction, and many diseases of the nervous system and birth defects.

"The 19th century was a time of great discovery in the field of genetics. A German Monk, Gregor Mendel, experimented with peas and flowers, in simple yet elegant experiments, and showed that there were predictable patterns of genetic inheritance. Breeders of horses and dogs had long known that through selective breeding they could develop animals according to their whim. Faster horses, dogs with greater ability to retrieve and so on, were now the order of the day. It was only logical that someone should entertain the idea of applying these breeding methods to humans.

"A German evolutionary biologist, August Weismann, is credited with being the earliest proponent of Eugenics, that is, an applied science of genetics in which the genetic makeup of a population could be improved by applying those same concepts that breeders had already been using. A number of social scientists and scholars picked up on that and eventually Eugenics became a policy that was embraced, as you all know, by the Nazis before the Second World War."

Dr. Gottwald stepped away from the long chalkboard. He wiped his hands clean of the chalk dust with a nearby cloth. He continued.

"So the Nazis embarked on a program to purify the German population and make ready for an evolution, or return if you will, of the Aryan race. This was based on the idea that a superior race of people, more intelligent, stronger, and healthier had emigrated from the Far East to northern Europe and was the foundation of the earlier German population. So the Nazis went about systematically euthanizing children and adults with severe birth defects or mental retardation, justifying their actions by explaining that those undesirables were draining the limited resources of Germany and tainting the genetic pool of the Germans.

"Their theory and practice of Eugenics was based on the Weismann Barrier, named after our friend that I mentioned earlier, August Weismann. He had postulated that no acquired traits could be passed on from one generation to another except through mutations of the genes on the chromosomes from the sperm and the egg of the parents. He felt that other cells of the body could not contribute to inheritance. He even snipped off the tails of mice for five generations to prove his point. After snipping and snipping mouse tails for five generations, no mouse was ever born that now had no tail! What an experiment! I don't think I would have wanted to be one of those mice!

"What he didn't know about then was that there is a separate set of chromosomes that is located in the mitochondria in the cytoplasm of the mother's egg. We are still learning some incredible things about these chromosomes and their genes. Because the genes are located outside of the nucleus, and therefore not part of the chromosomes from the sperm, these chromosomes and their genes are only passed from mother to daughter."

Sam enjoyed Dr. Gottwald's presentation. The professor's words and descriptions conjured up images of some things he had studied before. The idea of mitochondrial DNA however, was something he had only heard of or read about in passing. Now, as this class approached the end of the seminar day, Sam's tired mind started to wander.

As a kid Sam had been fascinated with biology and the diversity of all things great and small in the world. He would collect rocks and fossils, catch fireflies at dusk and keep them in a bottle by his bedside, and on some warm and sunny days lay on his belly in the fields by his house and peer into a world of insects and grasses, leaves, and worms, dirt and beetles. As he grew older he became immersed in books and articles about scientists and explorers and archaeologists and detectives. Some of his favorite grade school books were the Dr. Doolittle series, Sherlock Holmes stories, and Treasure Island. He dreamed of exploring the world, of digging up fossils and ancient artifacts. And he fantasized about finding a cure for diseases.

College had been a memorable experience for him. One day years later, he remembered, while sitting on his sofa at home fingering the pages of his senior college yearbook, he had delighted in recalling detail after detail of those wonderful years.

As he loved to explain to friends, the collegiate experience for him was like a crucible into which raw, molten steel was poured. From there it was transferred into molds which formed thick, rectangular blocks of hot metal which was then pushed back and forth through roller after roller in big machines, flattening the steel into thinner and thinner sheets until the desired gauge was produced. They were now ready for production. The sheets would be rolled up onto drums and allowed to cool before transport to their desired destination.

But Sam didn't have a specific "desired destination" after being molded by his college experience. Coming from an educated family, Sam knew he was expected to study and to make something of himself. Petries before him had done well in education and business. He had aunts and uncles, cousins, nephews, and nieces who had positioned themselves well financially and politically in business and government. The earliest "destinations" that Sam had frequented in his freshman college years were a popular bar called the Salty Dog and a few of the sorority houses just off campus at Cornell University in Ithaca, New York.

Sam attended Cornell in the fabulous Sixties and Seventies, the decades wherein, if you remembered them, you hadn't really been there. It was a time of tension and turmoil, of happiness and free love. It was a time to express oneself in so many different ways. It was the time of the Vietnam War, of women shucking their bras, of the Black Panthers and the Weathermen, of alcohol, marijuana, and LSD. There was great music and incredible changes in styles, from haircuts to colorful clothing. The art world blossomed. Everyone partied. Hell, life was one big party.

Everybody was committed to something. They were committed to getting stoned. To protesting the War. To traveling and seeing the world so that they could change it for the better. To having sex as often as possible and with as many people as possible. To finding all new sorts of cultures and experiences from Africa to Tibet, and from Japan to the Southwest American Indians.

In one sense everyone was so serious, "so fucking serious," as Sam remembered his friends say. The adjective "fucking" was used in so many different ways to express so many different ideas and shades of meaning.

"Can you fucking believe it?!!!!"

"Fuckin' A".

"Fuck this shit."

"She is so fucking beautiful!!"

"Is this the fucking place we're supposed to meet them?"

"I saw this huge, I mean HUGE fucking cockroach!"

Sam was not one to use profanity lightly. He seldom used four letter words when trying to tell a story or explain something. Not that he felt above anyone else or felt smarter or more educated. No, that wasn't the case. He just loved the English language and reveled in using the right words with the right meaning for the right feel or the right sound. To him, it would shorten, cheapen, or somehow diminish the impact of whatever he was saying if he resigned himself to using the simplest of simple words to try to convey what he was feeling. It just wasn't right. It just wasn't him.

He couldn't bring himself to just say, "Fuckin 'A, man!" No. If he was to agree with someone on something, it meant that he had thought some things out and had some opinion or experience or proof to back up his affirmative support.

Rather, he would reply with something like, "Yup that is such a phenomenal idea. It reminds me of how the Athenians would get together at the market place and argue their ideas publically until they either reached a consensus or put the idea to a vote."

"She is so fucking beautiful!" would only cheapen his perception of the object of his admiration and desire. He might use the word "beautiful" but then elaborate on that with sensitivity.

"She has that quality in her face that makes you want to look at her for hours. She's not picture perfect, and she has that slight flaw in her right eyebrow, where she must have had a bruise when she was little. But that little irregularity begs me to lose myself in her eyes, and watch her lips as she forms her words. My time is her time, my world stops when she notices me and talks to me."

Not to say that Sam was an effete snob or an aloof intellectual. Often, when questioned about his "clean" speech, he would explain, "I like to talk, I like to express myself. I don't like to just use shorthand or shortcuts to get my point across. Still, there are times when four letter words or swearing are the only thing that will do. If I were to accidentally drop a large concrete block on my big toe, well, there are only a few words that will do. And I can tell you it wouldn't be shucks or golly. I think in that instant, 'holy fucking shit' or 'Oh, fuck!' would be quite appropriate."

So, Sam had had no specific destination to which to springboard from college life to the eventual real world, as those over thirty loved to remind his generation about. To Sam, the "real world" was drinking with his friends at the Salty Dog in Ithaca, dancing to the sounds of Buffalongo, and careening to their break song, "Dancin' in the Moonlight". That song, originally written by them, was eventually sold to King Crimson who rearranged it without the half step slide up to another key. Even now, Sam could remember back to that song reverberating in his head as he danced with one friendly girl after another, swirling them around and around, while alcohol and THC molecules played hide and seek within their brains. When the band took a needed break the dancers would all go outside into the warm summer evening and suck face, fondle and grope each other, and smoke weed.

Now here he was in Utica, New York, a physician practicing back in his hometown after being away for years of study and a stint in the military. He had worked a long time as an emergency physician and recently made the decision to retire from the chaos and stress of St. Clare's Hospital's ER. His personal and professional life were now more stable, and in the last couple of years was building up a good osteopathic general medical practice. He was very satisfied with that decision and new path in his life. Life was good.

CHAPTER 6

A Deathbed Confession

Zofia looked at the windowsill. There, in a thin tall vase stood a lone flower, a rose, silhouetted by the window frame. She could see a darkening sky beyond the glass pane. Earlier there had been azure blue skies with wispy white clouds liltingly floating above the horizon. As the sun descended below that horizon, a gray pallor slid over the skyscape and thick dark puffy clouds replaced the earlier, delicate ones. These were storm clouds. This evening they seemed almost menacing, foreboding. No thunder yet, no lighting, but Zofia sensed that this change in the climate might nevertheless elicit some unwelcome surprises.

A clump of phlegm lay stuck in her throat. She tried to swallow but couldn't seem to raise it up. She leaned over to her left and reached for a small brown medicine bottle of expectorant, on the side table. She took a couple of sips straight from the bottle, bypassing the spoon that lay nearby.

She tried now, weakly, to cough and bring up that nasty mucus plug that was threatening to choke her. She reached for her throat with one hand and tried again to cough.

The door opened and in came Sam Petrie. Seeing his mother gasping and holding her throat, he quickly came around to her side of the bed and began gently rubbing her back.

"Are you ok, Mom? Can you talk?"

Zofia made an attempt to mouth some words but it was quickly evident that she couldn't breathe. Her tongue had slipped back in her throat and was blocking her airway.

Sam gently put his arms around her waist, at the same time lifting her up and sideways on the bed. With one swift compression, inward and upward over her stomach, his doubled hands pushed into her abdomen. Out came a burst of air and some mucus. She started to cough and took a few deep erratic breaths. She settled back onto the mattress and Sam helped her to rearrange her pillows to let her sit up at about a forty-five degree angle.

"My, my, Sam. So that's why we sent you to medical school," Zofia said, attempting to make light of her choking and Sam's Heimlich maneuver. "So you could squeeze your mother until she popped!"

"You were choking."

"I know that. And I'm thankful. I just wanted to calm my nerves with a little joking. I haven't had that happen before. I really felt as if I might not make it."

She took another deep breath and lay back down on the bed, her head propped up by a few pillows.

"Well, now I can breathe. In that sense I'm better. Now, but…well, you know, I don't have to tell you, that as time goes on, I won't be getting better. As Dr. Koscinski explained, I will get weaker and weaker. After a while I won't be able to swallow or breathe too well. I'll be losing more weight. And eventually I'll stop breathing."

Sam felt more than a little uneasy, listening to his mother describe truthfully and objectively what lay ahead and in store for her. He had seen enough patients with a similar diagnosis during his hospital neurology training to know that the final outcome was not nice and it wasn't very comfortable.

"Mom, I know what A.L.S. is. The doctor went over this with you and Dad a few times already, right after the neurologists made the diagnosis. Lou Gehrig's disease. And I don't need to be reminded. Remember, I'm the doctor in the family."

"A.L.S. Amyotrophic Lateral Sclerosis. What an odd name. It almost seems as if I could have had a choice on how I wanted the disease to present itself to me." She folded her arms now and looked ahead as if she was seeing some items in front of her, things that she could choose from. She feigned looking from one item to the next.

"Hmm. Lateral? No, what about central or anterior? So many choices! And sclerosis, why that means that something has become very hard and tough. Well, I may be a tough old bird myself, but I'd like to have this thing be soft and delicate. I think I'll have the amyotrophic anterior puffball. Yes, that's it, an A.A.P.!" She put her hands together like a little child and rocked her head back and forth on the pillows. She let out a little giggle that soon became a gentle sobbing. She took a few deep breathes to compose herself.

Sam put his arms around her. "I love you, Mom. Dad loves you. We all love you. We'll be here for you, everyday, for whatever you need."

"I know that. Thanks. I know I'm lucky to have you all."

Her face took a solemn turn as she lowered her hands. Her eyes closed as she took another deep breath. "Sam. You know I love you, don't you?"

He was surprised at the question. He took her hand and squeezed it gently. "Of course I know. And I love you just as deeply. You're the best mother that anyone could ask for. You…"

"Please, I have to get this out. It's very hard for me. I need to tell you some things. Some very important things. Important to me, and maybe important to you, too. I need to know that you understand that I love you with all my heart, I have always loved you and I've never kept anything away from you. I've never kept any secrets of anything away from you."

Sam didn't quite understand what she was getting at. He thought that she might possibly be reacting to medications, or to some depression, or to the difficulty of accepting that she was dying. He listened respectfully and compassionately.

"I'm so ashamed. And so angry with myself. But I did it to protect you, to protect us. And now here I am lying in bed with this goddamned 'puffball' disease and I realize that I have to tell you. It's so difficult and I'm ashamed for not having told you a long time ago. But as a mother who has inflicted pain on someone else, I feel so guilty. I need to get this off my chest…and you need to understand it all. And I'm asking you for forgiveness."

Sam was truly confused now. He was certain that his mother was suffering from some deep-seated depression. "Mom. Relax. I know this must be awful tough on you as it is on Dad, and me and Helen and the kids, and everyone in our family. But you're a wonderful mother, a wonderful person. You don't need to apologize or explain anything."

"Please, I need you to forgive me."

Not knowing what else to say, Sam softly, and with sincerity, replied, "I love you. Whatever you think you might have done, it's in the past. I forgive you. We all forgive you."

She settled back once again onto the pillows propped up behind her. She closed her eyes and took a few deep breaths. She composed herself and looked directly into her son's eyes. Sam sensed the faintest hint of fear in those beautiful eyes as she started to speak.

"My dear little boy, Sam. My one and only child. My little Samuel who I have brought up all these years with all my love.

"Remember, I used to tell you that I loved you so much that I would never give you away, no mater what was offered to me."

Sam remembered, with a smile. He had heard her repeat this funny little scenario many times as he was growing up.

"They could offer me a diamond as big as you were, even bigger. I would never give you up, never. I loved you more than anyone could imagine."

He nodded his head, remembering her telling that vignette many times over as he was growing up.

"So please understand that I love you dearly from the bottom of my heart. I would never want to hurt you. I would never want to lie to you. I would never want to keep anything away from you. And now I need to get this off my chest, as I am dying, and you have a right to know. I feel so guilty. I am asking you to forgive me for not telling you all of this sooner."

"Mom, please, you're working yourself up. Look at you. Your hands are shaking. You're not making any sense to me. And I told you, Mom, what ever it is, I love you, and I forgive you, whatever you did."

"It isn't what I did, Sam. It was what I didn't do. And for that, as a mother, I feel ashamed and guilty."

Again she took a deep breath. Not able to contain herself any more and knowing that she had built up this moment to the point that she had to directly confront Sam with the truth, something she had harbored within herself for years.

"Sam. You are not who you think you are. You are not who we told you that you were. You were adopted. I took you as my own child and adopted you when you were a very little baby."

This was a shock to him. Never in his life had he even imagined that he was anyone other than who he thought he was. William and Zofia Petrie were his parents. He had been told many times that he had been born in England right after the war and that the three of them had immigrated to the United States shortly thereafter. He sat next to his mother, at the edge of the bed, in silence, pondering what she had just said. After a short while he spoke.

"This truly does come as a surprise, uh, a shock to me. I don't know what to say. I think you could have told me this earlier. I mean I'm a grown man now with a family. But even years ago, when I was younger, a teenager I mean, I would have been able to handle it. I mean, lots of kids are adopted. But I don't know why you're now so emotional or ashamed or feeling so guilty about it. It's OK. I'm OK with it. I love you. There's no need for you to feel guilty."

"Oh, Sam! You are such a wonderful, loving child. I love you so much." She grabbed some tissues from a box on the side table, and wiped away tears that had welled up in her eyes. "I do so appreciate your understanding. But even though it is so hard, now, to tell you that, the guilt that I carry with me goes far beyond that. Far beyond keeping from you the fact that you were adopted. Only a mother who loves her child as much as I love you can understand the pain, the shame and guilt that I'm carrying."

He looked into his mother's teary eyes with a quizzical look. His expression told her to continue with her explanations. He sensed that there was more.

"The world I lived in as a young woman, in Poland, was a terrible time. It was a crazy time. I was one of a group of volunteers involved with a woman in Warsaw who was helping to protect and hide little Jewish children from the Germans. She was a health worker. Sendler was her name. Irena Sendler.

"One day she came to me and asked that I care for a young boy whom they had just secretly taken out of the Warsaw Ghetto, where hundreds of people were dying every day. You were that little boy."

Sam listened in silence. Incredulous.

"Your mother was a young Jewish girl who had fallen in love with a young reserve officer in the Polish army. He had been a watchmaker in Warsaw before being mobilized into the service just before the invasion of Poland in 1939.

"So young people back then, in love, were not any different than young people nowadays, although not so open. But we weren't prudes either. One thing must have led to another because your mother, your real mother…"

Zofia stopped for a moment. She cleared her throat and again took a slow, deep breath and sighed as she exhaled. She corrected herself.

She continued, "… your birth mother. She got pregnant and then she had you. She was arrested by the Germans and taken to the ghetto while she was carrying you. You were born there in November 1942, on the sixteenth. That much Miss Sendler told me.

"You were only one month old when you were secretly taken out of the ghetto and I got you. I think you might have been drugged and hidden in a toolbox or some other box on the sanitation truck and taken out under the eyes of the Germans. Or maybe they were bribed. I don't know. And I didn't care. You were this lovely little bundle, this cute little boy, not so healthy looking, kind of skinny. But you could cry! Oh, could you cry!"

"What happened to her? What happened to…my birth mother?" Sam didn't want to offend Zofia, quickly realizing that she was sensitive to the use of the word "real".

Zofia hesitated for a long while. Sam could feel the quiet, almost like a distant drumbeat. Her pause was so quiet, it was deafening.

"Like so many of the people of the Ghetto, after the Warsaw uprising of the Jews in 1943, they were sent to the German concentrations camps. Places like Treblinka and Majdanek. Not everybody though. Before the uprising some of the Jews were sent other places including to the one place most people hear most about…Auschwitz, west of Krakow."

Sam was quiet. He then said quietly, "So, she died in Auschwitz."

Zofia put her hands to her face. She started to sob. Sam felt a sadness come over him as well, and mixed emotions flooded through his mind. So much in such a short space to time. His parents were not his parents, he was adopted. He was from another ethnic group. His family history was not his real family history. You're not who you think you are, Zofia had said to him.

She sat up suddenly in the bed. She stared at him directly, with seriousness and a look resembling defiance in her piercing eyes.

"No. She did not die there. She survived that horrible place. Somehow." Again she paused, collecting her thoughts.

"She survived that. And she survived the war. I received a letter from her in the early part of the 1950's when you were about ten years old. I was shocked. I didn't even know how she could have known who I was or how she got hold of my address. I only learned later that Irena Sendler had put the names of all those little children she and her group saved into glass jars and buried them. There were the Jewish names of the children, the Christian names that they were given, and names of the people or families to whom the children were taken for safekeeping.

"After the war, Irena and her friends tried to find any surviving Jewish parents or relatives and tried to reunite the children with their families. It was sad but obvious to learn that most of the parents had been killed."

"But not her.... not my mother," Sam muttered.

"Not your mother," she repeated. "I later received a long distance call from a woman who identified herself as the lady in the letter, your mother. She wanted to take you back. She wanted us to meet and to have me give you over to her."

Sam looked up at Zofia. He waited.

"I told her that I had raised you as my own son. I told her that it would be a shock to you, and that I couldn't give you up....even to her, even to your .... birth mother.

"I was now your real mother. I had nursed you when you were sick. I had held you when you were hurt and crying. I had changed so many diapers, warmed so many bottles of formula. I had taken you to school every day. We celebrated so many Christmases and birthdays together. I had built up so many hopes of a wonderful future for you. I was not about to give it up because...she...wanted to take you back, to take you away from me."

She buried her face in her hands and started to cry.

"I am so ashamed of what I did. I feel so guilty, and I've kept that guilt in me all these years. But I would do the same thing again, even now, even after telling you these things. Even after realizing what an awful person I am for having kept you away from...her.

"I told William what I had done. He advised me to keep quiet about all of it too. He said, let them come, they'll have to step over my dead body before I let anyone take Sam away from us.

"I was afraid so many times that someone would come to the house or to the school and take you away from me. Or that some lawyers would send me a letter, taking me to court to rip you away from me. I have carried this fear, this guilt, this shame inside of me all these years.

"I know it was, and is, so selfish, but I did it because I love you so much. We had such a good life here to offer you. I didn't know if you would be taken away to some strange home and probably to some strange country. Maybe even back to Poland. Back then it was still controlled by the Communists. I dreaded even the thought of you being taken like that."

After a while Sam asked, "So, did you have any further letters or calls from her?"

"No calls. There were letters, some, sporadically. Always the same thing, her asking for us to meet, for us to give you up. And then the letters stopped after a while. That was it. I didn't have any other communications with her. Or anyone."

"So you don't know where she is or what happened to her?"

"No."

"And what about my birth father. Do you know anything about him?" Sam asked.

"There was nothing in the letter or the phone call, later, about him. A lot of young Polish soldiers died. They died in the initial invasion by the Germans. Many were captured and beaten, overworked or starved to death in the concentration camps. The Soviets sent many of them to Siberia. A lot of survivors joined with the British and were killed in the Normandy invasion or fighting the Germans under General Anders until the end of the war. It's anyone's guess what could have happened."

"He was a watchmaker," Sam mumbled. "I'd like to see the letter she sent you. Do you still have it?"

Zofia looked at him, with furrowed brow. "I do. I have it in the attic with other letters that I've saved over the years. Sam. I know this is a complete surprise and a shock to you. Forgive me for what I've done. I have suffered so long and so hard and I've had to live with my decision."

"I wonder if she might still be alive."

"Sam. Please. Don't. She's probably dead. I'm sure she must be dead by now."

"She would be close to eighty years old now. A lot of people are alive and well at that age."

"Sam. Please. Don't get started with this. Please just leave it alone. For me. You might be opening up a whole can of worms that is better left alone."

Now Sam looked directly into Zofia's eyes. With a tinge of disbelief in his voice he asked, "Are you telling me everything?"

"Everything. Everything I told you is the truth. There's nothing more to know. Leave it alone, Sam. Go on with your life. I'm sure she would have wanted it that way. And William and I want the best for you. Leave it alone."

They didn't talk any more about this matter. As the weeks wore on, Zofia slowly deteriorated, her breathing became more labored. It was more and more difficult to complete her sentences. The proud, active, humorous, strong lady that everyone had known was now slowly fading from them. Yet she bore this change with dignity. She had told her family not to feel sorry for her, that they needed to accept this as the other end of what she called "the spectrum of life". She was being blessed now, in death, by being surrounded with a family that loved her, as she had been all of her life. She had a strong belief in God, and this gave her strength and the gratitude for what God had given her as she grew and experienced and lived her own life. She had signed all of the necessary DNR papers, making her wishes specifically known to all family members that she did not want any resuscitation measures done to her, except to naturally ease any discomfort.

She died peacefully while in a coma. There were no apparent signs of pain or stress. One morning, with William, Sam, Helen and the two grandchildren, Nathan and Elaine by her side, she took a few last, deep breathes and then stopped breathing. Forever.

Sam stared at his mother's face. Her eyes were half opened and her dry tongue showed through her slightly opened mouth. He could see now, vividly, how much weight, how much muscle mass she had actually lost over the year as she was slowly dying.

He walked over to the window of the bedroom and looked out onto the freshly cut lawn and the clear blue skies. A vase which husband William had filled every few days with fresh roses made Sam remember the lyrics of one of Zofia's poems:

Silently closing the door
The doctor turned around and said,
"She won't be staying with us anymore"

And on the sill the flower slowly faded,
And all of the petals were torn,
They fell like rain to the floor
As she went.

CHAPTER 7

Zofia's Funeral

It was as if Sam was being taunted by a forbidden fruit. Ever since Zofia had sternly advised him not to try and find out about his birth mother, he was obsessed with thoughts about her. What was she like? What was his own real family history through her? What had she endured? What had happened to her? Were there any other relatives? And the final question that burned like an ember, refusing to be extinguished by reason or resignation...could she still be alive?

Zofia's funeral was attended by people from all over the Mohawk Valley. Some people came out of respect for Sam, who was well known in the area for his many years of work as an emergency physician at St. Clare's Hospital in Utica and now as an osteopathic physician in private practice. His adoptive mother however, was also well known in her own right.

She hadn't been shy. Zofia was a very caring person and had been involved with many civic and charitable organizations throughout her life. Shortly after she and husband William had left England, where they had met and married, they settled in West Utica on Lenox Avenue. A large community of Polish immigrants had settled there after the war. The couple joined the Polish Community Club on Columbia Street, where Zofia was able meet others who had also fled their now Communist controlled country and were building a life in the New World.

Zofia and William went to weddings, parties, and dinners almost every weekend when Sam was a little boy. Every "Sylvester", or New Year's Eve, they would listen to a Polish band playing polkas and waltzes or a polonaise. They ate soup and salad, and herring and bigos and pork cutlets.

They drank wisznowka and vodka and danced into the early morning hours, exhausted but happy.

Zofia was a congregant of Holy Trinity Church on Lincoln Ave, in West Utica. The church had been built by Polish immigrants at the turn of the 20th century and was long a hub of that immigrant community's heart and soul. Weddings and funerals, holy communions and holidays were celebrated or commemorated at Holy Trinity. The priests were visible at all social functions of the Polish community.

Down the street at Bazan's Bakery, one could buy fresh bread or Polish cookies, *czasteczki*, and specialty cakes or tortes filled with fruit preserves and topped with crushed almonds. Nearby was the Skiba V.F.W. Post and the Francis Street Veteran's Club where the kombatanti, or Polish World War II veterans, would meet for a drink, socialize, have a meal or a party. Zofia and William Petrie were "regulars" as they mingled with her "people".

Hers was a quiet ceremony at the Ryzek Funeral Home, near her beloved church. The open casket was surrounded with flowers sent by friends, admirers, and well-wishers. It was hard for Sam and his father to stand for hours and greet all of the friends and acquaintances that came to pray, offer their sympathy, and pay their respect.

The light in the viewing room was subdued with large candles placed at either end of the casket. People came and went, stopping at the padded kneeler to say a prayer for the soul of their departed friend. One couple that came and stayed for the entire evening was Saul and Eva Bielewski.

The Bielewski's had been very close friends of the family for as long as Sam could remember. They were like an aunt and uncle, *wujek* and *cioca*, to him. They had been a regular fixture at the Petrie home for all kinds of parties and celebrations and family milestones, as Sam was growing up.

Now Zofia lay in quiet repose, the life extinguished from her frail body. No longer would anyone hear her warm, confident, joyful voice with its enchanting, mild sing-song inflections that made it a pleasure to hear her speak. And when she spoke, people listened. She was caring and courteous but she could also be loud and brash and very direct when she felt it necessary to speak her mind. She loved to laugh and she loved to joke. More often than not, there was a smile on her face. At times she would hum as she worked at some household chore. Oftentimes she would stop what she was doing and just sing a song, to cheer up herself and everyone else around her.

In her hands William had placed her diary, locked, with its little key still in place. In her right hand she was clutching her favorite ink pen, a gift from William when they first met at a department store in London, as if the final chapters of her life were not yet completed.

CHAPTER 8

How William and Zofia Met

William spoke some Polish, having learned the melodious, yet at times difficult, Eastern European language while stationed in Germany during the war and England afterwards. He knew enough of the language one day after meeting Zofia in the famous London department store, Harrods, where she was working, to invite her to a USO dance. He had been walking through the various departments and had chanced upon seeing what he thought was the most beautiful girl he had ever laid eyes on.

She had shoulder-length auburn hair with slight curls that framed her oval face like a picture frame. He gazed into her huge brown eyes as hers met his as well. He was thrilled by her momentary pause as she peered directly at him in a most inviting way. A broad smile broke out across her face as she displayed the most perfect gleaming teeth and lips he had seen in all the long months he had been soldiering through France, Germany, and England. One would not think that seeing a woman's teeth would conjure up any feelings or images of beauty or stimulate any fantasies in a young soldier's mind, but dental care had been neglected in Germany and was well known to be atrocious in England. The famous actor, Terry Thomas, could have been a poster boy for the dental situation in England, with his crooked teeth with a large gap between his two upper central incisors. No, Zofia did not look like the actor's relative. She was instead a picture of health. She had smooth, unblemished skin and beautifully rounded cheeks that flushed and got rounder as she smiled at William, which was often, both then at their first meeting and all through most of the rest of her life.

William had stumbled upon her as he was aimlessly walking through Harrods with no particular items in mind. This was just one of his many "walks" that he loved to take wherever he was whether in destroyed Berlin or partially rebuilt London. He found himself staring at this wonderfully bright, smiling young girl with a thick Polish accent. She put the finishing touches of frosting on a large, artistically decorated cake. He watched as she deftly finished making a large red rose off to one side of the top of the cake, put the tube of red frosting on the table, and coquettishly licked a scrap of frosting off of one finger. Her gaze returned to William.

He hadn't stopped staring at her. Now he felt foolish, like a young boy looking through a pet shop window before Christmas, watching a cute little puppy that he would have loved to take home with him. Yet this was no cute little puppy, and he was not longing for a pet. He was startled to feel stirrings in his heart as he had never felt before in his entire life.

William was a very handsome young man and must have struck a gallant pose in his neat military uniform and cap. He was no stranger to women and had had many girl friends as well as fleeting romances. But at this moment, as he stood staring at this young woman with frosting on her finger and a light, lilting giggle, warm smile and gorgeous eyes, he knew that this woman, this moment, this feeling inside him, was different than he had ever experienced.

"Are you buying a cake for a lady friend?" Zofia asked playfully as she put the final touches on the cake with various colored frostings. "I can help you."

William, who was never shy and never at a loss for words, was nevertheless taken aback by the suddenness of her request. Like someone lost in a dream, with water splashed on their face and coffee firmly offered to wake them up, he stood looking at her, then at the cake she had just so expertly decorated, and then back to those gorgeous eyes that pulled him in.

William, a student of Greek mythology in his younger days back home, was instantly reminded of Ulysses and the story of the Sirens and their inescapably beautiful singing. However, whereas the Sirens would bring sailors and Ulysses and his crew to their destruction and death, this woman standing before him and smiling with the warmest, most inviting eyes, had most definitely awoken in him a spark of joy as he had never felt before. It felt right, so right. He knew instantly, and without any further words, that he wanted to spend the rest of his life with her.

While slogging through France after the successful Normandy invasion, and on into Germany, he had given up thoughts of a future. At times he was living as if in a dream. He watched as friends that he had trained with in England died on either side of him, by bullet or bomb. He saw new recruits, fresh up from the rear, not survive their first day on the front lines, they just hadn't learned how to keep their heads down. In Germany, in Dachau and scores of other Nazi concentration camps that the Allies liberated, he saw emaciated, starving, dying people with eyes sunken in their heads because there was no more body fat to give shape to their orbits. He sorrowfully watched as many of these poor victims of the Nazis were given food, which they greedily gobbled up. Some would vomit or cry out as they clutched their stomachs, not having tasted, eaten or swallowed a real meal for months or years, suddenly lay down and die.

William had seen so much. He had seen more than he could ever imagine, or ever want to imagine, courtesy of the Second World War. He had memories and experiences he would much rather have forgotten.

Now here was this young woman, this cute little Polish girl with a trim figure and angelic voice and taunting smile, bringing out emotions that he hadn't felt in a long time. He felt hope stir inside of him now, a strong feeling, like waves washing over his very soul, crashing over the rocks and sharp, jagged coral reefs that were the hurt and pain and hopelessness that had built up in him over the past few years. Washed away almost instantly were the memories of despair, loneliness, anger, confusion, shame, and the stink of rotting flesh and of death. Zofia embodied in him hope and promises of a life renewed. He was unmistakably, without a doubt, absolutely and most certainly in love. This was no infatuation or a young man's lust based on fluctuating hormones. No, here was a magical moment where two people meeting for the very first time, were bound together in mind and spirit. Here was the indescribable moment of love and commitment and hope that poets and artists and writers had been trying to express in their art forms for centuries. Successful to varying degrees, those artists could have used William and Zofia as their models.

Zofia had looked up at this handsome young man standing before her when she had offered her assistance. She was also suddenly taken aback by a most unusual feeling within her as she looked into his pale blue eyes and comfortably accepted his inquisitive stare. His right cheek was slightly rounded, with a dimple as it accepted the slightly upturned curve of his lip as he offered a half smile. She felt her pulse quicken and she unexpectedly took in a deep breath as if to drink in the sight of this exciting young man standing in front of her.

She had been working at Harrods for the past year, shuttling from one department to another and most recently assigned to the cakes and cookies department. She had assisted customers from all walks of life and in all shapes and sizes. There had been fat ladies in the lingerie department, young couples in the toy section, aristocratic well dressed middle aged men with hat and cane in the meat and poultry department. There had been young, sometimes handsome, dashing young men in the men's wear department. In a most professional and courteous manner she had assisted them all. Of course she had her own personal opinions on all of these patrons, sometimes good, sometimes bad, and sometimes even rude thoughts. But never had she entertained even the slightest thought that she might wish to become more acquainted with any of them. William, on the other hand, was an entirely different matter.

She originally had found an apartment in the Polish section of Swindon, where many Poles had immigrated during the war. She later moved to Hammersmith in west London and shared an apartment with her friend, Agnieszka. Zofia had come from a different world than the people she catered to at Harrod's. During the last year of the war, she had fled westward into Germany and beyond as the Russians advanced through Poland, crushing the German army as they went. She was able to cross into British occupied Holland and eventually made her way to London. She walked with lines of refugees and rode on horse drawn carts when she was lucky enough to be offered a ride. Once she found a bicycle at the edge of a wooded area that was still serviceable with inflated tires. She slept in the forests or in abandoned homes.

But she was never really alone. This part of her life she had kept apart from Sam. She had always started his life's story in London. She had told her little boy that his life started there and that William Petrie was his father and that she was a post-war bride. She did tell him as much as a mother might tell her son about their courtship and their marriage and their plans to move to America to resume a "normal" life. There was a large gap in the early part of Sam's history that she had kept from him and only revealed that to him as she lay dying at home, shortly after the Petrie family reunion.

As for Zofia, life would never return to any real semblance of normalcy. She had lost her country, a country that was originally overrun and destroyed by the Germans and their Nazi fanatics from the West, with an invasion on September 1,1939. About 5 years later the Russians began scoring victory after victory against the Nazis, who had also invaded their country, and pushed back across Poland in 1945 from the East, liberating Zofia and her people, only to become just as ruthless an invader. The communist regime, set up in Warsaw after the war by Stalin and his cronies from Moscow, set about rounding up Poles who had fought as partisans in the hills, or in the underground resistance, or as soldiers who had fought with the Allies. They were called "bandits" by the newly installed Polish communist government. They were arrested and charged with treason against the new communist order. There were trials and executions and many men and women were sent off to the cold Siberian work camps never to be heard from again.

One of these most famous victims of communist repression was Witold Pilecki, a handsome young cavalry officer in World War I, who fought in the Polish army during the September Campaign, or German invasion of Poland in 1939. He formed the Secret Polish Army, one of the earliest underground movements against the Nazi occupation. He voluntarily let himself be captured so that he could be sent to Auschwitz where he saw first hand the murdering of Poles and the extermination of the Jews. He was smuggled out of Auschwitz with the help of the Underground and wrote the "Witold Report" which convinced the Allies that the Holocaust was real and actually happening.

CHAPTER 9

Zofia and the Polish Priest in Warsaw

Zofia had been attending business school in the Polish capital at the outbreak of the war and the German invasion in September, 1939. For the next few years she was able to find work as a secretary at a large Polish fuel supply business in the capital, Warsaw. Its new manager, a German named Otto Bauermann, had been placed there by the occupying authorities. As she told friends in later years, she was "never interested in politics" and had no interest in the intrigues and clandestine operations that were taking place all around here. Yet even with her naiveté to things political it was impossible for her to ignore the horror that was taking place around her.

There were times when she would walk the streets from her apartment to work, watching as the city awoke from its restless sleep. There were people and German soldiers and officers, riding on the few still operational trams, and merchants at their tables or kiosks, selling vegetables, kitchenware or shoes. All seemed safe and routine. They had survived another day without murder or reprisals.

Then suddenly she might turn a corner and see a dozen people hanging from street lamps, executed by the Germans in response to a raid by the "bandits" or Polish underground. For every German soldier killed, the Nazis would round up 10 people off the streets and, after brutal interrogations, would hang them the next morning. It was not unusual to hear gunshots in the distance somewhere in the city on an almost daily basis.

Zofia described a scene once, in later years, to Sam when he was already an adult in America, that haunted her and caused her sometimes to have nightmares. She had left work at the Polish fuel supply company on a Friday, having just been paid, and was walking home. She decided to take a different route home because she wanted to stop at a small pastry shop, Cafe Blikle, on Nowy Swiat Street and buy some sweets to take home to her parents and her sister. The day had gone well and she was pleased with how quickly and efficiently she had completed the many clerical duties she had been given that day. Her boss, Mr. Bauermann even complimented her on her "professionalism". She thought to herself that all Germans couldn't be bad. She was treated well and with respect and she actually enjoyed her work.

Zofia turned the corner of a huge apartment building off Nowy Swiat, hoping to stop off at the cuckiernie confectionary store for some *paczki*, fruit filled donuts dusted with powdered sugar, and some cookies. Her eyes riveted suddenly on a macabre scene unfoldng before her eyes. There in the middle of the sidewalk was a pile of people laying in contorted poses on the ground or against a wall. Some were still moving. She could hear a few sobs and some moaning. There were German Wermacht with rifles and machine guns ready, cordoning off the scene of execution from the shocked and angry Polish bystanders. There was an acrid smell of gunpowder mixed with the sweet, meaty odor of blood that lingered over this pile of victims. Zofia could see the holes and chinks in the plaster of the walls where the bullets had finally stopped.

A thin, young officer with a pointed nose and a large cyst on his left cheek, dressed in a neat grey German uniform and shiny black boots, took out his Lugar and proceeded to shoot each victim in the head, the final coupe to ensure that they were all dead. After a few more shots, he took off his officer's cap and wiped the beaded sweat off his forehead. It was a warm day, and this simple, offhanded gesture made it seem as if he was hard at work.

He returned to his task, firing once again, another bullet into each body, man, woman, and even a young boy who couldn't have been more than ten years old. Satisfied that his work was done, he motioned with a flick of his hand for the soldiers to disperse the crowd. This they did with efficiency, as they had apparently done this many times before.

Zofia now had lost her appetite for sweets. She only wanted to run home and tell her parents of one more horror that was slowly squeezing her city, her people, and her country, into the depths of a hell that she could never have imagined. Instead she walked quickly and with determined steps further up Nowy Swiat and entered into a nearby church to pray for those just murdered Poles.

In the distance she could see the Royal Palace, off Castle Square, near the Warsaw Old Town or Stare Miasto. She felt confusion, anguish, and anger develop within her in one great wave. Her head was pounding with rage and her heart was heavy with grief. What was happening to her life? To Poland? Would she one day be put up against the wall, as those poor souls had been, and shot as well? Her parents? Her sister?

Poland had had a long and glorious history of kings and queens, of art and music. At one time Poland had been the largest country in Europe. Her fertile fields had produced so well, and such an excess of grain that there needed to be a system of brokers and merchants to deal with the money generated. At that time there were three social classes: the clergy (who had no business skills), the aristocracy (who couldn't manage money as lending and the charging of interest for profit was seen as the crime of usury), and the peasants (who owned no land nor titles, and hence no political or economic influence). To that end, Polish kings in the Middle Ages had invited Jewish bankers and accountants from other countries, where they had been persecuted, to come to Poland and run businesses. Poland offered them religious tolerance and even social autonomy. They could have their own districts in which to live, to thrive, to practice their religion, have their own schools and synagogues, and their own police and civil administration. By the middle of the 16th century three-quarters of all European Jews lived in Poland, and the country was called "Paradise for the Jews". They settled in Krakow in the Kazimierz district and later in other cities throughout Poland. Then, in 1795, during the last Partition, Poland was divided up among Prussia, Austria-Hungary and Russia. It did not regain independence and status as a country again until after World War I. The country had arisen from the ashes of repression and political annihilation and enjoyed democracy and a thriving economy. Life between the two World Wars, Zofia often told Sam, as he was growing up, had been good.

Zofia walked into the dark church. There were candles lit off to one side at an offerary. There was no one in the church. It was quiet except for the sound of her own soft footsteps on the stone tiles. She peered into the darkness and saw a large wooden cross with a beautifully carved figure of the suffering Jesus. The eyes had been made to appear half open and as Zofia walked down the aisle she felt as if he were looking directly at her. She settled into a pew off to one side and sat quietly, not knowing what to think or what to do next. She had never been so confused, so undirected, so unfocused in all of her life. A thought ran through her mind like a wisp of morning mist across a barren field just before the sun rose to burn away the moisture; like tears wiped from one's eyes.

One thought arose, as if the statue were speaking to her. "As your Jesus hangs here in perpetual agony, having followed the commands of his heavenly father to surrender to his fate as ordained by scripture and God, what have you done to make yourself worthy of this sacrifice? What have you done to redeem this world, to redeem Humanity?" Zofia was shocked by these thoughts. They came not as distinct words or pictures, but as feelings. She just knew in her heart and understood what these messages meant.

"Am I to take up a weapon and kill these Germans as they have killed us?" she wondered. She knew she was not up to that. She was no warrior. She was no hero. She was just a scared young girl who had only recently finished school, had been a girl scout, loved going to parties and to dance all evening and be flattered by the good looking young boys who vied for her company and to steal an occasional kiss.

She was so deep in thought and prayer and wrestled with so many conflicting, passionate feelings of anger, hatred, revulsion and fear that she didn't hear when someone approached the pew and sat down next to her. Suddenly aware of their presence, she turned to see a priest kneeling sitting next to her, hands folded in front of him, a rosary in his hands.

"Are you well, my child?" he asked sincerely.

"I am not, Father. I am so, so sick." She shook her head and covered her face as tears streamed from her eyes and covered her cheeks. "I am sick of everything that I see here in Warsaw. I am sick of lying to myself that everything will soon be all right. And I am sick of the killing, and all the horrible stories I hear of what is going on all over Poland. Of people disappearing. People being tortured and hung and executed." She was sobbing now but knew she had to keep talking and get this awful tension out of her mind or she would collapse.

She tried to compose herself and slowed down her speech somewhat so as not to stumble over her words and thoughts. "Of what is happening to the Jews as they are rounded up and sent off, never to return. And I hear terrible stories which I can't imagine are true. That the Nazis are slowly killing our people to make way for their own Germans. And the Jews are being murdered all over Europe and their property, their money, everything, is being taken away from them, to clean all of them off the face of the Earth! I can't believe that. I just can't believe that anyone can be that cruel.

The priest shifted in his position in the pew. He glanced around to see that no one else had entered the church. Satisfying himself that they were alone, he replied.

"It does seem that God has abandoned us at this moment. But I don't believe it for a moment. Our loving God seems to make his appearance usually during the worst of circumstances."

She looked up at him and stared between her tears. It truly did feel to her that God had abandoned them all. The priest continued.

"When life is good and everything seems to be going our way, we don't give much thought to God. We don't seem to need him. It's like an old friend that we haven't communicated with for a long time, but only call on when we need his help. And sometimes when we are in trouble or in need, that old friend of ours just seems to crop up right at the time that we need him the most. I think of God like that. He's always around, we just don't need him at the moment. But He's there, off to one side. Like the loving Father that he always has been and is, all we have to do is ask His help and there He is, ready to help his in His way and on His terms."

"What am I to do, Father? I pray, I go to church with my mother and father and my sister. I try to be a good person. I've had my Holy Communion and my Confirmation. I am a good Catholic. What more am I to do?"

The priest smiled and managed a faint chuckle. He shrugged his shoulders. "Oh, child. I too struggle with those questions myself every day. Look at me. I'm a priest. I've studied the Bible, I am loyal to the Church, to the Gospels, and I have pledged my life to God. Yet, I ask these same questions as you are right now.

"We are in the darkest times of our lives, here in Poland. But also in Europe and all over the world. It's as if the whole world has gone crazy. As if all of the devils of Hell have been unleashed and the rest of us are suffering terribly. It seems as if there is no hope, that all we can do is surrender to what is happening around us, hoping only to have one more scrap of bread. Hoping to live just one more day."

Zofia was not sure that she liked this conversation. The priest seemed to be depressing her even more. She sat in silence, unable to react or respond to him. He went on.

"Have you heard or read about Maximilian Kolbe?"

She thought for a moment. She had not. She shook her head.

"He was recently killed by the Germans in Oswiecim, at the concentration camp that the Germans call Auschwitz, west of Krakow.

In an instant she remembered. There had been leaflets circulated all over Warsaw on walls and in the streets of the murder of a young Polish priest at the Nazi death camp near Oswiecim. It was reported that Polish prisoners had escaped from Auschwitz. To make sure that others would not be so inclined, the German deputy camp commander had ten men picked to be starved to death in an underground bunker. One of those unfortunate men broke down and cried out for leniency, asking that his life be spared as he was an innocent man with a wife and children. From a group of prisoners observing this off to one side was a Roman Catholic priest, Father Maximilian Kolbe. He stepped forward and offered to take the man's place. That man, Polish army sergeant Franczisk Gajowniczek, was spared. In later years, Zofia would learn that he had survived his internment at Auschwitz and the war, and lived until 1995.

Zofia listened as the priest described Kolbe's torment and remembered reading that Father Kolbe was the last to survive the starvation. Polish underground leaflets reported that the Germans wanted to hasten his death and so injected him with carbolic acid. Supposedly the priest willingly offered his arm for his captors to inject him and therefore kill him.

"And so, Father, will this be the fate of all of the rest of us? We can stand up against the wall to be shot by the Germans, or we can give ourselves up to them like lambs to the slaughter, to let them inject us with poison?" She was crying as she spoke.

The priest hesitated for a moment, carefully choosing his words. He didn't want to incite this emotional distraught young girl into doing something irresponsible that would put her and others in danger.

"There are ways to resist the evil that is all around us," he began.

"And how is that, Father? I somehow get my hands on a gun and shoot every German I can find? I'm just a young girl, I don't even know how to fire a gun let alone kill someone. And isn't that a sin?"

"These are awful, perplexing times for all of us, me included. Yes, killing is a sin, but I feel that, often, God forgives us when we act in self defense or self-preservation."

"Father, are you suggesting that I go and kill some Germans? I tell you right now that if you gave me a gun I would go out right now and shoot one of those murderous…murderous Germans." She put her hands to her face and cried again.

"I hate them, I hate them, I hate them," she cried.

"No, Zofia. No. I'm not suggesting any such thing. There are many ways we can resist this evil. Father Kolbe showed, with his own sacrifice, how there can be a glimmer of light and hope, even in the darkest of hours. We have to honor his memory, what he did, by following our conscience and what our faith has taught us."

Zofia looked up at the priest. Her eyes were red and filled with tears. Her eyelids were swollen from all of the crying and rubbing of her eyes as she tried to see him more clearly.

He continued. "There are many forces acting in concert to defeat the Germans. All over the world. There are others who are rising up to the moment, with weapons in hand, ready to sacrifice themselves for the good of others. You, my child, must find your own way and with your own conscience how to add one more little glimmer of light to this horrible, diabolical nightmare that we are all living through. We must all become protégées of Father Kolbe."

"And how would you have me do that, Father?" she asked, finally able to control her sobbing.

"I have some people I'd like you to meet. They are doing wonderful things, right under the noses of the Germans and, in the process, saving lives. Do you think you might be interested in helping save the lives of some little children?"

Zofia looked into the priest's eyes. They were direct, calm, and hopeful. She could feel a renewed sense of purpose in her heart. The anger, the fear and hatred, were soon replaced by inner warmth and an energetic zeal, a realization that she could make a difference. She would make a difference, however small that might be for such a young girl in occupied Poland during the greatest nightmare of its existence.

CHAPTER 10

Saul Bielewski

It wasn't often that Saul Bielewski talked about pivotal events in his life. He wasn't shy or hesitant to engage in a discussion on all kinds of topics. Obviously, as an educated man with opinions, based in fact or experience, he just didn't seem to dwell on the past. Still, there were moments when friends would see him sitting somewhere, eyes drifting to the horizon, as if he was replaying significant milestones of a secret life.

People around Utica knew him as a thick-accented Polish Jew who had come to Upstate New York in the 1950s to set up a watch repair shop and jewelry store on Columbia Street in Utica. A young man in his 30s, he had somehow survived the Nazi occupation of Poland and eventually immigrated to the United States for a "better life," as he often said.

Now in his 80s, Bielewski looked 20 years younger. With a resonant voice, muscular physique, and a quick step, he was a commanding figure. Sometimes alone in thought, sometimes laughing boisterously at one of his own jokes, he also spoke his mind directly. No subject was taboo. He would just as easily wax eloquently about the day's politics or the economy or discuss music or sports. Even religion was fair game, and while a member of the postwar Jewish community of Utica, he just as easily traveled in and around the Polish Catholic immigrant circles of the city.

It was not unusual to find Saul noshing on a sweet buttered fresh bagel with whitefish at Goldman's Bakery on Oriskany Street. Or attending a wedding at the Polish Community Club behind the West End Brewery, drinking Luksosowa vodka and *wisznowka* cherry liqueur while savoring *golembki* and *bigos*.

Bielewski was a shrewd yet honest and respected businessman. He had been an active member of the Downtown Utica Merchants Association (DUMA), the Jewish Community Center, Temple Beth El on Genesee Street, and on the board of the fledgling Sitrin nursing home. He was an expert watchmaker and repairman. People from all over upstate New York sought out his skills. He could fix any timepiece from pocket watches to tall grandfather clocks. The famous Fountain Elms, historical home of the Munson and Williams families, on Genesee Street often contracted with him to fix or adjust their 19th century heirloom mantel timepieces.

Before the advent of cheap digital watches and the eventual takeover of timekeeping by cell phones, people relied on Saul to keep them running on time. He was like a conductor making sure that the people ran on time, just like the trains. Another of Saul's attractions at the shop was his hospitality, his wit, and his penchant for making a nice hot cup of fresh coffee on a small portable electric hot plate. This he offered to anyone who opened the door. Before the little bell attached to the front door stopped dinging its announcement of a visitor, Saul would ask, "How about a cup of fresh, hot coffee?"

It was an original in itself and predated Joe DiMaggio's pitches for the Mr. Coffee countertop coffee maker. Friends would often stop throughout the day, share a cup of coffee and catch up on the news and local gossip. Not that Utica didn't have news outlets. Over the years people had learned of the Kennedy assassination, Americans landing on the moon, the Vietnam War, the Grenada invasion, and the 9/11 attacks from a number of diverse news sources. Earlier in the 1950s, people read the Utica Daily Press or the Observer Dispatch. The area boasted of two television stations, WKTV and WUTR. A few radio stations like WIBX and WBVM were local favorites.

The watchmaker had seen Samuel Petrie grow up from a young boy playing Little League baseball at the Goldbas playground on Oriskany Street to a respected emergency physician at St. Clare's Hospital. Saul was a chaperone for Sam's Boy Scout troop when they spent a summer's week at Camp Ballou in Frankfort, New York. Saul had gotten to know Zofia Petrie through the Polish Community Club, and they had become good friends, although there was a palpable emotional wall between them. Zofia was an energetic, open personality who readily shared her thoughts.

She had learned some things about this Mr. Bielewski, but he could be somewhat standoffish if she asked too deeply about his past.

Over the ensuing years Zofia and William came to know Saul better. The relationship grew closer when the watchmaker married a newly immigrated middle-aged Polish woman, Eva, in 1956. The Petrie's often saw Mr. and Mrs. Bielewski at community social functions including at the Polish Community Club or "Dom Polski".

Saul and Eva fell in love with the young Sam from the moment they saw him. As they all got to know each other better, Saul or Eva would often ask about her son, and Zofia, the proud parent, would willingly oblige. They eventually became frequent visitors and later, fixtures, at the Petrie household. Sam eventually came to call them his wujek and cioca.

Zofia shared with them most of the major milestones in Sam's life as he grew from a feisty Little Leaguer to an honor's high school student at Utica Free Academy, to his first dates, to learning how to drive a car. William, as well as Zofia, proudly bragged about their son being accepted to osteopathic medical school in Des Moines, Iowa and later how he finished his training in emergency medicine and some of his adventures while in the military.

One day Sam met his old friend Saul Bielewski at the Columbia Bar and Grill. They shared a table, some beer, and fresh cooked potato chips. They made small talk for a while, catching up on some gossip and discussing some local news about City Hall and the mayor, about the debate over building a new police station, and about the declining tax base in Utica. Saul always had an opinion or two to offer on any and all of these topics. He had the luxury of a steady stream of patrons who came to his store not only to buy jewelry or to have a watch repaired, but also to share some of their own insights into the community goings-on.

Sam noticed however that Mr. Bielewski was a little more introspective today, not so quick to offer a comeback.

"Saul, you seem to have something on your mind today. It's like you're having a separate conversation with yourself. In your head. Sometimes you listen and sometimes you respond."

The old man gazed at Sam. He grunted a rough guttural sound of apparent acknowledgement.

"And sometimes you sit there, eyes focused off to the side somewhere, as if there is another room you go into. And you say a few words there before coming back here, to this table, to us. Is everything O.K.?" he asked sympathetically. There was no resentment or rapprochement in his voice. Only genuine, albeit mild, concern.

"The blessing to an old man is that they can have more than one conversation at a time. As you say, in my head, or in another room in my head," the watchmaker replied. "Someone my age can stand behind the graying cover of time and offer up the lame excuse that it comes with age. But these thoughts come not from age but from ages ago, when the world was a different place. And these thoughts are not easily controlled by me."

"You're talking about what happened during the war?" Sam asked. He suspected that Mr. Bielewski had been through an awful lot during the Second World War. Growing up with Mr. Bielewski often a guest at his house, Sam heard stories from that time. Sometimes he would listen with fascination, and often with disbelief. At times when there was too much detail discussed between Saul and his mother and father, Sam felt anger, disgust and even fear. A few times he had nightmares after hearing some of the stories.

They seemed like fairy tales, like the Brothers Grimm tales or Little Red Riding Hood. His father had asked Mr. Bielewski to tone down his descriptions after it was learned that young Sam had had some unsettling nightmares. Mr. Bielewski apologized to the father and to young Sam as well. "I know I shouldn't talk about these things. They were a long time ago, and maybe it's not good to go over what is passed. I know, for myself, that when I think back too often, I get sad. I too sometimes can't sleep when I think of what happened."

Yet curious young Sam disregarded his father's concern for too much graphic detail. In private, over the years, when Sam had time or was home from college or medical school, he would stop by Mr. Bielewski's store and visit. Eventually the conversation would return to the years of Nazi occupation in Poland.

"Things must have been rough, then," Sam would begin. "Especially for the Jews."

Mr. Bielewski nodded his head. "The Jews did suffer tremendously, this is true. But they were not the only recipients of Nazi brutality. So many others suffered at the hands of those monsters."

"True. But the Jews were singled out as scapegoats by Hitler and his supporters. They were the ones who were killed right away when they went to the death camps, gassed right away."

"Some were, and some weren't," Mr. Bielewski replied as he sat nursing a beer. "Some actually supported the Nazis when they first came to Poland. Some thought that the Germans would be their protectors against the Poles, allowing them to set up their own government within Poland with their own courts and police and all. And that they did."

"You make it sound like the Jews welcomed the Nazis into Poland." Sam said.

"Well, yes and no. It gets pretty complicated. Suffice it to say there were a lot of good and a lot of bad on all sides. Some bad Jews, some good Germans, some bad Poles, some bad Ukrainians, some good Russians. Virtue and honesty is not something that you find in only one people. Everywhere you look you find good people and bad people, no matter where they were born or how they worship God."

"The Jews were thought of as being worthless, subhuman, parasites, to be eradiated from the Earth," Sam interjected. "They bore the brunt of that kind of a policy. That's a well known fact."

"Careful about your facts, Samuel." Bielewski replied. "Sometimes facts get in the way of the truth. I lived through that period. I saw and heard a lot. Some of what I saw or heard from others, or later learned about, are not common knowledge, even today."

"You mean about people denying the Holocaust?" asked Sam.

"No. The Holocaust happened. I know because I was a witness to it. But when people say 'holocaust' they think only of the Jews and repeat that six million of them were murdered by the Nazis. And they stop there, never delving deeper into what happened to others."

"Isn't that horrible enough? I know that a lot of other people were killed by the Nazis, but nothing like the systematic murder that took place with the Holocaust." Sam added.

"Of course it was horrible. The unjust murder of even one human being, of even one Jew is horrible. A crime. One too many. And to multiply that by six million doesn't make it any less horrible. You can't dilute it down like too strong a drink by adding more numbers to the mix, to make it more palatable."

"But how is it that no one knows of or speaks of, the rape and murder that took place all over Poland at that same time?" Mr. Bielewski appeared slightly agitated as he continued. "Some done by the Russians early in the partition of Poland into a German part and an eastern Russian occupied part."

The watchmaker paused for a palpable moment. Sam could feel the lapse of time and became impatient after a minute or so. Just as he was about to offer an observation, the old man continued.

"You know that Poland had its own Holocaust?" he asked Sam.

"I know that there were a lot of people killed by the Germans, but they were resisting the Nazis, a lot were partisans."

Mr. Bielewski sat up in his chair and put his hands, palms down on the table. He looked directly at Sam. With a calm steady voice he said, "Six million Polish people died during the Nazi occupation. One million of those people were Polish Jews. The other five million were Poles from all over. They were mothers and fathers, and grandparents and children. They were lovers and actors and shopkeepers and priests and nuns. They were rounded up at times, on the streets, and papers checked. The next morning one hundred people would be found hanging from telephone poles across the cities.

"Many Poles were sent to the concentration camps for minor offenses or under any pretext and slowly starved as they were forced into heavy work, beaten, sometimes shot, sometimes given an injection of Prussic acid into their hearts. Sometimes they were experimented on and died." He slumped back into his chair and took a sip of beer.

"I thought it was the Jews who were experimented on, in Auschwitz," Sam offered.

"Tell that to the Polish pilots who were experimented on in ice cold water, measuring how long they could stay afloat in freezing water until they died. Or the Poles who had all sorts of bacteria injected into them to see if they would survive or die. Even children were used.

"And many Poles were executed, on the spot, for hiding Jews in their homes. The entire family would be executed for that.

"You see, Sam, you stop after you say 'Holocaust', as if only, or mostly, the Jews suffered during the occupation. It is a very complicated story. But Hitler's plan was to start with the Jews, and other undesirables like the gypsies, homosexuals, political opponents. But he needed room, Lebensraum, for his German people, for his Third Reich, in anticipation of a Fourth Reich.

"The official idea was to Germanify Poland and to eventually work and starve the Poles into submission and death as well."

Sam had never heard of this before. "First the Jews, then the Poles?"

"Yes, but there was an official plan to this all," the old man said. "There were three types of Poles, to the Germans. There were the Volksdeutsch, people who were of German extraction and could claim some German background and might generally be sympathetic to the Nazi cause. Then there were those who could be seen as Germans, would learn and speak the language and be brought around to support the Germans. The third or last group was the true Slavic Poles who would be turned into slave labor and slowly worked to death and starved.

"The Germanification of Poland was tried in quite a few small Polish towns. These were emptied of their citizens, who were sent to their death in the concentration camps and German families moved in. Polish children, who appeared to have Aryan characteristics of blonde hair and blue eyes, were taken away from their Polish parents and sent to Germany where they were given to German host families. These children were brought up as Germans. Children, who didn't pass the screening tests for Aryan characteristics, were sent off to the death camps almost immediately."

Sam listened intently. "I didn't know that."

"Most people don't," Bielewski replied. He continued. "Things were just as bad on the Russian side. You know about the fifteen thousand Polish military officers who were murdered by Stalin's NKVD, the forerunners of the KGB?"

"Yes, I did learn some things about that," Sam said. "Stalin wanted to get rid of the officers so that they couldn't fight against him again in the future."

Mr. Bielewski nodded. "Stalin wanted to destroy these people because they were all educated, professional, university trained. They were a large element of the intelligentsia. To kill them off would mean that there would be no military officer corps, and without an intelligentsia, it would be easier for the Russians to spread their propaganda with no educated rebuttal or response."

Sam at down at the table next to Mr. Bielewski. He interlaced his fingers on the table, like both an inquisitor and an expectant student. Slowly, enunciating each word carefully for effect, as if to show that he really wanted a detailed answer and was willing to wait until the man was finished, "Tell me about Irena Sendler."

The old man looked up from his glass of beer, as if woken from a moment of private reverie. "So what, you're a historian now too, as well as a doctor?"

"I understand that this little old Polish lady in a nursing home had something to do with me and my mother, Zofia."

"How would I know about these things?" the old man asked coyly.

"You are such a bullshitter, buddy." Sam shook his head in feigned disgust. "Seriously, I'm very interested in this woman, Irena Sendler, and I know that you know a lot, an awful lot, about what went on historically in your generation, before, during, and after World War II, and what happened to Poland and afterwards."

Bielewski took in a deep breath. He sat there is silence for a few moments, contemplating what to say as he drummed his fingers on the table.

"How would you feel if you lost your country? Huh? Everything is fine, although there's political instability all around you for months and years. Germany and Poland bickering with one another over their borders.

"One day you wake up to find that one of your worst enemies has crossed your borders, invaded your country and you learn that your own military is no match for the tactics and the strength of your enemy." He took a big swig of his beer and continued. "You hear on the radio that the Polish army is holding out day after day, even at Wizna, which is like the Polish Thermopylae. Against all odds, 40 to 1 in some estimates, to the last man, outgunned and outnumbered, they hold out hoping that the Polish forces can regroup for a counterattack. But no, our own generals are not up to the task, even though the soldiers would fight to the last man. Even after the Russians invaded from the East, making it a two front war.

"The order was given for the entire Polish army to retreat. Bury your uniforms. Become partisans, go underground. Many soldiers fled east only to be put in prison compounds by the Russian army, while others fled through Romania and eventually to Iran, while others ran to Switzerland and France, and eventually to England to fight with the British 8th Army. It was not a glorious or honorable fight, like you read in the romance novels."

The old man took a long swig of his beer, emptying the tall glass.

"Can I get you another beer?" Sam offered.

"If I'm going to relive some of my painful past, and it is just as much my past as it is anybody's who lived through and suffered through that time, then I'm going to need something to soothe my nerves and ease the painful memories."

"I know just what you need." Sam motioned to Steve Valone, at the bar. "Give us a bottle of the krupnik, that Polish liquor you've got down on the bottom shelf over there, below the vodka."

Steve obliged them. He deftly poured shots into two small glasses in front of the gazing men. They sat in silence for a few moments, then lifted their glasses in a toast and quickly downed the clear, amber tinted, sweet, spiced liquor.

"O.K.," said Mr. Bielewski. "Now we can talk about that little old lady in the nursing home. What an incredible lady!" he said as he raised his glass in a toast to her memory.

CHAPTER 11

At The Columbia

Saul Bielewski's coffee pot hearkened back to the rustic days of locals sitting on boxes next to a cracker barrel at a town's only general store, trading opinions, talking deals and spreading gossip, tall tales and, sometimes, outright lies. Today however, Saul was not sipping coffee with his friends at his shop. And he was not repairing watches. Today he had stopped at a landmark bar and restaurant on the corner of State Street and Columbia for personal reasons.

It was just a few short blocks from his store. This was not a random visit for the sake of quenching his thirst with a Saranac Pale Ale, one of his favorite beers. And Mr. Bielewski was not a regular at owner Steve Valone's watering hole, the Columbia.

The watchmaker sat at one end of the bar munching on freshly cooked potato chips, a specialty of the bar. He sipped his beer from a tall pilsner glass. He fiddled with a small device in his left ear, connected to the thick black temples of his glasses. A frequency sensor was easily controlled by the tip of his left index finger. Saul Bielewski gently turned the tiny sensor until he could clearly hear the conversation at the table behind him. The sensor was a unidirectional, high fidelity microphone that amplified only those signals, to which it was pointing. Behind Saul, at the table under surveillance, sat Sam Petrie, Steve Valone and Carl Thurston. Unbeknownst to anyone, Bielewski had been watching and privately following Dr. Petrie, ever since his mother's death.

Sam Petrie and his two friends sat at a round wooden table in the corner of the Columbia. Silence. Occasionally one of them would take a sip of beer, look at the others, and then settle back in his chair. Now and then one of them would burp. It was still early in the evening and patrons were only just starting to come in.

Steve Valone, a merchant marine come home to Clinton, New York, was now a successful young entrepreneur. He had bought the bar with money saved while working on big ocean going cargo ships. He hoped to eventually sell the bar and had plans to build a more upscale restaurant in the New Hartford area, just outside of Utica. A recent downturn in the local and national economy, and the stiff competition he would face from many other fine area restaurants forced him to reconsider his plans for right now. As a result he was focusing on making the Columbia a popular community watering hole. He installed dartboards, chess and checkers tables, and a few big screen TVs. He had a large cooler built in the cellar below the bar to accommodate 40 steel barrels of various beers from microbreweries in and around Upstate New York and New England. He also made sure to offer the local brews: the Saranac line from the F.X. Matt Brewery and beers from the Ommegang brewery in nearby Cooperstown.

Carl Thurston was the first to speak after the long silence at their table. "Sam, I can't imagine how you feel about all this. It sounds pretty confusing to me. But she did love you, I'm sure of that. With all her heart."

"And her soul," offered Steve. He raised a glass of Ommegang Abby Ale in her memory. "And I can kind of see her motivation, too, old buddy. I mean, think of it. Would you just pack up all of your things and just leave here and return to people that you never grew up with, people you didn't even know. People you aren't even sure you would want to be with."

Sam winced at that last suggestion. He hadn't thought that far ahead in his anger, his confusion, being torn between anger at Zofia on the one hand and feeling guilty for feeling that way on the other hand. Finally, taking a sip of his own Saranac Black Forest brew he said, "I feel so numb."

"We hear you," the two friends replied in unison. They knew he wasn't speaking about having had too much alcohol. This was only his second beer of the evening and Sam was no stranger to drinking four or five beers in an evening and still able to keep a clear head.

At last, again, Sam opened up to Carl and Steve. "I spent the last few days of my mother's time on this Earth with her at the bedside.

"I had a preconceived notion that everything would go kind of like you see in the movies. The patient slowly gets weaker, breathes a little harder, and the voice gets fainter. The son sits by her side, holding her hand, and looks at her as she slowly fades away. Different than what I was used to seeing when I worked in the ERs. There people usually died pretty quickly. They either lost their color and became pale and cool and weak as they bled out internally or they'd come in with some severe chest pain and difficulty breathing from a heart attack or a blood clot to the lung. We'd start doing our resuscitation and their eyes would roll back in their head. They might even shake, like having a seizure. In no time they were turning blue as the oxygen in their blood ran out. Despite tubing them and pumping on their chests or defibrillating them, they would flat line. And that would be it. It'd be over in five minutes or so. All gone."

He took another sip of his beer. "My Mom didn't go that way at all. She even seemed to gain strength as she explained to me what she was feeling and why. As if she had to get everything off her chest before she could die."

"Maybe that's what it was," Carl suggested. "I do remember a close friend of mine, an older guy, who was dying day by day. Had Lou Gehrig's disease. His family was around him every day, at his house. He had a private duty nurse and oxygen and everything. He wanted to see his one daughter before he died. Even said as much. She was in Alaska and had hopped on a plane, trying to get to Utica as fast as she could. She made it home on a Saturday morning. I can still remember the big smile on his face as she walked into his bedroom. They talked a little, mostly whispers. He was so weak but so happy then with his whole family around him. He died that same evening."

"I told you how she started telling me all of this stuff," Sam continued.

"She had been a young girl in Poland during the war. In Warsaw. Nazis all over the place. I remember her telling me stories about soldiers and Gestapo. It was enough to make your hair curl. She talked of how the Germans would just cordon off a street, pick out a bunch of people and line them up against a wall and just machine gun them down. All that as a reprisal against the Polish underground. To keep the people in constant fear so that they wouldn't help the Resistance. She talked about people being hung from lamp posts and telephone poles, and blood in the streets from the shootings."

He took another long sip of his beer. "I remember her telling me that she was just a young girl, just wanted to keep her job as a secretary at some fuel or coal company. She told me she was never in the Resistance. She wasn't political, didn't really have much understanding of everything that was going on, just that her country was invaded and people were being murdered on a daily basis. That was enough for her. Like she told me once, she was no hero. She just wanted to stay alive. At home a few days ago, just before she died, my mother started telling me the story that I started telling you guys earlier tonight."

Carl and Steve nodded in unison. Sam went over his story again, this time in more detail.

"One day this young woman from the city's health department came up to her and asked for some favor. I forget what it was, but the two became good friends after a while. The lady got very interested when she found out that my mother would sometimes walk or ride by bike to the outskirts of Warsaw to visit some cousins and stay over the weekend at their house."

"This lady, Sendler, one day asked my mother to help her with a very dangerous task. She told my mother that she might even risk being arrested or possibly even shot for helping. My mother said that by this time she felt she had to do something, anything. She was really starting to get scared, she said, and wasn't sure if she was going to survive that occupation. Some of her friends had already been arrested and had hands or legs broken, or shot or hung, or just disappeared."

"My mother had a tough time talking about that to me. It was like she could see it all so clearly, like it had just happened last week."

Carl interrupted. "I've talked with some of the older people from around that time. Same thing with them. Not too easy to talk about. To them it's not history, it's something that really happened, and they still get those feelings, just like when they were there. Remember Mr. Bielewski? He went through a lot as I remember. And you know he was connected up with that underground stuff. He was in the Resistance there back in Poland."

"I remember him talking some, too," offered Steve. "He said it was unreal, when the whole world went nuts. He was a real young guy then too. He said he wasn't sure if he was going to make it out alive with all the people being arrested and disappearing and all the killing."

Sam continued, "There had been a real bad feeling about the Jews in the ghetto being put on lists and carted off by train to south of Warsaw. My mother called it aws vee en cheem, or at least that's how it sounds in Polish. I never was very good at Polish. She used to speak it some at home and with some friends. Like that. And my Dad only spoke the basics of it, so they always spoke in English. But that's what she said."

"So what about that place?" Steve asked.

Sam turned to him with a slight frown on his face, hesitating to answer, as if there were a bitter taste of something in his mouth. "The Germans renamed it Auschwitz".

"Oh, the Nazi death camp. Yeah, I had heard about that and other Polish death camps from back then."

Sam's eyes widened in disbelief. His face took on a stern demeanor. In a measured tone of voice he answered deliberately, "There never were any Polish death camps. Poland never ordered the construction of, or the operation of any 'death camps', as you called them, in Poland. You've got to remember, Poland was occupied by Germany, and then the Russians came in from the East. Poland ceased to exist as a country. Under Hitler and his cronies Poland renamed it 'the General Government'. Look it up on the maps from around that time. And the area around Auschwitz was actually annexed to Germany as territory of the Third Reich."

"How do you know all that?" Steve asked.

"Because I went to Auschwitz. I saw the bundles of human hair cut off from people, saved in a museum sitting on the grounds of Auschwitz. They've got thousands of suitcases with the peoples' names on them in big white painted letters, displayed behind large glass windows. Jews arriving there by train thought they would be eventually taken to Canada. I saw thousands of eyeglasses, too in the displays. And dark, grayish-brown bolts of cloth made from human hair, the hair of the Jews that the Germans brought there. The Germans sent the cloth back to Germany to make clothing. Imagine that. It wasn't enough for those sons of bitches to take their freedom, their clothing, their possessions, and finally their lives. They took their hair and wore it as clothing. Sick or what."

He paused and took a sip of his beer. The others sat quietly.

"So, don't talk that bullshit about Polish death camps or concentration camps. Because I know. I know. And now you know." The friends all nodded in solemn respect and understanding.

After another pause, this time longer, Sam continued.

"Anyway, information was coming back to Warsaw that the Germans were doing some really bad stuff at Auschwitz. Thousands of people were being sent down there but there weren't enough buildings to house all of them. And yet they kept sending more Jews, and non-Jews, too. From all over Europe.

"There were a bunch of big furnaces at the far end of where the trains stopped at the camp. Black smoke was coming out of it shortly after the trains arrived. There was one young Polish guy in the Underground Resistance, incredible guy, Pilecki, Witold Pilecki who, get this, volunteered to be captured by the Germans and taken to Auschwitz, so he could get inside and report back what was going on.

"In the cities the Germans would round up a large group of people and hold them with their hands up and at gun point. Could happen anywhere, anytime, without warning. If you were a Jew, or a Pole who was harboring or protecting a Jew, you might be shot on the spot. Or they might be taken down to Gestapo headquarters for brutal interrogation. Some were shot there or hung in public the next day. Others were sent to German concentration camps like Auschwitz..." Sam emphasized the word "German".

"That's fucking insane," Carl muttered.

"Yeah, sure was," replied Sam. "But as a captured Pole, this Pilecki was put in work details where they basically worked you to death, cutting down your calories on a regular basis, and so starved you to death. Or beat you for the slightest reason if they felt like they needed to make an example, and they might beat you to death. Or if they thought you were in some secret group or tried to escape or any other excuse, they'd have a two minute trial in one of the buildings and take you to the wall outside and shoot you."

"Fucking sick," Steve commented.

"Well, Pilecki was able to escape from Auschwitz and, in hiding, got out a report that went to the exiled Polish government in London. With his letter they were able to convince the Allies that the Germans were torturing and killing arrested Poles, but were exterminating more feeble Jewish men and women and most of the Jewish children almost as soon as they got off the transport trains."

"Well, what did they do about it, I mean the Allies?" Carl asked.

"Essentially nothing. In the U.S. a lot of people in the State Department didn't believe it. The British didn't do much with it either. The Soviets, with Stalin, I guess they didn't even give it a second thought. Wouldn't want to help the Poles anyway because they would have to contend with them after Germany was defeated. It gets real complicated and political. But I guess the overriding consensus was that the best way to put an end to it all was to win the war against Germany. I think that's one more reason, along with all the other reasons, why the Normandy Invasion was so important."

"I guess Bielewski was right," added Steve.

"How so?" asked Carl.

"It really was a time when the whole world was going crazy."

"So my Mom volunteered to help this Sendler woman, to do anything in any way. She didn't know what the friend had in mind for her until one day she was invited to the woman's home. There she met up with some of the lady's coworkers and she was brought into the inner circle."

CHAPTER 12

Zofia Meets Irena Sendler

The teakettle whistled and the china cups and saucers clinked as Irena Sendler passed out dishware and flatware. Four young and middle-aged women were seated around her embroidery covered dining room table. The tall windows overlooking the street below were closed and the sheer white curtains drawn. At the far end of the table sat a newcomer, young Zofia.

The ladies all welcomed Zofia. Tea was poured from a large brass samovar. Plates of dark bread were passed around.

Irena began. "Thank you all for coming here so late this afternoon. I know you all must be very tired from your workday duties. I also apologize that we have no butter or comfiture or cheese. And no sugar."

"We all need to be on a diet anyway," one of the ladies offered. A short wave of giggles swept around the table.

"Well, with the rationing and all of the shortages anyway, I feel we must make do with what we have," added Irena.

One of the guests, Maria, expanded on Irena's topic. She was a middle aged, slightly overweight woman with curly brown hair and thick lips and round cheeks. She had devilish eyes that would wink or dart back and forth as she spoke. One could never be sure if she was going to make some serious declaration or come out with a double entendre. "Well, I for one have nothing to argue about with the shortages and the rationing by the Germans in Poland. They give us plenty of ration cards. The only thing that I don't like is that the cards are so bitter!"

As they laughed, another pretty, young blonde, Agnieszka, added, "And they take so long to chew. I can hardly finish my month's supply of cards."

The group continued in this way for a while, savoring small morsels of the bland bread and the unsweetened tea offered to them. Jokes made way for news and gossip, very little of it uplifting or hopeful. Irena felt she should start their meeting before it got too late. She stood up to address them.

"Most of you already know each other and why we are gathered her today in my home. And some of you are new." She gestured to Zofia.

"*Witamy*, welcome," She said first in Polish and then reinforced it in English, as was lately the fashion.

"What I am going to talk about now is something that would be punishable by death if the Germans were to find out what we are doing. What we are doing here right now and what we will continue to do in Warsaw. If any of you would like to leave before I continue, please, without shame, you may leave."

She paused for a moment, letting her guests consider her words before continuing.

"As civilians we do not have the capabilities to fight the German occupation as do the Underground or the Partisans in the woods. Yet every Pole, every Polish man, woman and child, is still a soldier against Hitler and his henchmen. There is much that we can do to right the evil and the incredible suffering that the Germans are inflicting on all of us. So, Zofia, I particularly ask you, as the others have heard my speeches before and I assume will stay. You however will be entering into a very dangerous operation that could have dire consequences for you, your friends and possibly your family. I only know that if we do nothing, we will continue to suffer and many more will be imprisoned or executed or worked to death anyway. As long as the Germans are here, we feel that we have no other choice but to resist. So, again, Zofia, you are free to leave before I continue. If you decide to stay and work with us, there is no turning back. No half-hearted measures. You either sacrifice with us, or you may leave. Now." She said the last few words "may leave" softly and gently, as if talking to a child.

Zofia did not hesitate. She had seen enough, no, too much already. She knew she couldn't stop the daily insanity that she witnessed on the streets of Warsaw, but she was certain that in some small way she could help, would contribute to get rid of this Nazi evil that was destroying her country. She felt her spirits lift, a flicker of hope awoke within her heart as she redefined herself as a soldier. That was what Irena had called them, soldiers.

"I will stay. I want to help. I want to do something, anything I can to help us get these Nazi bastards off our backs."

She felt a renewed sense of energy stir within her. "I want to help to stop the killing."

All of the women silently nodded their affirmation of this desire. Irena stood up and addressed them, "We all want to stop the killing. And none of us want to become killers, like our enemies are. Zofia, these women before you, Maria, Agnieszka, Katia, and Kinga are all coworkers at the Sanitation Department for the city. We have all come together to fight the Nazis by denying them their ability to kill everyone that they have in their reach. Our mission is not to kill Germans, nor to make ourselves into gun-toting soldiers."

"Although a few of us wouldn't mind doing that, if we had the chance," offered Agnieszka.

"And the guns," added the up until now quiet Kinga. She leaned forward and placed both elbows on the table. She swept the long wavy reddish brown hair from one side of her face to reveal a stunning, youthful girl in her mid twenties, a hint of rouge on her prominent cheekbones and bright red lipstick on thin, smiling lips. "With a rifle or a pistol we could probably kill one or two Germans before they killed us. But Irena has an idea that will save more lives than we few would ever be able to do by killing with guns."

Now for the first time, Katia spoke up, "I was so afraid when Irena first started talking with me. I wanted to get up and walk out. But then, I thought, just like you Zofia, I wanted to stop the killing. I knew that I couldn't stop everything, but I could stop some of it. Even if it meant I might be killed myself. For me it's worth it. It's the only thing I can do." She stopped talking and looked down seriously at a decorated plate in front of her that now held a few left over crumbs of the bread Irena had offered. "It's like that loaf of bread. All we have left now are a few crumbs. We have to make do with what we have, with what we can. We are the crumbs now; we are foot soldiers of the larger scheme. We will do what we can."

The others all nodded in support.

Irena began to outline her plan for the group.

CHAPTER 13

The International Alliance and Eva

Nights could be quite cold in spring in the Bavarian forests. It was November 1955. Earlier this year, the Soviet Union declared that the war between Russia and Germany, starting with Hitler's Operation Barbarossa in 1941, was officially over. The first vaccine against polio, developed by Dr. Jonas Salk, was approved for use by the U.S. Food and Drug Administration. The Mickey Mouse Club made its television debut a month earlier, in October. West Germany was recognized as a sovereign nation.

There was a roaring fire in the large stone fireplace (that took up over half of the wall of this rustic hunting lodge), which took out the dampness and the chill of the evening. Stuffed heads of all sorts of local game and shields, swords, halberds, and other various medieval armaments reflected the heat and the glow of the burning logs. It had been raining for days in this small village to the south of Munich where the five leaders of the close-knit, secretive group met. The locals here often complained of the bone-chilling dampness that could freeze the marrow and cause joint aches and misery until the warm days of summer would finally set in. One way to stave off this damp chill was to sit by a roaring fire, bundled up in a warm blanket, and sip spiced red wine.

The leadership Council of the International Alliance had come here to discuss business for the coming year. Investigators for the organization were scheduled to give a report to them of the killing of a young SS officer, Harvey Weinberg, and his two children, which had taken place not far away from here, in the fall of last year.

There were five men making up the governing body of the Alliance. They had risen through the ranks of this organization based on their family ties to the Nazi elite, because of their unwavering belief in and support of the ideals of the group, and because of their varied skills and ruthlessness. Four of them were of German descent and one was a young Frenchman, Rene Marcelle Gallois.

Gallois had made a name for himself during the war in Vichy, France where he had openly collaborated with the French authorities and their German allies. He was responsible for providing many valuable clandestine services to them, including the procurement of drugs such as morphine and the newly produced amphetamines, international currencies, and prostitution. He had grown up on the streets of Marseilles, a ruffian who never turned away from a fight, even if it appeared that he was outnumbered or outmatched. He earned the reputation of a man who was persistent and never gave up.

The other four men on the Council were all descendants of the architects and rulers or ardent supporters of the Nazi Party. After the killings, arrests, diaspora, and fragmentation of the Nazi leadership, the survivors felt that any new representative governing body should consist of young men with very close ties to the previous leadership hierarchy.

One such man was Bruno Metzger, the Butcher. He was a nephew of Heinrich Himmler, the architect of the SS. Metzger had lived up to his nickname many times during and after the War. He had been well trained by the SS. While still a teenager, he was promoted to low-level officer status of his regional Hitler Youth brigade in a crumbling Germany, just a few months before the war ended. He personally had killed a few Americans in the last months of the war in 1945, as the Germans tried to slow the Allied advance across the Rhine. He had crawled close to the front lines and shot three GIs in the back while they were on guard duty. His signature atrocity was to mutilate the faces of the dead soldiers with the SS knife he had been given during his swearing-in ceremony. With his commanding personality and ruthless commitment to absolute control, he quickly rose to the forefront of the Alliance as the de facto spokesman and leader.

Lothar Heinrich was a loyal and devoted nephew of Grand Admiral Karl Donitz, to whom had fallen the leadership of Germany after Hitler committed suicide in his bunker in Berlin as the Russians were closing in. Donitz was Hitler's personally named successor as Head of State and President of the German government, until he surrendered to the Allies in May 1945. With the support of this relative, Heinrich was readily accepted into the ranks of the International Alliance. Tall, thin, with a slight limp and a penchant for wearing a monocle over his left eye, he was a skilled organizer who could motivate people under his command with a warm smile and a firm hand on a shoulder. His demeanor could change in an instant when his orders were not immediately understood and put into motion. He would remove his monocle, convert his firm hold into a crushing grip, and peer into the eyes of his insubordinate as if signaling them for execution.

Wolff Heisenberg was another *wunderkind*, groomed by the Nazi cabala to lead the tattered Third Reich into a, hopefully, grand future. He learned during the War years to be a skilled administrator under the close tutelage of his family friend Albert Speer, Hitler's architect and Minister of Armaments and War Production. It was Speer who had recommended the young Heisenberg to the Council, knowing that he would be a formidable contributor to the development of the Alliance.

Manfred Haeckel was a boyhood friend of Bruno Metzger and the brother-in-law of Kurt Gruber, the founder of the Hitler Youth Movement. Before he died in 1943 shortly after a stroke, Gruber had instilled in Haeckel the importance of influencing the next generation of Germans, and groomed Haeckel for a post-war position in any revitalization of the Nazi party, which he took for granted, would happen. Manfred and Bruno had served in the same division in 1945 and he personally witnessed Bruno's atrocities against the Americans. He made a point of letting everyone know of Bruno's courage and brutality.

The five men stood in front of the fireplace, glasses of mulled red wine raised in a toast. They were all dressed in double-breasted suits with cuffed and pleated trousers. In one corner of the room a turntable provided subtle background music by Mozart, the famous German composer.

"Gentlemen, we are gathered here tonight, as we have every year at this time, not only to honor the work and the lives of our relatives and loved ones, both living and dead, but also to honor their contributions to the future of a Fourth Reich and the rise again of Germany and the Aryan Race!"

"To Germany and the Aryan Race!" they all repeated as they raised their glasses even higher. They swiftly downed the wine and then, in unison, threw their glasses into the back of the fireplace.

"*Heil Hitler!*" one of them shouted as he clicked his heels in the Prussian military fashion. The others repeated his salute and one added a "*Sieg Heil*" (hail to victory). Herr Metzger gestured for the others to sit down on the sofas or chairs arranged in a half circle around a small table on which were situated a punch bowl with the same spiced wine they had just used in their toast and a large tray of sandwiches. Metzger remained standing, his back warmed by the fire.

"Thank you all for coming, as you have done every year for the last eleven years. And thank you for your commitment and your contributions, with your influence, with your energies and your connections...."

"And our finances!" Heinrich interjected. They others laughed at his comment.

"Yes, this is true, Lothar, and thank you for reminding us all," Metzger nodded in agreement.

"Our great work takes labor, commitment, time, and, as our good friend Lothar here reminds us, also money. Lots of money. And we have had a steady stream of money coming in for the past decade because of our ability to organize and to keep our eye on the ball, as the American baseball phrase goes."

He took a new glass off the table and filled it with wine from a ladle in the punch bowl before him. "Feel free to partake of the wine and appetizers. We will be having a wonderful dinner shortly in the main dining room of this wonderful Bavarian Gasthaus. I am sure you agree that our recent purchase of this property for the International Alliance to use for our meetings, training sessions, and research initiatives was a wise decision. We will get to the business reports and the treasurer's report a little later. We will review how well we have been doing in amassing money from our international sales of drugs and weapons, and the gambling, prostitution, and slavery rings through our partners from all over the world.

"But I wish to indulge your patience right now on a very special report that will be given by two of our agents who have uncovered some monumental news concerning our struggle and our long term goals." He turned to one side and motioned with a flick of his finger to a security guard standing by the entrance to the great hall.

"Allow them in, please."

Two middle-aged men were ushered in by the unarmed guard who also was dressed in an evening suit. In their forties, the men were clean shaven. One man was blonde with blue eyes, with a sharp chin and fine facial features. He was lean, muscular and in excellent shape as could be seen by the way he proudly carried himself into the room. He could easily have been a model for a Nazi propaganda poster of a "typical Aryan man". His companion was also physically fit, but shorter, with broad shoulders and a chest that jutted out as his shoulders were thrown back. He had short brown hair and a thin mustache covering his upper lip. Neither man smiled as they accepted a hand offered to them by the Metzger. Each clicked their heels as they bowed slightly to their host.

"*Meine Herren*, I introduce to you Herr Kohl and Herr Steinberg."

The couple bowed again as they turned to the group seated before them. They again clicked their heels.

"These two fine soldiers of our cause were given an assignment to investigate the murder of our young SS officer and his two exceptional, beautiful children last year, only a couple of hours drive from here. Our organization was very interested in those two young boys, and we had plans to study them to see if they somehow possessed the hereditary material from which we could reconstitute the Aryan race. Obviously there was something very special about their parents, something very, very special." He put special emphasis on the word "very" as he stared into the eyes of each and every one of the Council members in front of him. He paused for effect.

"Herr Kohl, please, if you will." He offered his place in front of the fire as he sat down in a plush chair off to one side.

"*Meine Herren, vielen Dank fur die Gelegenhiet mit Euch zu sprechen.* Thank you. As Herr Ober has said, we were assigned to investigate not only the particulars of the murders in the Bavarian Forest last year of the SS officer and his two young boys, but also to find the perpetrators before the police did. We hoped to get information on why this heinous crime was perpetrated and by whom. We felt from the beginning that this was a planned operation involving more than just the people at the scene of the murders, and that there was something that these people knew that we had to get our hands on."

One of the Council members interrupted. "Yes, yes. We know about the murders. Horrible. And a great loss of two gifted young boys. But the German police and detectives went over the remains of the car, the ashes, tire marks, all of it. Our people had access to the investigation. In the end it was concluded that this was a robbery that must have gone bad, and the man, or men, who did this wanted to cover up any evidence by burning the cars and the bodies."

Metzger stood up and addressed the group. "Yes, and it was I who fabricated that cover story and fed it to our operatives in the Bavarian police. The purpose of that ruse was to stop the police and have them close their investigation, so that we could start ours. And that is why these men are here. Please, continue." The host sat down.

"*Jawhohl, Herr Ober.*" Kohl continued. "My colleague Herr Steinberg and I went back to the location of the murders, which is along a small road deep in the forest off the main highway. We were able to find a sign, crudely constructed, with the word detour and an arrow painted, directing any vehicles to turn to the left and onto the small road north of Ingolstadt, at Appertshofen, that led through the woods to the little town of Zandt.

"We went to the few lumber stores in and around Appertshofen and asked if anyone remembered someone buying plywood and paint of the colors that the sign was constructed from. We did eventually find one fellow who remembered two young men, with apparent Polish accents, who bought materials such as those used in the construction of the sign. We were able to locate a little hotel in the area that also remembered two young Polish men who had identified themselves as sign painters who were looking for a warehouse where they could rent space for their work. We searched and inquired until we found that place and spoke with the owner. He gave us a description of the two Poles and the first name of one of them, a fellow by the name of Mariusz. After a few more months of trying to fit the pieces of the puzzle together, we were able to local this guy in Torun, in Poland. We eventually apprehended and interviewed him."

"Torun? North of Warsaw? That town is noted for its gingerbread!"

"And it's also the birthplace of that fucking Polish bastard mathematician, Copernicus, that those people always parade out, as if they all were as smart as he was." They all laughed at that comment.

Metzger interrupted Kohl, adding, "And what this man was able to tell us was a fascinating story."

Kohl continued. "Well, this one fellow is, or was, Mariusz Robecki. The other is a man by the name of Rafel Bielewski. Mariusz we got and questioned. Rafel had quickly emigrated to the U.S. We're now in the process of trying to track down his whereabouts.

This guy, Mariusz, told us that the two young boys were the target of their operation, that it somehow became apparent to their handlers that the boys possessed a superior form of heredity that they feared might be used to reconstitute a master race. He told us that their mother, a young Jewess, now retained possibly the only remnants of that same heredity and that she was being protected somewhere."

"A young Jewess? Protected? And by whom?" one man asked.

Kohl and Steinberg looked at each other, as if to decide on who should answer the question. Steinberg stepped forward. "He told us that the mother of those two fantastic young boys was being hidden and protected by the Polish underground organization, Zegota."

The room was silent for a long moment. In a burst of outrage, Manfred Haeckel slammed his open hand on the sofa armrest and stood up. "Zegota! Those fucking bandits! They were the ones who took all those little parasite Jew bastard kids out of the ghetto in Warsaw. They tried fucking us over in Auschwitz with their attempts to organize resistance in there. They disbanded a few years after the war was declared over. Some of their leaders were arrested, tried, and executed by the Polish communists as enemies of the State. At least that's one good thing I can say about the communists. They are Jew haters, too!"

Kohl continued. "Mariusz also gave us some names of some of the surviving members of Zegota. We've been slowly locating those people and are having them dealt with. And he also gave us the name of the mother."

Again there was silence in the room.

"Her name is, or was, Eva Pilecki. We're sure that she is hiding under a new name."

The silence in the room, as the cliché goes, was deafening.

"Pilecki. That bastard Polish bandit. She's related to him?"

"We think that she was from another family with the same name. Or that she was a sister," offered Kohl.

"That Pilecki. He gave us trouble all through the war. Got himself voluntarily arrested in a street sweep, and sent to Auschwitz. He smuggled out information to the Underground about *die Entlosung*, the crematoriums, and the selection and the Sonderkommandos. Prick! And then he was smuggled out of the camp, survived it all, and told the Allies about our program. As fate would have it though, he was tried by the Polish communists in 1949 and finally executed."

"Thank God for that! Justice finally won out!" one of the now angered members shouted.

CHAPTER 14

At the Horned Dorset
Inn in Leonardsville

Carl took a sip from his lead crystal water goblet. "Why are you so insistent on trying to find her? Your mother told you to let it go! She's right. What will you gain by that? You'll probably find some grave somewhere, if you're lucky, where you can read some strange name. Again, if you're lucky. Actually, this sounds more like a never-ending goose chase that goes down some rabbit hole to nowhere."

"And what if she actually is still alive?" Helen Petrie added. "You saw the guilt, the anguish that Zofia went through in telling you about all of this. How do you think your birth mother would feel, now, an old woman, confronted by the fact that she not only gave her only son up, but also that she wasn't able to get you back? I can only imagine the raw feelings and unpleasant emotions that this would bring up."

They were seated in the main dining room of the famed Horned Dorset Inn in Leonardsville right on Route 8, about 20 miles south of Utica. They could see a beautifully arranged flower and vegetable garden through the high, arched Palladian style windows. There were fresh wild flowers and flickering hurricane candles situated strategically about the room to add life and color to the bright off-white walls. Fresh white cotton cloth covered the quaint dinner tables. The dishes and silverware and napkins were set out as is customary in all the finest French restaurants.

Sam sat in silence, listening, taking it all in. He knew that they were right. It was selfish of him to think that he could just make a trip or a few phone calls and find his birth mother. That he could just walk up to her, put his arms around her and say, hi Mom, I'm home. He knew it couldn't be that way.

Yet he had an overriding obsession with wanting to know who his real mother was. What was she like? Did he have other relatives? What had she gone through? Had she wondered all of these years what had happened to him? She must have.

There was a burning desire within him to make that connection. Not that it would make everything all right. That wasn't the point. She had given him up so that he might survive, at a time when things looked grim for her and everyone else.

He wanted to let her know that he was all right, that her sacrifice was worth it. He was alive, and doing well. He wanted to thank her for making it possible for him to live.

Because of her sacrifice, he was doing quite well. He had a wonderful life with fantastic adoptive parents. He was very satisfied with the way his life had turned out. He was happily married with two wonderful children. He had great, close friends, like Carl. He was in good health and financially secure. What more could he want?

Sam cleared his throat and looked at Carl, to get his attention. He produced a small packet of letters from his sports coat and untied the string binding them.

"Helen and I have been rummaging through the attic off and on since...." he hesitated, "...Zofia, my mother...died. In one corner of a large suitcase filled with some stuffed toys, my grade school report cards, and other personal stuff, I found these letters."

There was a pause as they all looked at the yellowing envelopes. A few of the letters bore engraved grey or burgundy or green stamps, reminiscent of typical, uninspired government art. A few were colorful and large.

"These few letters are the only contact I have to my birth mother. Apparently she had traveled quite a bit in the 50's. They were sent from Paris, London, Iran, and Israel. The last letter came from Nepal."

"Nepal? What was the date on that one?" asked Carl.

"1954," Sam replied. "I was 10 years old then."

"That was a long time ago, Sam," his friend said. "A long time ago."

"A whole life time ago."

They all nodded in agreement.

The waiter came over and took their orders.

"I'll have the bouillabaisse with the lobster, scallops, shrimp, and oh my, the mussels, and clams and cod and cherry tomatoes and fingerling potatoes, all in a saffron fennel broth," Helen read. "That sounds just wonderful!"

The waiter turned next to Sam. "I'll have the Chateaubriand with the Béarnaise sauce. With the green beans. And can we get another order of the Horned Dorset onion and cheese dip?"

"Certainly," replied the waiter. He turned finally to Carl Thurston, who was apparently mesmerized by the menu offerings.

Carl gently shook his head, finding it difficult to select a choice for his dinner. "This is quite the menu. And no chili or cheeseburgers or fries."

"If that's what you want, I can speak with the chef and see if he can accommodate you with something to your liking."

"No. That's all right. I don't want to be a bother. This all looks so good." After a pause he closed the menu book and matter-of-factly said, "I'll take page two!"

They all laughed. Carl was known to do that on occasion when the friends were out dining and Carl was stumped on ordering.

"Seriously, I'll take the Sea Scallops with Saffron Risotto and Ramp Puree. And can you bring another cup of black coffee?"

They finished their exquisite meal with coffee and some of the desserts, which the restaurant was famous for, including Dark Chocolate Bombe and a chilled orange soufflé with Grand Marnier sauce.

Their dinner conversation was eclectic. They talked about their hunting trip to Montana a few years before, when the seemingly relaxing outing became a nightmare during which Sam and Carl were almost killed. They reminisced about Carl's daring rescue of Sam when he had been kidnapped and held prisoner in the cellar of a farmhouse on the outskirts of Leonardsville, not far from the restaurant. Carl brought up Betty Stolarczyk, the wife of their Montana outfitter, who had come back to Utica to help avenge her husband's murder, and died in the process.

Sam turned the conversation back to their earlier discussion.

"You see, we're not normal, regular people. We've been through all these other things and here we are, stuffing ourselves with some of the finest food and wine and desert anyone could ask for. And we survived it all."

"What do you mean 'we survived it all'?" interjected Carl. "You mean this meal? I'd go through another meal like this again, in a heartbeat. In fact, even though I'm stuffed like a Christmas sock, I'd plow through another meal like this any time. I'm not so sure about right now," he said as he patted his stomach. "But soon. Maybe in an hour."

"You know what I mean, Carl. And you know that I mean to go through with this. I just have to find out what happened to her. Christ, it's my mother we're talking about, my real mother. Not some fictitious character or a distant relative or something. This woman gave birth to me...to ME!"

"O.K., calm down," said Helen. She had been sitting patiently listening to her husband for days now, muttering about or commenting on how he was torn between finding out about his mother and leaving it all alone.

As the three sat and talked over plans, the waiter returned and asked if anyone would like a refill on his or her coffee. He deftly filled their cups with piping hot freshly brewed coffee from a shiny silver pot.

"I couldn't help but overhear you discussing plans for a trip and your mention of Nepal," he said. "Nepal is my home. That is where I and my family came from quite a few years ago."

"How interesting," Helen replied.

"That it is," added Sam. "What brought you here to the U.S. and to, of all places, Leonardsville?"

The waiter finished refilling their coffee. "I am here in Leonardsville because of my job. I love it here. All of the staff and the owners. They are real good people. But I came here to Utica through the Refugee Center. Life was very difficult for us in Nepal."

"But I hear that Nepal is a beautiful country," said Carl. "A lot of people go there, especially to Katmandu, to climb the mountains and hike around."

"And to smoke the hashish," added Sam. "Or at least they used to in the 60's and early 70's."

"I don't know about hashish but, yes, my country is a very beautiful country. Wonderful mountains and waterfalls and beautiful forests and many colorful monasteries and villages. But you can't eat the scenery and you can't make much of a life there if you can't get a good job to provide for your family. It's worse too, when others take away your land because you don't belong to the privileged classes."

"I've read that there is a very rigid caste system in Nepal, similar to that in India," said Helen.

The waiter nodded. "That is true. I and my people come from a lower caste. We are not allowed the opportunity to send our children to schools for anything more than a basic education. And we can't get good jobs with the government or in private businesses except the lowest paying ones. So, because of the prejudice against us and the persecution we endure from the Brahmin classes, I and a group of my friends decided to ask at the U.S. Embassy for political asylum. Soon after we were given our visas and we came to New York, and to Utica."

"I wonder if you might be able to help me with something," Sam asked. He opened one of the letters from the bundle they had been talking about. "This particular letter was sent from Nepal, as you can see from the stamp, and there's a return address that's difficult for us to read. Can you help with that?"

The waiter took the envelope in his hands and focused on the return address.

"Yes, I know the area where this letter came from. It is a mountainous region of western Nepal. Very beautiful. Many people have been going there for years, to hike from village to village, through the many trails that are there. And this letter was sent from one of the Buddhist monasteries."

"Monastery?" asked Carl.

"Yes, a monastery. Many of the monasteries and temples are open to travelers. It is a way for the monks to make some money, for some of them to have contact with the outside world, and also to gently introduce people to the culture and ideas of Buddhism. Sometimes people go there and live in the monasteries for a long time. From all over the world. They relax, get away from the pressures and challenges of the outside world."

Carl lifted up his cup of coffee. "Well, there you have it, Sam. We've been looking for a place to go, to relax, and to put this all in perspective. And now we learn that Nepal might be a great place not only for us to explore but also to possibly let you find out some more about your Mom."

Sam looked at Helen.

"Don't look at me, Sam. This is your quest. I'm not going to stop you. If you feel that you need to find out about your mother and maybe get a lead on what happened to her well then, all well and good. Who knows, you might even find out that she lived out her final days there."

"Or that she might be still alive there," said Sam.

"Or that, too, Sam," Helen remarked, "but she would probably be somewhere approaching 90 years old, and might not be in the best of health, if she were still alive."

The waiter, who had stayed by their table as they deliberated, offered to help them with arrangements. "I know some people in Nepal who are in the tourism business. They help to arrange tours for groups of Americans, like you, to go on vacation, and to visit different places. I can give you some contact information if you would like."

"Maybe you might even go with us, as a guide. You know the language, the area, the customs?" Sam asked.

"Thank you so much for the offer. I cannot. I am needed here at the restaurant and I have many family commitments at the moment, so that could not happen. If you have a business card or your phone number, I will see if I can get one fellow who puts together group trips in the area where that letter came from."

Sam and Helen and Carl thanked him for the dinner and also for his offer to help them.

As they left the restaurant, the waiter returned. "I'll try to get you some answers and information in the next few days."

CHAPTER 15

An Expedition Is Decided Upon

True, they had had too much to drink at the Columbia. Sam had commiserated with his friends about his shock, his anger, his confusion, and the jumble of thoughts that went through his head after Zofia had confided in him about his past.

Carl Thurston had come to the rescue again to calm his friend down. He had made sure that Sam had a steady supply of Scotch to quiet him down and ease his pain. Somewhere during that evening Carl had recommended that he and Sam take a trip, a vacation somewhere, to ease his mind.

"I hope you don't mean Montana again," Sam asked sourly. "I don't know if I can go through another vacation like that. As I remember, we nearly got killed, and half of Montana would have been burned to the ground if it wasn't for you."

"No, Sam. No Montana. Not this time," Carl answered somewhat sheepishly. "But it's the same idea. You don't make some rash decisions based on how you feel now, or on how much Scotch you've had to drink tonight."

"How much Scotch did I have tonight"" Sam asked with a noticeable slur in his voice.

"At least one," Carl quickly lied.

"Yeah, at least one…and one, and one, and one and…" said Sam.

"Yup. Something like that," Carl nodded. "How about heading off to Nepal and Tibet and the Himalayas. We talked with that waiter fellow at the Horned Dorset. And Helen was on board with it. And those letters

111

you guys found, from Nepal, from Eva, your Mom. You told me the waiter called you back and gave you contact info on some travel agent over there that would set things up for us. We could stop off in Paris for a day or so, and then go on to Nepal. You can't make that long trip in one day. We've always talked about going to Katmandu and Lhasa, checking out the mountains and the monasteries and the food. Remember, you had that buddy of yours from Maine who went there and told you stories of how great it was."

"Yeah, I do remember. He went in the 70's when all the globe trotting hippies went to India and Nepal and Tibet to find 'nirvana'." Sam sipped some Scotch from his glass. "And hashish too, lots of marijuana, hash, Thai stick, all that stuff. That was long ago. Don't do that shit any more, remember? Not cool. Not wanted."

"No, I don't mean smoking shit like years ago in college. No, I mean taking a vacation, like hiking and enjoying the scenery, and relaxing. Maybe a beer or two, that's all. But getting away for a while and getting your head screwed back on where it was before."

"Where is it now?" Sam asked.

"Way, way out in left field," Carl replied. "Way out."

"I'd have to close my clinic for a few weeks," Sam thought aloud.

"So, have the patients rescheduled and justify it as sick time that you need to get yourself back together." Carl offered.

"Left field, huh?"

"Way out."

CHAPTER 16

A Reunion - Lisa and Carl

Carl was alone after lunch in their hotel room in Paris, near Montparnasse. Sam had wanted to take a look around Paris and do some shopping for Helen and their children, Elaine and Nathaniel. The adventurous doctor had become excited when he discovered that this wonderful city of love and romance and history had kiosks strategically located throughout Paris where one could rent bicycles and ride through the streets and then find another drop-off in which to magnetically replace the bike only to return later and take out yet another bike. Sam was like a little kid, excited about pedaling along, weaving in and out of the traffic, and going wherever he wanted without the need to find a parking spot for a car or ride the crowded subways.

Carl, on the other hand, was not very good with bicycles. Even as a kid he had rarely ridden them. He felt safer using the "shoe leather express" instead of a French velocipede.

Carl picked up a pen and hovered over some hotel stationary he had found in the drawers of the escritoire, or writing desk, in their room. He paused for a moment, trying to gather his thoughts before putting ink to paper. It had been over three years since he had last seen Lisa, but never did a day go by that his thoughts didn't drift to some attribute or aspect of her, or his intense love for her. One common cliché people use to describe the vividness of their most important memories is that "it seemed like only yesterday."

Yesterday.

Carl smiled a half-smile as he remembered the poetic phrase that Lisa had given to him in their last moments together, in Leonardsville, before they were violently separated. He was reminded of the lyrics from a song that she had given Carl as a password, so long ago.

"Oh, you'll never, ever find tomorrow, 'cause
The yesterday you saw was just a little bit of today."

Carl was living "a little bit of today" every day. With Lisa in his thoughts he was always "in the moment". He carried that 'yesterday', their desire, the sweeping emotions that flooded their hearts as they kissed and held each other for that last moment before they were forced to let go of each other, before they would be discovered and killed.

Despite all of his confusion and conflicting emotions at the little farm house in Leonardsville, Carl know that she loved him dearly and deeply and that every word of love and passion that they had spoken between themselves was true.

That truth was only underscored and reaffirmed after his meeting with special agent Bolton of the Syracuse FBI office. He remembered and had replayed that meeting in his head many times over the past three years. Agent Bolton had kept up the ruse, as planned, to protect Lisa. Only after Carl Thurston recited the words of the poetic code that Lisa had given him in their final moments of desperation, did Bolton's demeanor change.

At first seemingly unfazed, the veteran FBI agent cautiously questioned Carl and Sam, who had driven to Syracuse to corroborate their story. Satisfied with Carl's story and his well-intentioned involvement with Lisa, he proceeded to open up to the policeman and the doctor. It was then and there that Carl learned the true story of Lisa. He came to understand her pain, her anguish, her loss, and the source of her drive, determination, and sacrifice. He loved her even more now, if that was possible. He remembered his own commitment to her.

Agent Bolton had advised that Carl forget about her. She would be a different person after she completed her undercover assignment. He cautioned Carl that he might not even recognize her afterwards.

Agent Bolton had not explicitly said the words that police often used when referring to someone who had experienced the profound and sustained stress of living their cover, monitoring their every word and action until they became that persona, that shield, that they could not let down for even one moment. This might otherwise spell exposure and certain death.

Damaged goods.

Those were the damning words. Carl had worked for many years in the Utica police department, the U.P.D., and had seen the havoc and personal deterioration of a man that occurred after having gone deep undercover for a year or more. Psychiatric problems, drug abuse, divorce, and suicide were often the result.

Damaged goods.

Lisa had been undercover as a mole in the FBI's sting operation for three years and more. Surely she would be damaged goods. But Carl had made a commitment to her, to himself and to their love. He would wait for her, however long it took.

He picked up his pen and started to write on the hotel stationery: "My dearest Lisa, I don't know if you'll ever read this letter, or if I will ever see you again. I don't even know where you are or what you're up to. I hope you're safe. I hope you're OK. I carry you in my heart every day. I also carry the hope that someday, soon, we'll be together again, this time for good, forever. A real reunion."

Lisa picked up the phone in the Hotel Ritz lobby. She asked the hotel operator for an outside line. Looking around, she saw no one nearby, no one watching. She punched in the codes for international calling and dialed the number from memory, fearing to ever commit the number to paper. Lisa knew that she was taunting death, her own execution. But just like the high an addict experiences right after having made the decision to score some drugs, before even making the deal, and well before even snorting or shooting up with the drug, she felt that same exhilaration. She was almost giddy, like a naughty little girl who felt tingles all over, knowing that she might get caught.

She could hear the phone ringing above the beating of her heart. She tightened her grip on the receiver, her expectations mounting.

"Hello?" said a familiar voice on the other end.

A feeling of relief washed over her. She brought the mouthpiece of the receiver closer to her. Her lips quivered and she licked her upper lip with her tongue. She drew in a deep breath.

"Hello? This is Officer Thurston. Can I help you?"

She suddenly hung up the phone. She slammed the receiver back onto its cradle on the wall with more force than she had wanted to. She turned around, to see if anyone had reacted to the noise.

Carl felt the hackles in his neck rise. He wasn't expecting a phone call from anyone in particular that day. It could have been a wrong number. Sam was out shopping for gifts for Helen and his kids. He wouldn't have hung up without saying a word. The two of them were traveling together in Paris on their way to Nepal.

Carl and Sam had both purchased International calling plans and had all of their calls through their cell phones routed to wherever they were outside of the United States. The arrangement had come in handy, during their flight over to France, when they were waiting to board their connection in Dublin to Paris.

Helen Petrie, with the help of William, had been going through her mother-in-law's possessions, especially old boxes and crates and old papers and letters in the attic. She had found a few more letters from an Eva in Nepal also dating from the late 1950's. Helen updated her husband with bits of new information that might help him on his quest to trace the whereabouts of his biological mother.

There was something in the silence, the lingering before the abrupt termination of the call, which fueled Carl's curiosity to a razor sharp focus. Did he detect a sigh, a deep breath just before the caller hung up? Normally he would just shrug the incident off, relegate it into the dustbin of "no importance". He had an instinctual feeling with this call however, that the call to him was deliberate. It was not a wrong number. It was not a mistake. In the few seconds that the caller and Carl were connected an ethereal switch had been turned on, a connection made, in the policeman's mind.

Carl believed, and had often verbalized that, "there are no coincidences, no accidents. All things happen for a reason. It might be something trite; it might have nothing to do with the case you're working on, or anything to do with you at all. But all things fit into that big puzzle of Life, somewhere. If you can figure it out, if it works for you and you solve the case... Well then, bingo! You got it!"

Lisa hurried back to her hotel room. She felt anxious now, hoping that no one had seen her making the phone call. She hadn't dared to use her cell phone.

A cell phone had been given to her by the drug lords and capos that she worked with, and for and....on. Those smart phones were the latest models with the latest apps, filled with games, unlimited texting and data contracts, and the latest technology. Included in that technology was the ability of the lords to monitor every call or text or data that was received or transmitted. It was like having an electronic leash around your neck. You could venture out and explore and try out just about anything. Conference calls, online gambling, order a pizza, or buy something on eBay. But say something offensive, or worse yet incriminating, proving that you were disloyal or possibly a threat, you might be signing your death warrant.

Lisa knew, however, that she had to contact Carl. The International Alliance was planning its annual meeting in Upstate New York, right near where Carl lived and worked. Was it the convenience of the location or the urgency of the moment that forced her to take such bold action and possibly expose herself, and him, to discovery and almost certain death?

Was she simply giving in to whatever remained of her love for Carl and her desire to see her life of danger, and depravity, and constant threat of being exposed, finally brought to a close?

She struggled with that for a long time. It would be so "safe" to just have her call up her FBI bosses and ask to be taken away to safety and into a witness protection program. She could live in peace; quell the horrible, shameful memories that roiled within her brain like scalding water boiling over the brim of a kitchen pot, those painfully unwelcome thoughts and memories of the past few years of her life that haunted her almost every night.

Knowing what she now knew of the diabolical plans that the International Alliance was about to be set in motion, and the dangerous terrorist and criminal organizations that were being recruited, she felt she had no choice. She had seen and heard enough of the plans and understood that she, and she alone, held the power and the key information to topple the Alliance.

She made her decision. In so doing she realized that her resolve now was just as strong, if not more so, as when she finally stopped feeling like a victim after the murder of her family.

She remembered walking into the FBI office where her husband had worked and announcing that she wanted to help apprehend his killers. She remembered vividly how the director tried to dissuade her, asking her to go home and leave the job to the professionals. She recalled applying for and getting a secretarial job at the FBI office and how she took the Civil Service Exam to become an FBI agent. She had to explain, justify, and fight every step of the way to get through the agency training.

After many discussions with her superiors, and badgering, and persistence, she finally convinced them that she could do at least as good, if not a much better, job of infiltrating the local drug cartel as any man. Also, as an attractive woman with training, skill, and the drive for revenge, she might be able to go places and get information that no man could get.

After pacing around the hotel lobby and out the front door to the street, she returned to the bank of hotel lobby phones off to one side of the ornate receptionist area that the Hotel Ritz Paris was so well known for. She picked up the receiver once again.

"Hello, operator? I'd like to have an outside line."

"*Mais bien sur tout de suite!*"

CHAPTER 17

At The Jardin de Tuilleries

She waited until he picked up the receiver. "Hello, Carl? This is Lisa. I'm calling from Paris. I need your help. We need to talk."

Carl was overjoyed to hear her voice again. It was like a dream come true. "This is unbelievable! I'm in Paris right now! Where are you?" he stammered.

He quickly explained why he and Sam were there. They would scratch the Nepal trip, do an about face and take her back to the U.S., right then and there.

"No, we can't. I love you more now than ever before, and hearing your voice lifts my spirits and gives me hope like I've never felt before. I need to get off the phone right now, though, I don't have much time. I'll explain it all as soon as we meet. I can't believe you're so close! We've got to meet somewhere right away."

They would rendezvous at the Bel Canto, near the Hotel de Ville, a place she had frequented before. She enjoyed this elegant restaurant, not because she was an opera lover, but because of the exquisite menu and a chance to hear the waiters, from the Paris Conservatory, belt out classical songs from Mozart and Verdi, and other composers. She had dined here alone often, while Gallois attended his meetings with the Alliance. This had been a place to ruminate, to ponder and contemplate. Now it was the first step in meeting Carl and making plans that would determine her fate as well as the fate of many others.

Carl had arrived at the restaurant before Lisa. He specifically asked for a table in a dimly lit corner but where he could see the entrance to the establishment. After a short while, during which he ordered an espresso and a smoked duck filet salad with raspberry vinaigrette, he saw her walk in.

As happily surprised as he was, he didn't want to make his presence known to her right away. Reflexes stemming from his training as a police officer, who had been in many a dangerous situation, caused him to sit at his table, in a low profile, and unobtrusively observe her. He wanted to make sure that she was alone before attempting any contact with her.

After a quick glance at the menu, and her order taken by the waiter, she stood up and walked towards the restrooms. Again Carl waited, but saw that no one, either male or female, seemed to be following her.

He stood up from his corner table and walked slowly towards the bar in the adjacent room, knowing that there was also access to the rest rooms from there. He waited in the dark hallway. No one else came. He heard the door to the ladies' room open. There before him stood Lisa.

"Lisa, it's me. Carl." he said in hushed tones.

She grabbed him firmly by the arm and rushed him into the ladies room, locking the door behind her. She threw her arms around his neck and buried her face into the side of his neck. He could feel her trembling and her grip on his neck and shoulders tightening. Her body was heaving rhythmically, and her breathing heavy, as she apparently was stifling sobs.

He held her without saying anything. Gently, he kissed the side of her head, her cheek, and her neck. Slowly he rocked her from side to side, not wanting to ever let her go. He could smell the fragrance of a sensuous perfume that she had dabbed behind her ears and on her throat, feeling certain that she had chosen this special scent just for this meeting.

"We don't have much time, Carl. Please. Listen to me." She continued holding him.

"Lisa, I love you. Not a day goes by that I don't think of you. Let me help you, to get out of here. We could walk away now! I will protect you with my life."

"Oh, Carl, you don't know how much those words mean to me. And believe me, I want to. I think of you all the time. I've written countless letters to you and then immediately destroyed them, so I wouldn't blow my cover.

But now all of that has changed. I've gotten deeper into this whole mess than I thought I would."

"Then let me help you," Carl interrupted.

"Listen. Stop. This thing is so big, it's international. This is so big, it's incredible, it's mind boggling."

Carl was confused. He stood there in silence, looking into her big, sweet brown eyes. He wanted to lose himself in them. Like Ulysses fighting off the sounds of the Muses, standing bound to the mast, Carl regained his bearings and listened intently.

"I worked my way up to the major players in the International Alliance. This is an organization that not only controls most of the major drug operations in the U.S. and most other Western countries, they are funneling billions of dollars into their plans which, when done, supposedly will reconstitute the Nazi Third Reich and the Aryan Race."

Carl stood there dumbfounded. There was a lot of information to process in so short a space of time, from when he first saw her again, after three years, to now being confronted with information on an organization that went beyond terror.

"You're in danger!" he nervously exclaimed. "You're way too deep into all of this! We do need to get you out of here now!"

"No. No. I'm O.K., at least for now. I need to go to a few stores and buy anything so that I have a few bags to prove that I was acting out my gender stereotype... shopping!"

They both laughed nervously at that. They kissed a warm, sensual kiss. They hugged and held each other.

"In an hour I'll meet you at the Jardin des Tuilleries. I'll explain everything to you there. I know what the International Alliance bosses are up to. I know their schedules and most of their plans. I need your help to bring them down. This is the most diabolical scheme I've ever heard of. We need to stop them. With your help, we can. Here, on this napkin I drew a map of where we'll meet. There's a statue of a lioness near the statue of the Good Samaritan, on the park side toward the Louvre. Once you get there, destroy the drawing and wait. I'll be there. We have to be careful."

"And we can't do this in public," he said. Carl wrapped his arms around her waist and planted another warm, long kiss on her eager lips.

They pressed their bodies even closer and ground their hips in rhythm, as they ran their hands over each other.

"Oh, Carl. You've been a beacon of light through all this darkness, this hell I've been living through. At times I even thought of taking my own life. I knew however that you were there for me. You promised me that, and I believed you!"

"And I meant every word of it. And I mean it now and to eternity. I love you with all my being. I'll do whatever it takes to bring down this International Alliance, and to bring us back together. I'll sacrifice everything that's dear to me, my life if needs be, to bring you away from this horror, from that hellhole you've been existing in. I will bring you home."

"Home." Lisa said the word slowly and carefully, as if it was a foreign word she was just learning and cautiously wanted to sound it out.

"Home."

Carl passed the statue to the Good Samaritan, as directed by Lisa's crude drawing, and turned towards the Seine River and then rounded his first left to a smaller pool with a central fountain. There was a great tree, a Judas tree (one with large long seed pods, tan brown, as she had described for him), hurriedly, in the restaurant. The tree stood near the statue of a "tigress", with a pheasant in her mouth, ready to feed her two nearby cubs.

He read the placard describing the lion's statue:

Cain Auguste Nicholas
Paris 1822-1894
Tigresse Portant un Paon a Ses Petits
Bronze 1873-1876
Place au Jardin des Tuilleries en 1884

There were faded green painted metal chairs situated throughout the park, courtesy of the Paris Department of Parks. Carl settled back into one of these comfortable chairs and sat there, impatiently, waiting. A wave of mixed emotions washed over him and roiled within him.

In one sense, he felt so happy, so lucky. After three long years he had finally made contact again with the one person that he loved more than anyone on this earth. And yet he felt as if he had seen her through a thick clear glass wall. He was so close to her yet unable to express his own feelings churning within him. The meeting had been so brief, as the last time. It was as if he was given the world's most beautiful treasure, only to have it immediately snatched away from him, yet with hopes of possessing it once again.

She casually approached him, wearing a dark green trim jacket with a dark sweater with a high collar that peeked through a colored scarf that was wrapped loosely around her neck in the Parisian fashion. She had a charcoal gray pleated skirt and black tights, and shiny dark brown leather boots with buckles on the sides that went to her knees and flared open. She had a small matching purse, dark green, slung over her shoulder and under her arm. Without glancing at Carl, she turned down the small dirt walkway in the garden and walked past Carl without a nod or acknowledging his presence.

She stopped and looked around to her right and left, turned and slowly walked back towards Carl. She looked him right in the eyes. A flood of emotions seemed to come from those eyes. He wanted to stand up and wrap his arms around her there, hold her tightly and hold her as long as he could to make sure that this wasn't a dream. He wanted to smell her hair, plant kisses on her forehead and her cheeks and eyes and hug her again. He wanted to hold her and let her know that his love had only grown in the years since he had last seen her at the Leonardsville Farm. He knew however, that she would have to be calling the shots and so he sat in silence, staring at her without expression.

She turned to him in a matter of fact way and asked, "Do you have a light?"

She brought out a cigarette case. He fumbled in his pockets without taking his eyes off of her and offered her a match. She lit her cigarette and stood there for a while and inhaled deeply.

"May I join you?" she asked.

He was surprised at the emotionless of her question. He understood full well that they had to act this way in public for fear that they might be noticed. She sat down in the green metal park chair near him. She took another drag off her cigarette.

Lisa looked around again cautiously as she smoked. After a pause, she said, in hushed tones, "Carl, I have thought of you every day since we last saw each other."

He started to say something, and to reach a hand out towards her.

"No, Carl, put your hands down. We can't show that we might know each other. It has to appear that we've just met as strangers."

Carl sat back in his chair. She continued.

"Carl, I have some incredible information I need to share with you, and I need your help. I started out working with the drug cartel in New York State, which led me to Montréal and to René Gallois, the head of the North Eastern division for narcotics. But it's gotten further than that, and I've gotten deeper. I wish I could tell you everything that's happened, but I can't. Some of it is very important, some of it would probably even sicken or anger you, and some of it even makes me ashamed. I had to do a lot of different things in order to keep my cover and to get as high up as I could in the organization. And now I've put it all together and here we are. The International Alliance."

"International Alliance," he quietly repeated.

"Yes," she nodded and continued. "The drug cartels and a lot of security departments and spy agencies are involved in the grand scheme or organization called the International Alliance. It's in essence, a rebirth of the Nazi party and their goal is to develop into a Fourth Reich.

"It is on track to be the most wicked, diabolical, strongly organized and well financed secret organization the world has ever known. And I need you to help me to stop it. We need to pool our resources, my knowledge of the group, and your contacts. We can do this. We can bring them down."

"But why not just walk away from it. Now. I could take you away from this right now," he pleaded. "Let others handle it."

"No. I can't. It wouldn't work. If I leave now people will be suspicious. They'll hide in the woodwork; change their plans, their schedules. They'll probably kill off a bunch of people just to sever some connections, and wait a while longer to consolidate their power. And their plans. And when they're ready to strike out again, they will. But we won't be there to know what's happening. And when they do strike, it'll be too late."

"All right then, what can we do?" he asked.

She briefed him on the most important aspects of what she had learned about the International Alliance, about Bruno Metzger, Manfred Haeckel and their Board of henchmen. Lisa detailed, as succinctly a she could, what she knew about their next grand international meeting of regional members, allies, contributors and major political and financial sympathizers.

The annual meeting of the International Alliance was this year to be held outside of the small town of Oriskany, New York at the Turning Stone Resort. Ironic it was that the first victorious battle of any significance, of the American Revolution, was fought nearby, at the Battle of Oriskany. Lisa understood the symbolic significance of the location, that here was the "keystone" to their success. She opened her notebook and took out a page, obviously torn from a book, and read a synopsis of the Battle of Oriskany to Carl:

In August, 1776 a small army of local militia, commanded by General Nicholas Herkimer, had marched for 2 days from today's Little Falls to a wide ravine with a stream running through it, near the Indian village of Oriska. There they were savagely attacked by Indians of the Iroquois Confederation and their British allies as well as Tories; settlers loyal to the British Crown.

The American colonists, the Tryon County militia, had come to rescue the beleaguered soldiers at Fort Stanwix, at the site of present day Rome, New York. the British invasion of New York, and the siege of Fort Stanwix, was part of a grand scheme to split New York State, the "Keystone State" via a three- pronged attack coming from the West with General St. Leger, from Montreal in the North by General Burgoyne, and from New York City in the South with a force commanded by General Howe.

The plan fell apart first with victory of the Americans under General Herkimer. Up until that battle any time American rebel forces took to the field against the well trained, well armed and well disciplined British troops, after one volley of musket fire the Americans broke and ran. Here now for the first time supporters of Washington and the Revolution could dream of the possibility of standing their ground and giving resistance. The next great battle was a few weeks later at Saratoga, just northwest of Albany. Due to the brilliant fortifications constructed by General Thaddeus

Kosciuszko and the invigorating news of the Oriskany success, and the skilled leadership of Benedict Arnold, the British were soundly defeated.

"What goes around, comes around," Lisa said as she looked with longing eyes into Carl's. She would make her stand against the International Alliance in Upstate New York, as the brave patriots from Tryon County had done two centuries before. They would plan; they would execute those plans, and through their actions, topple a mighty empire, an Alliance of power, greed, deceit, obscene decadence and murder as never before seen on the face of the Earth.

"Carl, you need to go on with Sam to Nepal. Don't tell him about us meeting today or what I've told you until you get back to the U.S. He needs to do what he needs to do. You said he's on his own personal quest. And nothing is going to happen for the next two weeks anyway. Make your contacts, like we planned. I'll get in touch with you as soon as I'm in New York, as soon as I can."

They embraced again. Neither Lisa nor Carl wanted to be the first to break their hold on each other. Who knew if this might be the last time they saw each other alive. Would this reunion be their last?

CHAPTER 18

The Killing of Rene Gallois

Gallois was furious. Yet while seething inside with anger and rage he, as was his character, expertly feigned an outward manner of control, of calm, and a display of command of everything happening around him. Having been notified by one of his men that Lisa had used the hotel phone that morning, he quickly reviewed many of his earlier suspicions about her.

He had been introduced to her during his visit a few months earlier to Upstate New York. His direct pipeline, his connection to the entire Northeastern U.S., had been through Carlos Quinterra and his organization. That relationship had been irreparably severed with the death of Quinterra in a helicopter crash. There had been no one left who Gallois could solidly trust.

He had traveled to Utica and interviewed the remnants of the local cartel. While some of Quinterra's "soldiers" had scattered and vanished, fearing an in depth investigation into the crash and the farmhouse at Leonardsville with its stores of cocaine, some remained loyal and were cautiously taken under his wing. The rest who knew too much were, with the help of Bruno Metzger and the Council, systematically ferreted out and terminated. This not only prevented further leaks of information to the authorities, but also cemented loyalty of the few remaining Quinterra men who joined him.

Her cell phone rang. "Hello?" Lisa answered. There was no immediate reply on the other end. She could hear faint deep breathing, like a snake, hissing in the distance, pondering its next move.

"I need to see you in your room. Wait for me. I'll be there shortly." It was the unmistakably monotone voice of Rene Gallois.

Even though she had heard his voice countless times before, it still brought out feelings of disgust and revilement. This was one part of her that didn't need acting, but it did take a lot of conscious energy to control and hide her feelings of hatred and loathing.

Back in his own room at the Hotel Ritz de Paris, Rene Gallois paced the carpeted floor in his stocking feet. He was angry. Agitated. What a fool he had been. He had only too easily accepted Lisa into his fold. Admittedly, he had fallen for her beauty and her charm. And her willingness to please. Now he realized she had been only too willing.

One of Gallois's men had seen Lisa in the lobby using the hotel phone, making a quick phone call, and had thought that odd. Everyone in Rene Gallois's entourage had cell phones given to them. All of Gallois's people were explicitly told not to use any other phone to call anywhere or anyone. This allowed Gallois to keep total control and review over who called whom, when, and where. To do otherwise would be treasonous. And here was one of Gallois's women doing just that. The man had reported her actions to Rene Gallois immediately.

Lisa opened the door to her suite and allowed Rene to enter. He was dressed in dark, pleated dress pants with black suspenders over a white cotton shirt. He wore no tie. It was apparent that he had quickly left his hotel room to hurry over to her, as he had many times before at other meetings when he needed to have his carnal appetites fulfilled before moving on to some other project or meeting or business deal. Tonight however, he was in no rush to kiss and fondle, grope and undress Lisa, as he often did as soon as he entered her room.

She sensed something in his behavior, his body language. It smelled less of raw sex and desire. She felt the presence of power, cunning, control. Of evil. She didn't like this atmosphere. Instinctively there rose in her a fear, a need for self-preservation.

He stared at her with cold eyes, his face expressionless except for the slightest hint of a sneer, an upturning of the right side of his mouth. He reminded her of a cobra, coiled with head erect and motionless, waiting to strike, as it stared blankly ahead, mesmerizing its victim before the fatal lunge.

"Who did you call today," he asked matter of factly. His head and eyes remained motionless, without blinking as he spoke.

Lisa turned away from his gaze, trying to collect her thoughts, searching frantically for a believable reply.

"What do you mean, Rene? When? I called a few different people today. The hairdresser at the hotel."

He slammed his fist down on the nearby table. "Don't fuck with me! Who did you call this afternoon? You were in the lobby and you used the hotel phone. You know you are only to use the phones I gave you. Only those. No calls to anyone else."

She stared at him in silence. She drooped her eyebrows and pouted, hoping this display might cool his anger, as she contemplated her next moves and replies.

"I'm so sorry, Rene. I had forgotten the phone in my purse up here in my room. I needed to call the hairdresser to make an appointment so that I could get in, so that I could get an appointment to have my hair styled for tonight's dinner. Remember, you told me that tonight's meeting was very important and that I needed to look my best for you. Remember?"

"Yes, that I did," he replied. He seemed calmer now, as if her explanation might have sufficed. "Ah, how could I have been so stupid, of course? Sorry, it's just that there is so much riding on these meetings we are having here in Paris, the connections, the business deals, and the upcoming meeting of the entire Alliance in New York. Upstate. I hope I didn't upset you or frighten you. Come here, let me hold you."

He advanced towards her with open arms. He enveloped her, holding her close to his chest and lightly squeezed her to him. He took her firmly and deliberately by the hand and led her to the bedroom.

At first he was gentle, even loving. He teased her earlobes and then her nipples with his teeth, ever careful not to bite or nibble too hard. His stroking of her breasts and her thighs and her vagina had become rougher and rougher as they rolled from one position to another. His saliva moistened fingers glided into and out of her vagina and her anus. He pumped her wet womanhood with his hand and fingers and eventually entered those same channels with his rock hard penis.

She gasped and moaned as he took her again and again. She was surprised by his boldness and eventually by his abandon and his aggressiveness. His steady advances onto and into her surprised and even excited her. While there was obviously no love lost between Lisa, the huntress, and Rene, her prey, she couldn't deny the reflex waves of pleasure that were washing over her as he probed deeper and deeper into her body, and now, even into her soul.

He expelled his man juice into her with a guttural moan and one loud high-pitched sigh after another. He pulled his long, still stiff and swollen member out of her and continued to ejaculate a steady stream of steaming white semen onto her buttock and thigh. He knelt on the bed straddling her thigh and watched the volcanic eruption of his cum onto her hot skin.

He lay next to her now. He took in a deep breath and slowly exhaled. His eyes were closed as he savored this experience.

"It's good that we can be so open like this, and about so many things," he said.

Lisa wasn't sure how to respond to that. She heard his breathing become slightly more rapid and deeper. She was starting to feel uncomfortable again.

He tightened his grip around her waist. "Tell me again, who did you call this afternoon with the hotel lobby phone."

"The hairdresser, I told you, silly." She tried to sound coquettish.

Ah yes. But I spoke with the hotel operator as well. She told me that you had asked for assistance to get an outside line. You made a call outside of the hotel. The hairstyling salon is in the hotel here. You used them just two days ago, isn't that right, Lisa?"

Lisa felt panic rise up within her. She tried to sit up and to break Rene's embrace, but he tightened his grip even more.

"I remember back to when you joined me and my organization in Montreal. You had been an escort to Carlos Quinterra from New York. Poor fellow. He was killed in a helicopter crash, right outside of his farm. Leonardsville, right? What a tragedy!"

Lisa attempted again, gently, to loosen his hold on her and sit up.

"Carlos was dealing with a lot of drugs, doing a lot of business for me and for our cartel. He was a key player. Nothing happened after his death, no inquiry into his farmhouse. And then you showed up on my doorstep there, in Montreal, with some of his men, and I took you in, on their say so. All seemed OK, but now, now I'm getting a little concerned. Are you just sloppy, and stupid, and not doing what I told you. Or are you working for somebody else? Are you plotting to have me killed like Quinterra was killed? Are you working for somebody else...or maybe, are you working for the police, for the Feds, for the authorities?"

Lisa's mind raced around and around, as she searched for something to say to steer him into another direction of thought.

She was able to roll away from him and off the bed. As she stood before him, pacing, she tried to collect her thoughts and come up with a reaction, a plan, a response to his accusations. One minute she was like a chess player, calculating her next move. The next minute she felt like a cornered animal, in a cat and mouse game. Either way the stakes were very high. Either she would convince him that she was not a threat, not a security breach, not a traitor, or she would be dead....or one of them would be dead. She tried to remember what she had learned at the FBI Academy. Had they rehearsed any scenarios like this?

Gallois broke her stream of thought now as he stood up from the bed and slowly walked towards her. He buttoned and zipped his pants. She watched with fear as he slipped his black leather belt off. He doubled it up and held it in both hands as he came closer.

"What are you going to do with that, Rene? I told you the truth. I'm sorry if you don't believe me. I'm sorry if I made you feel uncomfortable or ungrateful."

"Shut up, bitch," he yelled as he struck a nearby sofa with the large belt. The dull contact sound of a thud startled her as much as the vicious tone in his voice.

"I'm going to show you what it means to fuck with Rene Gallois! I don't know who you are or why you're here or what you want. I'm going to beat you until you beg me to stop and beat you again until you tell me the truth!"

"I am telling you the truth! I called the hairdresser for an appointment. I don't know anything about a hotel operator. I used the lobby phone to call them directly."

Gallois unexpectedly swung the belt down and across, striking her on the left side of her head and face. She was able to lift up her left arm at the last moment and softened the blow only slightly. She reeled to her right from the impact and fell onto the bed.

Gallois began swinging wildly at her now, hitting her covered head, hands, belly, and legs with the strap. She yelped from the searing pain she felt as he continued his onslaught. He was a wild man unleashed. She had never seen him like this. She had never seen anyone like this.

She summoned enough strength, her senses awakened keenly by this threat of death, to roll off the bed and attempt to distance herself from him. He watched with a smirk of sardonic amusement as she ran to the glass doors to the patio and slid them open.

"What are you going to do now, slut? Call out to the manager or some Good Samaritan that you're getting the shit beat out of you? Or are you going to jump over the railing to the street and get away? We're on the 2nd floor. I don't think that will do you any good."

He paused for a moment, as if in thought.

"Of course, that might be a good option. Either I beat the fucking piss out of you until you're dead, or you jump out, over the railing to a quick and much painless death." He chuckled. "Not a bad choice, really. Death...or death."

He started again towards her, picking up his pace as he swashed the leather belt back and forth before him. Suddenly Lisa remembered a scenario from her FBI training days similar to this. Her mind raced now, reflexively calculating the man's rhythmic moves as he ran towards her. When he was within one pace of her, with his right arm raised, poised to strike yet once again, she grabbed him under both armpits with her hands. At the same time she rolled backwards onto her buttocks and back. She had flexed her legs in anticipation and was now placing both feet flatly against his belly. As she continued rolling backwards his momentum carried him further. She quickly straightened her legs, forcing him even higher off of her and over the balcony railing. It was over in a fraction of a second. The stunned Gallois didn't even have a chance to scream or let out a word of protest, as he silently sailed over the railing and into the cool airspace of Paris. A short moment later she heard a distant, sickening, low-pitched thud, as if a sack of potatoes had been thrown onto the concrete below.

He lay on the pavement below, not moving, with his head angulated and twisted to one side in a gruesome, anatomically incorrect position.

Lisa awoke abruptly early the next morning, sweat pouring off of her half-naked body. She lay on her hotel bed, scarcely covered. She felt the warm, wet clammy skin of a breast beneath her left hand. The nipple was hard, erect, as if she had been aroused by her own exploring fingers or by some sordid, sexual dream. Quickly the memories rushed into her consciousness as she became more alert.

She remembered. She had killed Rene Gallois. Last night she had been his plaything, his sex toy. He had been very energetic then, caressing her, fondling her, kissing and licking her, and pumping her like a jack hammer as she lay on her back or on her stomach or on her knees or splayed over the back of a sofa. She had never experienced him in such an orgiastic frenzy.

The morning sun shone across the wide balcony and through the sheer curtains into the bedroom. Lisa's hands now clenched the railing of the balcony as she looked out on Paris. The high-rise apartments, the skyscrapers, and the distant hum of traffic reminded her of just about any large city she had been to. While Paris was steeped in history and offered wonderful cultural, culinary and shopping opportunities that rivaled Paris or Tokyo or London, to her it was like a small boat out at sea with her once familiar shoreline of home off in the distance, too far to swim to. And now the city, to her, reeked of fear and death.

She was reminded of Long Island, which had once been her home. She imagined it lying there somewhere to the west, where the sun went down. So near in memory, yet so far in possibilities of ever reaching it again. In some ways she could never go back home. No, that home, and her life had been destroyed. Her fingers curled more tightly now as she let feelings of anger, despair, revulsion, and revenge wash over her. As if struggling in the waves of that far off imaginary beach, she could never get to that beach, to rise out of the crashing surf, nor to stand firmly and safely on the warm, comforting sands of home.

So much had happened in such a short period of time. She felt now as if standing in the center of a vortex, the "eye of the storm". She was so tired, tired of what her life had become, tired of the daily struggles to conceal her identity, tired of suppressing her true emotions as she floated along, like a lonely leaf on the winds of a tempest all around her. Suppressing the urge to lean over the edge and, like Daedalus' son who had tried to fly closer to the sun, fall back to Earth and to closure, to the peaceful serenity of death, she turned and instead threw herself onto the bed.

Over the next few hours Lisa struggled in her mind over what direction to take next in her quest to reach the top of the drug smuggling syndicate "food chain". She had gleaned a lot of surprising information from her two new friends, Conrad and Jozef, at the earlier Hotel Ritz meeting. Lisa had used her flirting skills, assisted by free flowing wine, cognac, and scotch, to put together enough information, without seeming to be overly interested or focused, to understand "The Next Step" that those men had alluded to.

Lisa went out, to find a quiet place to sort out her thoughts. She found a quaint little sidewalk café near the Louvre, the Café Des Beaux-Arts, at the Quai Malaquais, along the Seine River. She pondered her next move as she tried to relax and sipped espresso coffee along with a snifter of Louis XIII de Remy Martin cognac. She took small bites of a croissant.

After last night's incident at the hotel, she had urgently sent an encrypted report to her contact at the FBI in the United States, giving a detailed report on Rene Gallois and his position within the hierarchy of the North American drug cartel. She knew that she could stop now, finish her job. She had killed the target she had worked so hard to identify. She had earned the right to start a new life. It would be a fresh start, a new identity, a chance to live to a ripe old age without fear that someone or something was lurking near you, in the shadows, ready to expose you after the slightest mistake you might make in doodling on a napkin, or expressing an opinion, or making a phone call or an email.

Home.

Her mind drifted back to the previous evening's soiree and her conversations with the heel-clicking Conrad and his friend Jozef.

CHAPTER 19

Sam and Carl Go To Nepal

Nepal. The land of enchantment. Shangri-La. A mountain kingdom miles above sea level. Sam looked around him at the snow capped mountains and deep valleys that were the Himalayas. The crisp, clean air he drew into his nostrils was scented with the calming aroma of incense burning from a nearby monk's temple. It was summer here in this land of snow and ice, and even though he was warm enough from the long hike this morning carrying his heavy backpack, he could feel the cool breezes against his unshaven cheeks as he trudged to the monastery that lay before him.

A magnificent wooden structure of green and red with typical curves up at the edges of the many roofs, its foundation was made of large heavy stones, carved and fitted to perfection. The locals recounted legends to him that these stones were cut and carried from the higher elevations centuries ago, in a time when there were giants and wizards in the land. There were prayer flags and prayer wheels all over the surrounding grounds of the temple, dancing and whirling to and fro like waves of yellow cloth and little ballerinas. There were no trees or shrubs nearby, only the occasional gnarled and twisted arbor, clinging to life amidst cracks in the boulders of the nearby foot hills. The sun was low on the horizon as Sam trudged over the rocky plain that led to this monastic palace, his shadow casting a long profile over the uneven ground. He turned to see Carl, also laden with a heavy backpack, breathing heavily and looking obviously tired from their long walk from the last temple.

"Why couldn't we just take a taxi here?" complained Carl. At just over six feet, Carl resembled a Percheron more than an agile mountain goat.

He put his backpack down and quickly thrust a canteen into his mouth and greedily drank from it. Sam could hear the heavy breaths and sighs between each swig of water. Thirst temporarily quenched, Carl withdrew the canteen from his lips and wiped his sweating brow and mouth with a moistened hand.

"I never should have had that last drink at the Columbia," he said ruefully, shaking his head as he spoke.

"Goddamn alcohol. Goes to my head. As if our Montana trip wasn't enough. I had to go and open my mouth about this." He took another swig from his canteen as he continued.

"Nepal! Top of the world! Exotic place! Give us a chance to really get back to Nature, away from the corrupting influences of civilization. Hah! Right now I want to be corrupted! My feet hurt, I haven't slept in on a comfortable mattress for days, I smell like a curry factory and the beer here takes like yak urine." He took another swig and took in a deep breath of fresh air. "At least the air doesn't have the stink of cars and cigarettes."

Sam smiled as he looked at his friend. He remembered back to the family reunion in Utica.

Sam had been quite surprised, and frankly shocked, at the revelations from his mother at the Petrie family reunion. To learn that he was adopted was somewhat troublesome to him. Why had she not told him of that years ago, when he was a child. Other parents normally did that, gently introducing them to their personal story, explaining where the children had come from. But now, as an adult, to suddenly learn that he had been born of a Polish Jewish woman who had survived the Nazi death camps, that Zofia had refused to return Sam to his birth mother, was too complicated for him to handle. Too many questions. Too many emotions all competing for time and resolution in his head.

He loved Zofia, even now, even knowing that she was his foster mother, not his "real" mother, whatever that meant. His birth mother? Was she still alive? What happened to her? Zofia had sternly ordered him not to try and find out about her. So much had happened since the war and afterwards. To go back and look into the past now would not only be difficult, it could create some serious problems that Sam should not be involved with.

What did she mean by that, Sam thought. Had his birth mother been involved in something that would bring shame to him? Was she involved in illegal activities? Was she even alive and, if not, under what circumstances had she died?

So many questions and no answers. He remembered back to the time around when Zofia had died. He and Helen had gone up into the attic of her home rummaging through boxes and old suitcases and old wooden trunks that held many objects from Zofia's and William's past. There were books in Polish, porcelain dishware, magazines, clothing, William's military uniform, and stacks of letters, bundled with string. Most of the letters were written in Polish, and one bundle contained letters from William when he was courting her. There was one letter, separate from the others, stuffed within the pages of a Polish Bible. It was unopened. Thinking that odd for some intuitive reason, he and Helen had opened the letter but were unable to read the Polish cursive.

They had taken the letter to their family friend, Mr. Bielewski who translated it for them. The letter was from Sam's birth mother, asking that the boy be returned to her. Evidently, from its content, this was not the first time the mother had tried to contact Zofia or asked for the boy's return. The mother had again profusely and sincerely thanked Zofia for allowing the child to survive and to care for him as if he were Zofia's own.

The birth mother had a name.

Eva.

The return address on the envelope was the Kazimierz district of Krakow. Mr. Bielewski explained that this was a well-known Jewish community from the 14th century until after the Second World War when the Nazis exterminated most of Poland's Jews. He told Sam and Helen that he himself had lived near that area from before the Nazi occupation and so knew it and its history very well.

As she lay in her deathbed at home, Zofia had urged Sam not to delve into the past. Again and again, seeing that he was struggling with this new information about himself, about his past, about his mother, she tried to impress on him that "what was past was past". She even gave examples where others had tried to return children to their Jewish parents after the war. They hadn't known their real parents, were raised as Christians, not as Jews, some were raised in socially and financially better circumstances, and so on. Zofia tried to explain that there were too many heartbreaking stories and that she didn't want that to happen to Sam, whom she cherished.

The young monk sat quietly in front of them, legs folded in the traditional Lotus position, while his hands were placed, palms upward on either knee. His index and thumb were curled, opposing each other, like the closing of electrical circuit.

His head was bare, shaven to the roots. He couldn't have been over 20. He wore a saffron-colored robe over his shoulders. He had draped a burgundy wrap typical of his monastic order. Earlier he had been animated, joking, conversing in explaining some subtle aspects of meditation to Sam and Carl. Now the three sat quietly in the same pose, contemplating their lesson for the day. Each man's breathing was slow and rhythmic as proscribed by the methods of this Buddhist sect.

Sam was not used to sitting stiffly with back straight and legs bent. He wasn't able to cross his left foot over the opposite leg while the right foot went under the left knee. Instead he allowed himself to put the soles of his feet together and let his knees flop to the sides.

Carl Thurston, with his larger, stiffer frame had an even tougher time sitting into what approached some semblance of a Lotus position. Unlike Sam who comfortably plopped himself onto a large pillow on the floor Carl was sitting in a large, hand carved wooden chair with side arms and no back. He tried to settle into a comfortable posture; his arm supported by the wooden rests. These curled outward and upward. He mimicked the monk's electrical circuit by touching his index fingers to his thumbs.

Sam could hear an occasional grunt or groan as his friend shifted and fidgeted and experimented with various positions. The noises would stop for a while as Carl's large frame settled into another pose approaching ergonomic balance. There would be stillness and quiet for short while. Then the muffled protestations of his body's struggle against gravity would start again.

Balance. That was one of the key words that Sam had absorbed from the monks lesson today. Balance and meaning. "All things are in perfect balance, one with the other," the young monk had preached. "We are really only observers in the dance of life" as he called it. "In all of these things, these observations have meaning. The interface between things or events and their meaning in consciousness. What we do, what you will do as you learn to meditate is to find your own consciousness, that place between what you perceive. There. And its meaning."

Sam had tried to comprehend what the monk was saying. He had sat for a very long time, breathing rhythmically in and out. He inhaled through his nostrils, held his breath for about three heartbeats. And then slowly exhaled. He did this as he gently placed the tip of his tongue on his hard palate, just above his teeth. They had taught him also to inhale slightly quicker and exhale through his mouth, slightly slower. This was a cycle of breathing that brought the prana, or life force, into balance.

Sam's mind wandered, flitting to and fro, from one idea or one scene to another, like a butterfly erratically flapping from one flower to the next. In milliseconds Sam jumped from vistas of the Himalayas as they hiked from monastery to the next, to thoughts of friends back in his hometown of Utica. He settled momentarily on images of his wife Helen, who had urged that he and Carl make the journey. He smiled as he saw her face, her eyes and her upturned nose in his mind's eye.

At first the images flashed through his mind as if he were riding on a merry-go-round. There were faces and cars and buildings and clouds. There were flashes of light and stop signs and railroad tracks. His mind flew about like that butterfly on a warm summer field foraging from flower to flower searching for the vital nectar that was the essence of the insect's sustenance.

And then suddenly, like a jolt, he was sitting in his living room. He felt a rush of comfort and familiarity. Warmth, joy, friendship, and memories. Home. He focused on a large painting, a Parisian street scene in front of the famed cabaret famous for the original cancan dancing; the Moulin Rouge. He and Helen had once attended a charity art auction for the international emergency medical training organization, EMS Global, in Utica. They had been to Paris, visited the Moulin Rouge and delighted in the variety musical and comedy performance there. They had laughed at the French pantomime artist. They wondered at the skills and agility of the acrobats and contortionists. And they marveled at the beauty of the bare breasted, scantily clad showgirls in their shimmering, colorful costumes and oversized headdresses as they pranced about the stage. And how those beautiful young women had danced the cancan as a finale, to wild applause from an appreciative audience.

Helen had wanted that painting and Sam eagerly kept bidding until he finally got it, with its beautiful gilded frame, at a price he thought quite reasonable. Helen was so pleased when she hung it on their living room wall that she expressed her appreciation to him by performing some wonderful acts of intimacy, normally only shared quietly and discreetly by two people in the deepest love of one another.

Sam relaxed a little more as he shifted in his modified lotus position there in their room in Nepal. He next settled on an image of the Gretsch electric guitar in its floor stand in his living room at home. He had that guitar for over 35 years.

His father had bought it for him when he was still in high school. Sam always had a penchant for music. He loved the blues and classic rock 'n roll, and he loved to sing. In high school he had auditioned to be in a rock band. He'd been singing all of the latest songs off the radio and knew the lyrics to most of the popular tunes of the time. The sounds of Chuck Berry, the Beatles, the Rolling Stones, Sam the Sham and the Pharaohs, Sam Cooke, James Brown, and Billy Joel. He knew them all.

None of the other band members could carry a tune like he could or had a singing range as wide as his. Sam passed the audition with one stipulation: He needed to learn how to play guitar. Sam had gone home and pleaded with his parents to buy him a guitar. They refused at first, thinking that his interest in a band and the music would quickly fade. They thought that the guitar would just lean in a corner of the house somewhere unused.

Sam signed up with the Utica Observer Dispatch to make money with a paper route. He continued to practice songs with his band friends who are getting steadily more critical of him when he would show up without a guitar.

Every day at 4:30 AM, a delivery truck would swing by Sam's house and bring a stack of that morning's newspapers. He would untie the large bundles, fold each newspaper into a roll and push them into a clear plastic sleeve ready to be hand-delivered, placed in a mailbox, or thrown from the street onto a front porch while pedaling by on his bicycle.

Soon he had enough money to walk into Target, the large local department store near his home in West Utica, and bought himself a six string acoustic Kingston guitar, made in Japan.

He remembered that first guitar. Like a virginal experience, he thrilled to the feel of its fret board and the mellow sounds that came from the body as he gently strummed his fingers across the strings. He started with single notes, but with diagrams from a book, he was soon playing chords. His band friends were content with his strumming and they watched as he quickly improved. Soon his guitar playing was providing a solid, yet still amateurish background to his rich blues voice.

The four aspiring musicians played and banged on the guitars and drums in the cellar of one of the band's homes. Their repertoire expanded. Soon there was talk of performing, but Sam was the only member without an electric guitar or amplifier. He was a front man, the guy with the voice, but he was also the guy holding back his friends from pursuing their teenage fantasies of fame, money and girls.

Sam's parents were resistant to spending a huge sum of money on an electric guitar. His father finally gave in after seeing his son saving money and practicing three times a week after school. William had gone to a couple of band rehearsals and liked what he heard. On Sam's 14th birthday, the senior Petrie took his son to Peate's music store on the "Busy Corner" as they called the intersection of Lafayette and Genesee Streets in downtown Utica.

Sam's eyes settled on a dark brown sunburst-patterned Gretsch anniversary model guitar. It looked almost like the one he had seen George Harrison play with the Beatles on the Ed Sullivan Show. Mr. Petrie bought his son the guitar and a Fender amplifier. It was one of the best presents Sam ever received in his entire life.

He went on to play the guitar with his band all through high school and then played alone and with friends in college and medical school, and even now, at times, as a doctor. That guitar had brought him great joy. His band did make some money and local notoriety. And, oh, did they get girls. The memories!

Sam's mind now jumped from one item to the next in his living room at home. A book. A magazine. A painted, handcrafted wooden box from Poland. An album of family photos. A large ferocious looking Japanese warrior doll dressed in a colorful costume with a face painted whiteface with yellow streaks. This was a model of a Kabuki actor in a glass display case that he and Helen had acquired during a memorable trip through Japan.

All these things had meaning. Suddenly as if a dam had burst open, in Sam's head, he felt a wave of intense calm and understanding come over him. He felt as if a cosmic truth was being revealed, a lesson about life, perception, meaning, and value was being exposed to him.

All things have meaning.

All things have value and play some varying degree of importance in life, because the observer, he, Sam, was involved. All things were related and interrelated because they existed in the context, his context, his consciousness.

Now he understood what the young monk, Tanka, had meant when he said, "You are God. You are the creator of the universe. You have the unlimited power within you to create and destroy the universe. You are God and God is you. He is within you and outside of you. He is, you. One unity. There is no separation."

Sam understood. He felt a surge of thankfulness, of gratitude, well up in him as he absorbed this. Perspective and context. That is the basis of our consciousness. There is no other reality. And the resulting paradox is that therefore the realities are infinite.

CHAPTER 20

In The Monastery in Nepal

Sam and Carl retired for the night. They had spent most of the afternoon walking through the well-maintained gardens surrounding the monastery accompanied by the young Buddhist monk who was their teacher and yoga instructor over the last few days. They could have continued on their walk and reached the next village within a half day, but something compelled Sam to convince Carl that they should linger here for a while longer. Somehow this place seemed special. Sam couldn't verbalize it, but he felt drawn to this holy place in the mountainous foothills of Nepal.

Carl lay in a creaky, old bed on the other side of the small room that they shared. His soft pillow was covered with a coarse, burlap-like material and his blanket was made of thin wool, colorfully dyed with geometric shapes of all sorts on it. There were two thick squat candles on a table against one wall of the room. A small window allowed the light of dusk to penetrate the room as shadows from the flickering candlelight and statues of Buddha and other furniture danced along the floor and walls.

Carl was the first to speak as they snuggled under the covers for the night.

"What a day!" He paused, "I mean, I think that little prick is trying to kill me. My body doesn't bend like that!"

Sam chuckled quietly under the covers. He remembered how Carl had tried too hard to get his legs bent, one under the other, as the monk demonstrated a proper lotus position while he lectured them on the basics of meditation. Tanka, the monk, had even tried to help position Carl's large legs and frame into the desired position only to have Carl fall backwards, legs tucked under him as he rolled towards the stairwell and almost went down, like a massive Humpty Dumpty.

"Oh, you'll get over it. He really is a very good teacher. He did show you another way to sit and meditate that you were able to do. It wasn't as if he was out to murder you. I think you're being a little too dramatic about the whole thing. I think he's happy to have us here. I gather they don't get too many visitors like us here, and he makes a little money for his order by taking care of us, teaching us, and showing us around."

"And feeding us too," Carl added. "I do have to say that they do feed us well. I never thought I'd like vegetables that much. But, boy, they cook 'em up in so many different ways with all those flavors."

"And no meat! They don't eat meat. And I don't miss it. I think this is turning out to be one of our most productive stops on our hike."

"We'll see," Carl muttered. "We'll see. He did get interesting after a while...after he stopped trying to dislocate my hips and knees."

"There, see? All was not lost. We'll be here one more day and then strap our backpacks on and move on to the village down river and in the valley. I was told that there are shops there with all kinds of trinkets and cloth and brass stuff we can buy for souvenirs to bring home."

Carl grunted. "The only souvenir I think I'll be bringing home is a sore back and a sore butt. Good night."

"Good night," Sam replied.

It wasn't long before the two friends were in a deep sleep. Images of what they had seen here in Nepal, the people, the beautiful countryside, the rich colors of the clothing, and the smells and exotic tastes of the spicy foods, floated about in their dreams like the shadows on the walls from the wavering candlelight.

Sam was being nudged awake by Tanka. He held his fingers to his lips in a gesture of silence. Sam turned to the side to see that Carl had already been woken up and was silently putting on his shoes, jacket, and his shoulder pouch.

"I don't want to alarm you, but we have visitors. Very bad visitors. Not welcome people like you. We must hurry and go to shelter to avoid any harm."

It didn't take any persuasion for Sam to quickly slide out of bed and into his clothes. "Who are they?" he whispered.

Again the monk raised his finger in a sign for silence. "Very bad people. Bandits. Sometimes they just come and rob. But when they come in the night they sometimes come to rob and kill. They know that there are foreigners, like you, who come with lots of money. They might be looking for you."

Suddenly, with no sound at all, the monk was by the door motioning for Sam and Carl to follow him. They tip-toed down a hallway and down a couple of flights of stairs and through the primitive kitchen with its walk-in fireplace and two long, rough hewn, thick wooden tables.

They squeezed through a narrowly opened thick wooden door and were now outside of the monastery compound. It was dark, but the sky was clear. The stars shone down on them and sparkled like a jewelry-studded black velvet robe. Sam noted that the constellations he was used to in Upstate New York were absent from this night's sky. He marveled at how bright the night sky was and how many, many more stars there were here. There must have been three or four times the stars here compared to what he knew. His astronomical musings and comparisons were interrupted by the monk who firmly grasped Sam's arm and led him down a path hidden by bushes and small trees.

A short distance away, down the sloping hillside, they came to a dark stone building set unobtrusively into a hillside. It appeared to be more of a doorway than a building. The monk took out a large key from somewhere in his robes and deftly clicked open a large padlock. Taking the lock with him he opened the heavy metal door and slipped inside. Shots were heard, ringing out from the monastery above them, as Sam and Carl followed their guide.

There was a scraping of metal and a loud click as the entrance door was bolted by the monk. It was eerily quiet with total darkness within. Carl felt a momentary disequilibrium and claustrophobia until a diffuse yellow light flashed down a corridor before them as their guide turned on a large flashlight. Like the rabbit from Alice in Wonderland, the monk scurried down the dark corridor, his sandaled feet pat-pat-patting against the stone floor. Without a moments hesitation the two friends obligingly followed.

The hall sloped downward and turned into switchbacks as they hurried deeper down the walkway. The path leveled out at times for a short distance and there would be a large metal door, with huge locks and chains, in the middle of each landing.

The monk stopped at one of the large doors and with another key deftly procured from his robe, inserted the key and turned it. There was a smooth, effortless click from the lock. Sam thought this room must be used fairly frequently, unlike the huge lock on the entrance door from where they first came in. There must be another way into this place, he mused. The monk motioned for them to follow him in.

The room was soon lighted by candles and some small torches in each corner of the room that the monk had lit. The two Americans looked quizzically around this large room which was outfitted as an office and library. It was apparently also a small shrine with statues and paintings to various saints and lesser gods as well as to the Buddha.

Along the walls were countless shelves with stacks of books lying on their sides showing the edges of their pages, like sandwiches stacked one upon the other. Each book had its own cubbyhole and a little tag that was apparently a number in the Nepalese language.

There was one main table at one end of the room, of heavy construction with thick legs and darkly stained wood. In the center of the room were three longer tables with books and manuscripts strewn about haphazardly, identifying this as a room for research and study.

"Sit down," the monk offered with a sweeping gesture of his hand. "We will stay here until someone from the monastery comes for us. My people know that we are here, waiting until it is safe to come out."

"You did hear the shots, didn't you, as we came through that first big door?" Carl asked, breaking an uncomfortable silence.

"I did," the monk hesitatingly replied. He nodded his head and seemed somewhat perplexed and worried. "I did," he repeated.

"That doesn't seem like some routine break-in or robbery. For all we know, your friends up there might all be dead," Carl offered.

The monk started again to speak, "We have had robberies in the past but no one has ever used guns. Except a long, long time ago. I only know of these things, it was before I was born. Some people from Germany came. They were looking for information from us on, let me think, I guess you say the Aryans."

Carl sat up. He now offered a bit of historical trivia to Tanka's story. "There were some guys, an expedition, sent by Himmler and his SS guys, who went to Tibet and Nepal to see if they could find any historical records on the Aryan race. For some reason I can't remember, they believed that the Aryans, a superior race of people, started out here and then spread across India and into northern Europe and settled in Germany."

"They also came here," added the monk. "They stayed here for a long time, asking to see records from our library, as you see here. We have much information, records written from thousands of years ago that describe this Aryan race."

"So who were these people, these Aryans?" Sam asked, showing some interest in the direction the conversation was going.

Sam and Carl sat on thick, carved wooden chairs by the center tables and listened like students in a classroom as the monk started his discourse. Tanka seemed to relish in this role, possibly as a diversion to pass the time, or possibly so as not to face the idea that some of his fellow monks may have been murdered. He stood and paced slowly back and forth as he spoke, occasional stopping and pointing in one direction or another with a finger or his hand as he emphasized a point.

"It was a little before the war in Europe. A group of Germans came here, and also Tibet, asking about the Aryans." He turned and searched through some shelves behind the main desk by him. He pulled one thick sheaf of papers, bound with a dark green leather cover, from its resting place and, with some effort, placed it on the main table. The pages were about a foot long and six inches wide, looking more like an oversized receipt book than a journal. On each page was the crowded characteristic runic-like cursive of ancient Nepalese writing.

"We Nepalese love to write, and to describe in detail, events from the past. We come here and study all of these different records of what transpired hundreds and thousands of years ago. That is why there are so many books here.

"The Aryans were a group apart from the others of their time. They lived here in the region of the mountains many thousands of years ago. No one knows where they came from. But they were known as a very special kind of people."

"Meaning what?" Carl asked the monk. "How very special?"

The monk paced slowly back and forth, searching for the words to describe the characteristics of these people who he had only read and heard about.

"They were a people apart from others in the area. It is written that they were very strong people. They could walk through the hills for days with little water or food and go high up in the mountains without problem. They could...endure...a lot.

"They were supposedly very healthy people. It is written that they never seemed to get sick. That they grew older but only looked stronger and wiser and smarter until, after outliving most of the local Nepalese, would suddenly slow down and die. It was written that they would easily live one hundred years or more.

"It was believed that they had some type of spirit or blessing within them. Their children were exceptional in schools and in their strength and endurance, but if one of the women or men had children by a non-Aryan, the children would be special but their children, that second generation, would not be special, except for the daughters who would retain that spirit or that blessing within them to have this greatness."

"A matrilineal genetic trait," Sam interjected.

"Say again?" Carl asked. "Remember, a lot of us never got beyond the police academy."

"Genetic traits passed down only from mother to daughter. Some call it the Eve gene. We all carry genes from our parents, one half from each parent as the germ cells that they're made from divide in half. That genetic stuff or information comes from the nuclei of the sperm and the egg. When the sperm and the egg come together, voila! There is again a full set of genetic instructions to make up the baby."

"I got that part, Sam, that's basic Birds and Bees 101. What about this Eve gene?"

"Well, in the late 1950s and early 1960s, as I remember, more DNA was found in other parts of the cell, specifically in the mitochondria. The powerhouse of the cell where nutrition is converted into energy.

"It seems that this DNA is inherited only from the mother because she's the one that provides the cytoplasm, which has the mitochondria in it. The male adds only the genetic material from the nucleus of the sperm cell."

"So let me get this right," Carl started. "There are other things that we inherit from our parents, especially our mothers, that don't just fit into the pattern of half the chromosomes from each parent? And those other traits might be found in the DNA that comes from the mother, in her mitochondrial DNA. Is that right?"

"Yup. And I'm thinking that this stuff that our friend here is talking about, if true, would mean that Aryan traits, if they were passed on from one Aryan to another, would show up in both sons and daughters. If the females went 'off the ranch' so to speak, they would pass the Aryan traits to their sons and daughters but in the next generation those sons could not give the Aryan inheritance to their children, neither girls nor boys, because they couldn't pass on their cytoplasm and mitochondria, and thus their maternal DNA. They can only pass on the DNA from their nucleus."

"So, what happened, Tanka? You said that the Germans came here with guns," Carl asked. "Go on, what do you know about those SS guys. What did they do here?"

The monk had been sitting all the while that Sam spoke. He stood up and started leafing through the pages of the book before him on the main table. He turned each page tenderly and with respect as if they might turn to dust and vanish before his eyes. His eyes scanned each page and he stopped at a section that he apparently had been searching for.

"Ah, here it is," he said. "I will translate loosely instead of giving you every word, OK?" He continued without waiting for their replies.

"These Germans were welcomed at first. They seemed to be polite and generous as well. They shared news of the outside world, and gave many gifts to the Abbot and the monks. It is recorded that they gave flashlights and some medicines, some finely decorated silver spoons and even some money.

"They became very excited when we started showing them the texts, as I am doing with you here, about the Aryans. The writings tell that those people traveled frequently back and forth to the west, visiting and having families with tribes in their own regions of northern Europe.

"Those men became very upset and nervous however, according to the reports here, when they also learned that the Aryans had interacted and bred with tribes in the southern lands beyond India where the Ashkenazi and other Jewish tribes lived. They demanded that the Abbot give them the records detailing the Aryan's interbreeding with the Germanic tribes but also to destroy any records of the Aryan's involvement in what we now call the Middle East. This the Abbot refused.

"Again, according to the records, there was much pleading and attempts at bargaining. This later turned ugly as the Germans threatened to kill the Abbott if he didn't give in to their demands. They then took him hostage and attempted to find their way down to these passageways and this room, to retrieve the journals. Monks blocked their way with their bodies and a few were shot dead, as was the Abbott.

"By now, local villagers had learned of the treachery of these SS men. To avoid further violence and possibly their own deaths, the German group fled as quickly as possible to the lower valleys and eventually to the Indian border. They were never again heard of by our people.

"So, despite the tragic loss of our monastery's leader and some of our beloved monks, we have kept all of our records, and will safeguard them forever."

Sam and Carl sat quietly, absorbing all they had heard. It was quite a revelation. The Nazis had been wrong. Their SS officers, and especially Heinrich Himmler, had spent all kinds of energy, and money and emotion to "rediscover" the Aryan race.

There were Nazi scientists who measured thousands upon thousands of people in and out of Germany, before and during the Second World War, to try to define the physical characteristics of the Aryan race. But they couldn't bring themselves to believe that the Aryan race had also been commingled with the very people that the Nazis were trying to destroy, European Jews! And now, the true Aryan race had all but disappeared.

CHAPTER 21

The Nazis, the Aryans and Genetic Restructuring

From what Lisa had learned, the Nazis of the Third Reich even before World War II had attracted all sorts of people with very disparate agendas to support them. There were of course the nationalists who adored the Furher, and people who wanted to correct the injustices of the post World War I reparations and its crippling affect on the German economy. And there were the Jew haters, people who thought of Jews as sub-human and even categorized them as some kind of vermin or bacteria or parasite. In this mix were profiteers, not only from Germany but also from other countries, including the United States. The Nazis had supporters and made business deals with the likes of IBM, General Motors, the Chase Manhattan Bank, Henry Ford, Charles Lindbergh, and the first CIA director, Allen Dulles. Many of these relationships helped the Nazis in their rise to power in the 1930s and some even continued into the 1940s as war broke out, and afterwards.

There were the mystics, clairvoyants, magicians, and supporters of the Nazis who believed that the earlier, pure Germanic tribes were descendants of a superior race of human beings called Aryans. The Nazi hierarchy from Hitler and Goering, to Himmler and many others, were interested in the mystical history of Germany.

Heinrich Himmler, head of the SS, had renovated a castle at Wewelsburg, in Germany, that was to be the home of the "Center of the New World Order". He had sent a team of explorers to Tibet, under the leadership of Ernst Shafer, to seek out evidence establishing the origins of the Aryan race and documenting how they had eventually emigrated westward and to northern Europe, to become the early Germanic tribes.

Lisa skimmed through sections in a small notebook she had kept hidden in her suitcase. A few days earlier she had made a clandestine visit to the American Library in Paris, near the Eifel Tower. In her research she had come across an odd, unusual German name. She was astonished and sickened by the reality and the depravity of what she learned. She knew that this group, the Ahnenerbe, was a forerunner of the present day International Alliance. With help from the librarian, she had found articles and books on the organization and had xeroxed and cut and pasted select passages into her little notebook:

The Ahnenerbe was a Nazi German think tank that promoted itself as a "study society for Intellectual Ancient History." Founded on July 1, 1935, by Heinrich Himmler, Herman Wirth, and Richard Walther Darré, the Ahnenerbe's goal was to research the anthropological and cultural history of the Aryan race, and later to experiment and launch voyages with the intent of proving that prehistoric and mythological Nordic populations had once ruled the world.

In January 1929, Heinrich Himmler was appointed the leader of the fledgling Schutzstaffel (SS). He launched a massive recruitment campaign that took the SS from fewer than three hundred members in 1929 to ten thousand in 1931.[1] Once the SS had grown, Himmler began its transformation into a "racial elite" of young Nordic males. This was to be accomplished by a new bureaucracy in the SS, the Race and Settlement Office of the SS (Rasse- und Siedlungshauptamt-SS) known as RuSHA. Himmler named SS-Obergruppenführer Richard Walther Darré to lead the organisation, which determined if applicants were racially fit to be in the SS. This brought about a campaign meant to educate the new applicants about their Nordic past through weekly classes taught by senior RuSHA graduates using the periodical SS-Leiheft.

In 1937, Himmler decided he could increase the Ahnenerbe's visibility by investigating Hans F. K. Günther's claims that early Aryans had conquered much of Asia, including attacks against China and Japan in approximately 2000 BC, and that Gautama Buddha was himself an Aryan offspring of the Nordic race. Walther Wüst would later expand upon this, stating in a public speech that Adolf Hitler's ideologies corresponded with those of Buddha, since the two shared a common heritage.

NOTE: Before, and during the war, the Nazis had sent out many expeditions all over the world, from South America to the Canary Islands, to Iceland, various parts of Europe, and Tibet, looking for any archeological evidence or artifacts or writings that would shed light and insight on the Aryans and on the claim that "true" Germans were the descendants of a superior race of people that had inhabited parts of the world thousands of years ago, and had had significant influence on the development of many cultures spread throughout the world.

Medical experiments

The Institut für Wehrwissenschaftliche Zweckforschung ("Institute for Military Scientific Research"), which conducted extensive medical experiments using human subjects, became attached to the Ahnenerbe during World War II. It was managed by Wolfram Sievers.[12] Sievers had founded the organization on the orders of Himmler, who appointed him director with two divisions headed by Sigmund Rascher and August Hirt, and funded by the Waffen-SS.

Dachau

Dr. Sigmund Rascher was tasked with helping the Luftwaffe determine what was safe for their pilots—because aircraft were being built to fly higher than ever before. He applied for and received permission from Himmler to requisition camp prisoners to place in vacuum chambers to simulate the high altitude conditions that pilots might face.[1]

Rascher was also tasked with discovering how long German airmen would be able to survive if shot down above freezing water. His victims were forced to remain out of doors naked in freezing weather for up to 14 hours, or kept in a tank of icewater for 3 hours, their pulse and internal temperature measured through a series of electrodes. Warming of the victims was then attempted by different methods, most usually and successfully by immersion in very hot water, and also less conventional methods such as placing the subject in bed with women who would try to sexually stimulate him, a method suggested by Himmler.[13][14]

Rascher also experimented with the effects of Polygal, a substance made from beets and apple pectin, on coagulating blood flow to help with gunshot wounds. Subjects were given a Polygal tablet, and shot through the neck or chest, or their limbs amputated without anaesthesia. Rascher published an article on his experience of using Polygal, without detailing the nature of the human trials and also set up a company to manufacture the substance, staffed by prisoners.[15]

Similar experiments were conducted from July to September 1944, as the Ahnenerbe provided space and materials to doctors at Dachau to undertake "seawater experiments", chiefly through Sievers. Sievers is known to have visited Dachau on July 20, to speak with Ploetner and the non-Ahnenerbe Wilhelm Beiglboeck, who ultimately carried out the experiments.

Skulls

Walter Greite rose to leadership of the Ahnenerbe's Applied Nature Studies division in January 1939, and began taking detailed measurements of 2,000 Jews at the Vienna emigration office—but scientists were unable to use the data. On December 10, 1941, Beger met with Sievers and convinced him of the need for 120 Jewish skulls.[16] During the later Nuremberg Trials, Dr. Friedrich Hielscher testified that Sievers had initially been repulsed at the idea of expanding the Ahnenerbe to human experimentation, and that he had "no desire whatsoever to participate in these." (v:II pg:37)

Jewish skeleton collection: Beger collaborated with Dr. August Hirt, of the Reich University of Strassburg, in creating a Jewish skeleton collection for research. The bodies of 86 Jewish men and women were ultimately collected and macerated.

Lisa closed the little notebook and put her head down on her folded arms. She tried to stifle a cry but her body resisted, instead heaving in short, quick, convulsive bursts shuddering of her entire body. She bit her inner cheek to keep from making any loud crying noise. That didn't stop the tears that now came rushing out of her eyes like water bursting from a breached dam. She considered the monster that she was dealing with. After reading those notes again she was more determined than ever to see it all through. In the beginning she had thought only of her husband and her children. And now Carl had come back into her life, offering her salvation, a way out from this sordid life of deceit, fear, death, and moral bankruptcy.

She knew what she had to do. She would devote her energies, her cunning and skill, and possibly her life, to all those poor innocent victims of the horror that was the Nazi Ahnenerbe, and its modern day spawn, the International Alliance.

CHAPTER 22

The Adirondack Railways Trip to Old Forge and The Brightside

It had taken them six days to retrofit the rail car. They examined their work. Rafel and Mirek Rednicki and their three partners, calling themselves Team Jadwiga, were satisfied with the job they had done. In the limited time they had, the team had replaced the windows of the Adirondack Railways passenger car with bulletproof glass, and other refinements. There were holes through the roof of the car in three locations and trap doors with rubber gaskets lining the edges had been installed to make them air tight. Soundproofing had also been blown in through now plugged holes in the walls, ceilings, and floors to prevent unnecessary sound from escaping.

It was early evening. The train had left Union Station in Utica and made one stop at Remsen to pick up extra ice for the private party car. A small throng of other ticket holders including young couples, some with children, and senior citizens, a few with walkers or canes, also climbed on. Most were there for the Fall Foliage Tour, a major attraction, which was popular at this time of year. There was happy chatter, jibes, and joking as they made their way off the platform and up the steps to their seats in one of the six Via coaches outfitted for the public for the tours.

One passenger with a special package also boarded, unnoticed. He was alone, quiet, and barely nodded his head beneath the newsboy cap he was wearing. Wearing a dark brown leather bombardier jacket and black jeans, the young man had a small backpack slung over one shoulder. He sat alone at the rear of the car, near the door, appearing nonchalant. He opened a newspaper, seemingly intent on relaxing and reading alone.

Inside, in their reserved car, the Silver Spring, built by the Pullman Company in 1925, the honored guests of the International Alliance were having a wonderful time drinking beer, and schnapps, and other liquors, and devouring appetizers and sausages as if they had never seen such simple fare. The men were dressed in tuxedos and patent leather shoes. Some of them wore medals that glittered and shined from the small overhead chandeliers. Many of them had little gold swastikas pinned to the lapels of their dinner jackets. There were no women on board, except for two waitresses, who worked for the catering service and were not connected with the Alliance.

And Lisa.

As close confidant to the late Rene Gallois, she had previously been invited by him specifically to be at this upcoming meeting, with the leaders of the International Alliance. He had been insistent then, refusing to take no for an answer, despite her protestation that she would be the only woman there. She had initially shown reluctance to attend, but she soon acquiesced, making it seem as if she was giving in just to please him.

She also believed intuitively that if she protested too much, Rene might have become suspicious that there was an underlying agenda. Lisa was no stranger to living on the edge, to taking risks. Her recent actions, however, did cause her great internal debate and concern.

And now Rene Gallois was dead.

She had worked so hard and sacrificed so much. At times she even questioned how much of her own humanity and dignity she had destroyed in her quest to get to the top, of the leadership of this insane organization. She feared jeopardizing Carl's life. She loved him so much. It seemed almost unacceptable that she would place him so close to harm's way that she might be sacrificing him to her own ends. Is that how she saw it now?

Carl had been her little candle, a tiny light in the dark chamber that was her daily life. She interacted with some of the world's most horrible people, men and women, who engaged in some of the most awful things that any human being could do to people.

At times, Lisa had thought she might go crazy, dealing with these sadistic lunatics. To quiet the fear and disgust and loathing, she would cloister herself in her room or the lady's room or go for a walk. She would focus on Carl. She would see his face, his smile, his bright hazel eyes and the bushy brown hair that she had grabbed in tufts, so many lifetimes ago, when they were in each other's arms.

He had been the anchor that had kept her chained to reality. As she experienced one dangerous or awful situation after another over the years of their separation, like a small boat on the open sea while a treacherous storm raged all around, her vision of him had been there to steady her. He was the steersman in her little boat, the calm in her raging storm.

The padded saddle seat barstools and little round cocktail tables of the Silver Spring coach were strategically arranged so that the two waitresses could glide from one table to another and refill beer pitchers, wine glasses, or offer more plates of meat and appetizers to the guests. Bruno Metzger, the main speaker for the International Alliance, arose from his table at the center of the railcar. He clinked a spoon against a tall beer mug and raised his hand, palm stretched outward, motioning for permission to speak. The room suddenly became quiet, as if a switch on the wall had been flipped. Everyone turned to him and waited patiently as he cleared his throat to speak.

He gazed across the long, narrow room packed with two dozen loyal officers of the International Alliance. These were the movers and shakers and the kingpins of the money making operations that kept the wealth flowing into their coffers, allowing them to continue with their work. These Germanic lugartenientes and capos had control of, or significant influence on, and had fashioned alliances with, "Los Zetas" and "Narcotraficantos" in Mexico, the Columbian drug cartels of BACRIM, the Russian and Chechen mafias, the Afghani Juma Khan and their opium distribution and Taliban connections, the Israeli Abergil crime family whose specialty is distribution of ecstasy pills, and many other nefarious organizations throughout the world. There was almost no movement of drugs, no laundering of money, no major extortion scheme and no significant assassination of underworld figures that didn't involve the International

Alliance. Their efforts brought in countless billions of dollars in profit on a daily or weekly basis.

"Dear friends and colleagues," Metzger began. He used no notes to help him with his remarks or to acknowledge the guests. He knew each and every one of them very well, their personal histories, where they came from, and their responsibilities within the organization.

"I hope you are enjoying this pleasant outing provided by the Adirondack Railways as we go to Old Forge and then, by limousine, on to Racquette Lake and our final destination, The Brightside, a quaint, famous bed and breakfast on Racquette Lake. Please indulge yourselves in the drinks and the appetizers. Hasn't the view been wonderful as we ride up through the Adirondack Park on our way north?

"We will be having a short meeting as we leave the Remsen station and then we will have a sumptuous meal which has been prepared by the professional caterers from one of the finest restaurants in Utica. Afterwards I have a wonderful announcement to make, something very special that, I think, you will find absolutely amazing. It will be the dessert of the evening for us!"

The room burst out in applause and shouts of approval.

"But let me say that this will not be the last 'dessert' of the evening. When we arrive at The Brightside, there will be a sufficient number of exotic young ladies who will escort each and every one of you to your private room."

A murmur of approval wafted through the car.

"But what happens after you reach your hotel room is your own business. Our business stops at your door!"

There was laughter at his last remark, and the clinking of glasses on the table, as if, reminiscent of a wedding, someone should be kissing him at that moment.

"And tomorrow we will be dividing up into a few groups, as you know. Some of you will be playing golf with me, while another group will be taken part way up the windy road to Whiteface Mountain. You will then hike up the rocky path to the top of the mountain. For those who can't or don't wish to walk up, there is a tunnel bored into the mountain with an elevator which will bring you to the top. Lastly, some of you had asked to do some fishing and also tennis. Those groups have also been formed. So, I expect that all of your needs will be taken care of and we will have a wonderful day at the Brightside, compliments of our International Alliance. This is one very small way for us to thank all of you for what you have done over the years to further our cause.

"After our meal this evening I will be presenting you with some extraordinary information, and some surprises, which will make you all, I am sure, so very proud and happy of what we are about to accomplish, as we look to our future and to a new generation! To victory!"

Everyone stood up from their chairs and raised a glass or a mug and replied, "To victory!"

Dinner was served.

The dinner was concluding with dessert, delicious little pastries from Café Canole and a perfect cup of coffee from the Utica Brewing Company, as Bruno Metzger rose from his chair. He looked over at two of his closest, most trusted officers Lother Heinrich and Manfred Haeckel. Heinrich gave him a thumbs-up sign of support, encouraging him to start the evening's meeting.

"My dear colleagues, my friends. As we travel this evening to Racquette Lake and The Brightside, and enjoy this dinner and our camaraderie, bruderschaft, I want to now take this opportunity to inform you of some wonderful developments that have taken place recently. I have some extraordinary information to pass on to you. As this is highly confidential and, shall we say proprietary information, to use a business expression, I am asking that our beautiful young ladies, and our barman, please leave us now. We will ask to you to return in a short while to resume your services, as we continue our celebration."

With that, the two young ladies in hostess outfits and the young barman, who had been mixing their specialty order drinks, worked their way nimbly around the closely situated tables and chairs of the moving dining car.

Lisa took her purse and started to leave the car along with the waitresses. This was her chance to get out of the rail car. Metzger stood in front of her, blocking her from leaving. He had wispy white hair and paper-thin skin and a frail physique, yet the eighty-some year old had a gaze that commanded obedience and eyes of cold steel that might bore a hole in the hardest of metal. They showed no compassion, only strength, commitment, cunning, and a singular purpose.

"Excuse me, Lisa. I meant for the two young servers to leave us. You must stay. I want you to stay. Please, have a seat right here by me at the table. Let me pour you a little wine as well."

With great apprehension Lisa sat down at the small head table in the middle of the narrow railcar. The door was slid shut behind them. She could hear the lock click.

"Thank you, my dear, for staying. I think you will find this a very surprising and entertaining evening, for all of us, and also, for you!"

She felt very uneasy as she looked out at the small gathering of men seated before her. Her mind raced from detail to detail about her relationship with Gallois, and with others in the Alliance. After his fall from the balcony at the hotel in Paris, she had been interrogated and was deemed an innocent victim of Gallois' aggressiveness and sexual energy and attack on her, which ultimately led to him tripping over the railing and falling two stories to his death on the pavement below.

The speaker himself had been at the interrogation, with other Alliance officers, the morning after Gallois's death. He seemed sympathetic and understanding. It was Metzger who had brought out Rene Gallois' propensity for outbursts of violence and sadistic treatment in the bedroom towards women. The Alliance knew of instances of Gallois beating women during the course of his sexual dalliances. There were known to them episodes of female escorts suffering broken noses and fractured ribs or arms. During their questioning of Lisa, Axel Weismann recounted how a young Parisian girl was strangled to death in bed while Gallois had sex with her. The Alliance covered up the entire affair, disposed of the body, and manufactured a cover story that the young lady had last been seen leaving the hotel alone in the middle of the night. None of her friends or family had any further contact with her afterwards. They never learned what had happened to her.

As soon as the barman and the two waitresses had left, the doors on either end of the car were securely locked. Civilian clothed guards were stationed outside, on either end, to prevent anyone from attempting to eavesdrop on the proceedings.

Bruno Metzger began again. "As you gentlemen all remember, many years ago, in 1954, there was a young SS officer by the name of Harvey Weinberg who was part of an experiment to see if we could reconstitute, or fabricate or recreate if you will, those characteristics of our earliest Nordic heritage, that of the Aryan Race. I know you recall as well the expeditions sent out by Herr Himmler, all over the globe, to try to find a genetic pool or hereditary remnants of the Aryans, which we might somehow utilize to raise anew our Aryan genes.

"There were a number of avenues of research that were pursued with varying degrees of success. I refer to the judicious selection of young SS officers, chosen in the 1930's for their superior intellect and physical prowess and strength, with their blonde hair and blue eyes. They were chosen specifically to breed with select young German girls with correspondingly desirable features of intelligence, strength and looks. Their offspring were carefully chosen, schooled and trained and measured physically and psychologically and biologically, to see the effects of such selection.

"I am reminded of some of the medical experiments carried out by our much-maligned Dr. Mengle, who injected various chemicals into the eyes of select Polish children to see if minor physical details such as eye color could be modified. It was felt that this might be useful in a situation where a child who, through selection, was otherwise near perfect except for some minor detail. Thus, eye color or hair texture or some other feature might need to be altered, modified or reshaped so as to conform to the desired result.

"Experiments were also carried out on prisoners in the various camps, including Auschwitz, in which some of our finest SS men impregnated women from various backgrounds and ethnic groups to evaluate objectively to what degree our Nordic characteristics could be influenced, adulterated and weakened,or even enhanced or strengthened. To that end, Polish girls, Czechs, Russian women, even some Gypsies and Jews were used in these experiments. Those that bore children were allowed to live as we wished to have them care for their own offspring and to have the hereditary expressions come out as normally as possible, given the circumstances.

"There was one couple who provided our researchers with some very interesting results. A young Polish girl from the Warsaw area was enlisted in our eugenics program and was made the consort of our young SS officer,

Herr Weinberg. She bore him not one, but two, wonderful little boys, Fritz and Hans. That was in 1944. When I say 'wonderful,' I truly mean to say 'remarkable'.

"From the first few weeks after their birth it was obvious that these were not average babies. They were very strong, robust, and exhibited mental and physical growth characteristics beyond the usual milestones of development.

"They were raising their heads and even rolling over from back to stomach and back again within the first two weeks of life, something not seen until the first few months. They were verbalizing and even repeating sounds within the second month. By four months they were beyond crawling and were standing, even walking. Gentlemen, I don't mean to bore you with the details but tell you all of this only to underscore that these children were developing by leaps and bounds far beyond any achievements of any of the other children in that program.

"You might think that, with the official end of the war, and with the death of our beloved Fuhrer and so many of our top leaders, that any continuation of our goals would have been stopped, or at least severely hampered. You know however, that was not to be the case. Thanks to our friends in the Vatican, through the "Ratline", through our strong relations with our Italian fascist friends, and our American supporters, the CIA and our own General Gehler, we were able to fairly quickly reestablish our chain of command. Thanks as well to the support of our South American friends, Dr. Mengle and his researchers were able to continue exploring various scientific options for wound healing, optimizing health in our people, conducting longevity experiments and making even some attempts to genetically modify members of our community with strong Aryan features. Our scientists however had limited success, even with the finest specimens of Nordic youth, in manipulating the genetics of our volunteers."

The speaker paused for a moment to clear his throat and take a few sips from his beer glass. He then continued.

"Well, we watched these twins, these little 'wunderkind' as they developed over the years. It became obvious that there was something inherent in both boys that would explain their academic achievements in kindergarten and beyond. They learned the basics of some foreign languages in a very short time. Their grasp of mathematics by the second and third grade approached that of students in the Hochschule. Physically they were incredibly strong, healed from bruises and even a fractured wrist in one boy, in only a couple of weeks! Unheard of!

"The Alliance contacted the father, about 1953, through the cooperation of the local Bavarian school district. We wanted to study these children more thoroughly, to do biometric and psychological testing on them and, of course, obtain blood and tissue samples from them in order to study their genetics.

"As you are aware, science today has progressed so far today that we have identified all of the genes in a human being. We have the ability even to clone another human being. I know you have read that scientists all over the world have resisted doing this for moral and ethical reasons. Shall I boldly proclaim that we have no such reservations, not when it means re-establishing our rightful place in the world as the Fourth Reich and to redirect human evolution back onto the path it should have been following, had not the human race been bastardized by the mixing of impure genetics into our Aryan genetic pool.

"I regretfully remind you of the tragic murder of that courageous SS officer, Harvey Weinberg and his lovely twins, Fritz and Hans, which occurred, back in 1954. That sent a shock wave through our organization. Somehow, someone knew of our interest, of our goals. There was a traitor in our midst. A spy. A quisling. We never found out where that security breach came from. We did however recently learn that the murder of those two twins and their father was the work of Zegota!"

There were gasping sounds of disbelief at this last pronouncement. The Alliance members knew only too well of Zegota and how they, time and again, in so many hundreds and even thousands of ways, had saved Polish Jews during the war by hiding them and helping them to escape to other parts of Europe and to the Middle East.

Zegota had begun as a few separate underground organizations with various names, founded by Polish Catholics, sympathetic to the plight and dangers confronting their countrymen, and later joined with some secret Jewish groups. A few of the largest groups banded together and, throughout the German Occupation and even afterwards, helped in hiding and saving the lives of countless numbers of Polish Jews.

One man stood up, his face red with anger. Spittle flew from his mouth as he spoke, as if there was an awful taste in his mouth that he was trying to get rid of.

"Fucking Polish prick bastards. Goddamn Jewish kike parasites! We should have made a truce with the Americans and the British early on so that we could finish what we set out to do. There were enough powerful people all over the world in England and Ireland and the U.S. and the Middle East that were all sympathetic to what we were doing. We should have cleansed the German soil, yes, and the European soil from those fucking filthy bacteria!"

"Every last one of them," shouted another in agreement. There was a murmur of agreement that swept through the railroad dining car.

Metzger raised up his hands in supplication, regaining his hold on the audience. "I know how you all feel, believe me I do. We tried. We did everything in our power to bring about the destruction of the European Jewry and of the Zionists. We lost so many brave souls in our quest, so many wonderful heroes. Well, the time was not right. Fate was not on our side then.

But Fate has a strange way of returning and, sometimes setting things right. Now is that time. Financially we, the International Alliance, are much stronger. Our influence, our reach, is much more solid."

The speaker took a few steps away from his table. He turned, in silence, a half circle to the left, and then wheeled slowly to his right, slowly peering into the faces of the twenty or so Alliance member. The gesture had its desired affect. Glasses, forks, and spoons were politely put down and all eyes were on him.

"Gentlemen. I have the distinct pleasure of telling you now that we have in our custody the mother of those two murdered twins, those two young lads that would have been the hope of a new generation of Aryans. She is alive. It is the mother who harbors the genetic information that made them who they were!

"Only recently did we learn that she had actually emigrated to the United States, and to Upstate New York. And only recently did our people find this woman, and capture her! Her name is Eva Bielewski. We have her!"

A roar of approval and applause followed as everyone stood and clapped excitedly at this incredible news. Bruno Metzger stood, lips pursed and chin jutted forward as he placed his fisted hands on his hips. He had struck a Mussolini-like pose. His head bobbed up and down in affirmation.

"So now, my friends, our journey is only beginning! We will extract the genetic material from that mother and study it, clone it, and use it to breed a new generation of Aryan *ubermensch!*"

The air in the railcar was electrified by these last words. A chant started in one corner of the car and was quickly taken up by all, arms stretched out in the familiar salute to the Fatherland: "*Heil Hitler! Heil Hitler!*" the crowd repeated rabidly, until voices became hoarse.

The speaker wiped his lips with a napkin, took a sip of water and continued.

"And now we have a little bit of housekeeping to do before we continue on with our dinner and with our plans and with our wonderful trip to the Brightside Lodge."

He walked back to his table and stood behind Lisa.

"And so we have, with this news, a new beginning. A resurrection, if you will, as if sent to us by God. The Bible relates to us how God sent his son to us, Jesus, to usher in a new order. Well, we were given two sons, if you will, little Hans and little Fritz.

"Jesus had his supporters and followers, just as we do, our International Alliance. But he also had his enemies and, one in particular, his Judas".

At this point he placed his hands firmly on Lisa's shoulders. A shudder went through her as he spoke those words. She tried to move, but he pushed his full weight down on her, forcing her to remain seated in her chair.

"Our little friend here, Lisa, who we had embraced as a confidant of Rene Gallois and accepted by us, is our Judas!"

Gasps and whispers murmured through the car.

"Oh yes! Our Lisa is not at all who we thought she was when she came to us. She had been a close confidant of Carlos Quinterra, a very important business associate here in Central New York. But he died. Somehow. Under what some might consider peculiar circumstances. A helicopter crash near his farm at night!

"Lisa then was befriended by our beloved Rene Gallois. Only a few short weeks ago, during an evening romp in bed, she somehow overpowered this rather strong man and he managed to 'accidentally fall to his death' from the second floor balcony of the Hotel Ritz de Paris and break his neck."

Lisa was shaking now, thinking how she might loosen his grip on her. There was a door behind her but that had been locked. The windows were all closed and the train was moving. She had no weapon. She eyed the table for anything that she might use to fight with.

"I recently learned that our Lisa had been making phone calls to someone, while at our hotel last week. And I also learned that naughty little Lisa had a clandestine meeting with a stranger, someone not of our organization. This only hours before Gallois fell to his death…or was he killed?"

There were exclamations of shock and surprise from different corners of the car.

"Lisa, did you somehow use some martial arts maneuvers to overcome Rene Gallois? Or, did you have an accomplice?"

She slammed her hand onto the table, to get everyone's attention. She realized that her only chance was to somehow defuse the situation or to distract their attention long enough for her to attempt an escape.

"This is crazy! All of your accusations! I don't know what you're talking about. I loved Rene. I loved that man! He hurt me at times, and that night he was brutal. He used me and then he beat me and beat me again. You saw the bruises! I told you before, I don't know what happened but, as he chased me around the apartment, he stumbled and fell over the railing."

She felt her purse, on the floor by her left leg. As she weaved her head around while talking and shaking her head, she saw it. A black leather hand bag which she had brought with her. She had been warned and knew that if there was trouble and she couldn't leave the railcar, then this would be her only salvation. She only hoped that the plan she and Carl and the others had put together for tonight would work. She was abruptly jolted back to her senses by the clawing hands of the speaker's fingers digging into her shoulders and his piercing voice.

"You are a liar!" he shouted over her feigned whimpering. "You are a fucking liar and you will pay for this!"

He motioned for two bodyguards nearby to come up and restrain her. "We will deal with her when we get to Brightside. There, no one other than us will be witness to her final solution."

Outside of the meeting in the adjacent railcars no one noticed two young men, in synchronized fashion silently kill the Alliance guards posted on either door of the Silver Spring. No one heard the pistol shots above the clack-clack-clacking of the train as the 9 mm SIG Sauer SD silencers muffled the put-put report of the guns. The guards slumped to the floor.

Two other accomplices of the assassination squad then climbed up onto the roof of the railcar in which the International Alliance leaders were reveling. They opened the special hatches that they had installed during their renovations of that one railcar. Wearing respirator masks they carefully opened cans of Zyklon B and poured the blue crystals down onto the unsuspecting and shocked passengers below. They saw the people in the Silver Spring coach below look up in shock and surprise.

There were screams and shouting as men tried to stand on the tables and grab at the hatches, hoping to close them or to grab their assailants, to no avail. People start to cough and scream and vomit. They pounded on the windows and the doors, trying desperately to escape.

After what seemed like an eternity to the men clinging to the closed hatches on the railcar's rooftop, the screams and kicking and retching stopped. Lisa had dared to open her eyes only for seconds. Tears welled up in her eyes, not because of some chemical irritation from the Zyklon B – her eyes and face were covered by the respirator mask and a small oxygen cylinder that had been in her purse only minutes earlier. She had slid underneath a table, and lay quietly on the floor, as was the contingency plan if she could not get out of the railcar. She was to wait for one of the others to come for her. She knew that she only had about 15 minutes of oxygen in the small metal flask that she was holding to her face. She felt very weak now. She wondered if she was slowly succumbing to the effects of the cyanide in the car, despite her precautions to avoid breathing the gas. She noticed some difficulty in breathing now. Was she going to die alongside all of these awful people, these murders and cutthroats, and Nazi zealots who now lay strewn about the passenger car floor like so many discarded dolls?

If she were to expose her eyes to the remnants of the prussic acid which had killed everyone else in the car, the chemical would diffuse through her sclera and her eyeballs and into the cerebrospinal fluid that bathed her brain and the brainstem, which housed her breathing and circulatory centers. She too would succumb and be dead in a matter of minutes. She kept her eyes closed for fear of poisoning herself.

The tears came despite her accepting that this job had to be done. She realized that outside of actual concentration camp guards during World War II, SS officers, and Heinrich Himmler and Adolf Eichmann, no one had directly observed the grotesque murder of scores of people in a confined space with Zyklon B. Those Nazi overlords had the advantage of peering into the fake showers into which their victims were led by peering through thick sealed glass portals in the doors by which they could determine that there was no more movement, no further sign of life.

Her tears were not for these monsters that now lay before her, many with blood trickling out of ears, froth or vomit on their faces, eyes bulging and pants wet or soiled as sphincter controls were lost. She thought instead of the victims of these sadists. All of the people who had suffered at the hands of their fathers and uncles before and during the Nazi rule. And how many more people had suffered and died at the hands of these foul people in the decades and generations that followed, these men who now lay before her, cut down like so many blades of grass with their own poison? Her tears were for them. The children, the mothers and fathers, the entire families. It was fitting that these creatures, as she viewed them, were exterminated by an insecticide developed by German chemists.

Her mind became confused. Lisa passed out. The small yellow Israeli portable gas mask covering her nose and mouth and connected to the tiny oxygen cylinder dropped from her hand to the floor. The last image she remembered was looking into the eyes of a man laying face to face next to her. Bruno Metzger. His eyes were opened wide, as in shock and terror. She had no thought on that, only an observation and no energy to even think. Then stillness. Quiet. And darkness.

The door to the railroad car slid open forcefully. Two young men, wearing military grade gas masks, rushed in and looked quickly around. Almost immediately they saw her. All the other guests, all males, were dressed in dark grey or black suits. Lisa had been wearing a blue velvet evening gown with sparking diamond earrings and necklace. The men noticed her quickly and hurried over, picked her up, and took her out of the room into the cool night air. They slid the car door closed to prevent any further cyanide gas from escaping, on the off chance that there might be some hearty survivors of the Zyklon B attack.

One of the men strapped a non-rebreather mask to Lisa's head and face. He turned the control on the flow meter of the e-cylinder of oxygen to 15 liters of oxygen per minute. She lay on the floor of the passageway between railroad cars. She was limp and almost lifeless.

"She has a pulse. It's weak, but she has a pulse," the first man said to the second. "He pulled a cell phone from his pocket and dialed.

"How did it go?" came a voice from the other end of the call.

"Pretty well, I guess. The job is finished. We were able to get Lisa out, I've got her here, but she's not doing so well." He explained the situation and her condition.

There was a pause at the other end. "We'll meet you at the Old Forge Hotel, the train will be stopping there very shortly."

The two young men could feel the brakes already being applied as the train started its deceleration and arrival at the station.

"Get off on the side away from the Hotel. Got it? We're already here waiting for you. We'll be by the door of the passenger car closest up towards the locomotive side. Got it?"

"Yes. We're already there." The man could feel the train almost coming to a stop. "I think I can see you through the door's window."

It was dusk as the train reached the station and stopped. They had arrived at the Old Forge Hotel Station. The two young men opened the door and deftly carried Lisa off the train and to the nearby trees where their colleagues were waiting for them.

"She doesn't look so good," said one man.

"Is she dead?"

One of the young men shook his head, "No. She has a pulse, it's weak, but she has a pulse."

"And she's breathing," said another man kneeling by her. "We've got to get treatment for her, and we have no time to spare. Put her into the car over there and let's go!"

As they all piled into the two cars that had been parked beyond the row of pine trees by the railroad tracks, one of the young men asked, "Dr. Petrie, where are we going?"

Sam Petrie pointed ahead. "Drive there to the main road then turn left. We've got to go south for a mile, to Thendara and make a right at the entrance to the Old Forge Diamond Mine."

"Why there?" one man asked.

"It's the only place where we can get what we need to keep her from dying, which she might do anyway, unless we can get the right stuff to treat her."

"What's at the Diamond Mine? There's the Town of Webb Clinic in Old Forge. We could break into there. It's after hours. We wouldn't have to worry about police. They'll be busy at the Station trying to figure out what happened in the railroad car."

"No, we've got to go to the Diamond Mine," replied Sam. "Don't drive too fast. We don't want to draw attention to ourselves. The last thing we need is to have the police stop us now. It's her only chance. Damn it. I thought we had figured this thing out. She was supposed to leave the car before you dropped the pellets through the portals in the roof. I thought we had planned that she would excuse herself to go to the ladies' room. That mask and oxygen cylinder were only supposed to be used if things went wrong."

"Well, obviously, things went wrong, somewhat wrong," answered Mirek Rednicki.

"We did what we could. We guess she couldn't get out and we had some difficulty in getting in."

"What kind of difficulty?" asked Sam.

"One of the security guards that we had shot with our silencers wasn't dead. When we climbed down off the roof of the car, he grabbed Janusz's leg and started to fight with him. Tried to drag him onto the floor and towards the open door. I shot him in the head to finish him off. Then we had to throw him off the train so that we had room to maneuver, and to get into the car and find Lisa.

"And then a couple of people came out into the corridor from the next passenger car. A guy and a waitress. They demanded to know what we were doing. They had seen something going on. We told them to get back into their seats. Told them we were security agents and that everything was going to be fine. Go back and sit down. I told them we'd sort all of this out when we got to the station."

"Do you think they suspected what was going on in the next car?" asked Sam.

"No, I doubt it. They seemed a little tipsy, a little high. They went back to the other car."

Sam gestured ahead, pointing through the windshield of the car. "There's the road. Turn right here and go right to the front door. We've got to get in there, and fast."

They turned onto the asphalt road and drove along a short entry road through the pines. The second car followed them.

CHAPTER 23

At the Diamond Mine

"OK, now break the amyl nitrate ampule and stick it under her nose. She'll breathe in the fumes. That will give us a little more time as I inject this other medication into her."

Lisa was laying on a table with a folded coat as a makeshift pillow for her. Sam slid the catheter over the needle and into Lisa's antecubital vein. He adjusted the flow of the intravenous saline solution and watched the plastic collection chamber as the fluid dripped out and into the tubing. It went slowly first and then faster. He checked Lisa's arm to make sure that the skin didn't puff up, signaling that the fluid would be infiltrating the skin and not going directly into the vein. There was no swelling up and the saline flowed freely into her body.

Sam opened the Lilly Cyanide Kit box, as Carl and the others looked on, and took out the second, much larger glass vial. He broke off the tip of the vial and sucked the medication through a needle and into a syringe. He clamped off the saline flowing into her and injected the drug through the IV tubing and into Lisa's vein. Once finished with that he grabbed the final vial and mixed that as well into a syringe. After a short while he injected that drug into Lisa.

Her skin took on a darker, violaceous hue. "Is she going to be all right?" asked one of the men, Adam Karas.

"I don't know. It depends on how much cyanide she had gotten into her body. The cyanide basically is like a chemical tar. It gums up the enzyme systems in the cells that allow her body to use oxygen. As you know, without oxygen the heart and brain, and everything stop. And she dies. Just like the people in the train. These chemicals here, the amyl nitrite she breathed in, the sodium nitrite and the sodium thiosulfate. They take the cyanide and make it water-soluble so that her body can get rid of it. We'll see if it works."

"How did you know about this place," asked Janusz, "And how come a diamond mine has a cyanide kit here?"

"Well, as an emergency physician, I was asked a few years ago to help this company to put together a work place safety plan. You know, eye wash stations, first aid kits, automatic external defibrillators or AEDs, and CPR training. I learned that, in addition to having a so-called Diamond Mine like they have in Herkimer, they also do some mining for small amounts of gold."

"So they have diamonds here. And gold."

"Well, the diamonds are actually clear quartz crystals. They're really pretty. Come in all sizes, from really tiny to very big, bigger than a plum. People come up to Herkimer and here to Old Forge to pick away through the rocks and find these diamond-like quartz crystals," Sam explained.

"So what about this gold?"

"Well, people come up here for that too. The company has a sluice where people can come to pan for gold. Just like out West in the old days. But there is also a fairly significant amount of gold in the dirt and rock around here, enough to make it worthwhile for this small company to use cyanide as part of an extraction method to get gold out of the rock and dirt. In order to comply with OSHA safety regulations, the company contacted me to set things up, including getting this Lilly Cyanide Kit."

"So these kits are not that common? You wouldn't find one at the town clinic?"

"Most likely not. Lisa wouldn't have had a chance there." Sam inserted the needle and syringe into the IV tubing and administered the third, and final, medication. He noted that Lisa was breathing better, more deeply. Her eyes began to flutter and she started moving her fingers and arms.

"I think she's coming around," Mirek said.

"Yeah, she'll be alright," said Sam. Carl gave her a kiss on the forehead as she slowly opened her eyes and smiled weakly at him.

CHAPTER 24

Rescuing Eva - The Attack on Brightside

Everyone gathered around the table in the Diamond Mine company's break room. There was a topographic map laid out in front of them detailing the geography of Racquette Lake.

"There," Sam pointed, tapping his finger to emphasize his find. "There's the Brightside. That's where we have to go. That's where they've got Mrs. Bielewski."

"How do we get there?" asked Mirek. "The Brightside is on the south side of a long peninsula facing a large bay of Racquette Lake. I don't see any roads within miles. There is this road from the north, but we'd have to hike in all along this way, and then up through that small trail that runs along the length of the peninsula. That could take us hours. We need to get there now, and fast."

The others grunted or mumbled in agreement. Rafel added, "I'm sure that someone from the limousines that were supposed to pick up everyone off the train and get them to Racquette Lake has contacted them at the Brightside. They are sure to suspect that somebody might be going up there to get Mrs. Bielewski."

"They could already be packing everything up and heading out with her," added Janusz. "Everybody could be gone by the time we get there."

"Well then," Sam replied grimly, "we'll have to make some quick plans and just get up there as fast as possible." He leaned forward and studied the map more closely.

Carl Thurston entered the room and joined the group. "Can I make a suggestion?" They all quickly nodded their heads in agreement. They knew that Carl had been an expert tactician with the Utica Police Department, and he knew the Racquette Lake area from years of fishing and hunting up there.

"Right here in the Village of Racquette Lake is the boat launch for this bay. There are always some boats moored there this time of the year. I remember seeing a party barge there all the time, over to the left. I think it belongs to the guy that owns the little bar there right behind the general store. I know that owner. He might be able to get us some keys or contact the owner to get us keys. I suggest that you use at least two boats, maybe three, if we can get them."

Mirek interrupted. "OK. OK. Listen guys, we don't have much time. Like we said, those guys at the Brightside are most likely already on alert and will be expecting trouble. We need to muster all the help we can get if we're going to pull this off."

The group spent the next few minutes finalizing their assault plan and making an inventory on how many weapons they had and each man's job. Mirek passed out a few walkie-talkies allowing the groups to contact each other. They needed to coordinate their assault.

The main group would consist of five men who would take a boat and quickly drive around the eastern side of the bay to the inlet at the end of the Brightside peninsula. From there they would continue around and land on the north side of the peninsula. Their landmark to beach their craft would be Lookout Rock, which was the highest point there. There was a trail from that beach to the Brightside. This would allow them the high ground and a chance at a surprise approach from the north to the house. A second team of two men, in another boat, would break off from the first group and travel along the south edge of the peninsula. As they got closer they would cut their engines and row to a beach a few hundred feet east of the Brightside and walk along the water's edge to the boat dock. This would allow them to control any attempt by the bad guys from making an escape and also alert the other team to any approaching boats from the bay side and Racquette Lake Village.

Carl stepped off of the party barge they had commandeered for this part of the mission. Although they had driven the barge to the north side of the peninsula, and using the Lookout Rock to guide them, as close to the beach as they could, Carl still had to step into foot-deep water. His weight caused his feet to sink into the mucky bottom, making it difficult for him to lift his legs. Two of the lighter weight team members had to help pull him out of the quagmire and onto dry land.

"I guess I shouldn't have had those donuts this morning," Carl joked, as he shook water out of his boots and pant legs.

"I don't know how you could have passed that up," said Janusz.

"Don't you cops have a special digestive enzyme that metabolizes donuts and coffee?" added Michal. "It's like you have a special stomach or something."

"Yeah, donuts are a food group for cops, aren't they?" added Janusz, with a smile. "They're like a vitamin, right?"

"So is my fucking fist, asshole," Carl replied. "Enough with the trash talk. Let's get going. We've got to follow the trail...there's the marker on the tree for it." He pointed straight ahead, the marker shining under the bright LCD flashlight Carl was holding. "OK, from here on in, no light, and no talking, unless we have to whisper or tap each other to get attention, and use hand signals." They quickly went over some hand signals they would use.

Janusz clicked on his walkie-talkie. "Hello, Mirek, are you there? Do you copy?"

After a short, tense moment of complete silence there was a fuzzy crackling on his walkie-talkie. "Copy. Copy. We're on land on the southern beach and starting to walk to the Brightside and to the boathouse. How long do you think it'll take you to get to the top of the trail and the overlook point?"

"About 15 minutes, assuming we don't get lost or meet up with anyone," radioed Janusz. "There's a full moon, so that's to our advantage. That should help us to keep on the trail and speed our movement."

Mirek spoke, "No voice contact when we get there, but I'll press the send button two times to give you a quiet heads up that we're in position. Copy?"

"Copy. Over. Alright, let's go, guys."

The lights were on all over inside of the Brightside. Floodlights illuminated the sloping backyard of the Inn as well as the eastern part of the complex, highlighting two smaller buildings with a large wooden boat sitting on the ground attached by a walkway to one of them.

"That boat was outfitted as a bar a few years ago by the owner. It was an old touring boat that used to take people around the lake for drinks and dinner," Thurston explained. "There's also this third building just up the slope closer to us. That's a bunkhouse. No lights on. Hopefully nobody's in there."

"We'll have to check out each one of these buildings as we get closer, before we can get into the main house," said Michal.

"Have to be real careful then, and sneaky like little mice. We can't let any lookout see us as we go to each building. That means we have to get up to each building on its dark side to avoid being seen. That'll take some time."

Carl spoke up. "Alright then, listen up. Here's what we'll do. I'll stay up here on the high ground, so I can see the whole complex. I can let you know if anyone is sneaking around to the back and if anyone comes to the Brightside from the lake. Sam, Michal, and Janusz, stay in the shadows as you go to the main house and try to get a fix on what's going on inside. Remember the laundry room, from the map I drew? Go in that way. Adam, check out the buildings, one at a time, starting with that bunkhouse. Make sure there aren't any surprises. If we get company from the lake, which I expect we will, I'll come down to the west side of the main house and provide cover from there to the boathouse and the beach. Mirek and Rafel are on the east side, so we'll have a crossfire if we need it."

They heard two brief crackles on the walkie-talkie. This meant that the other team had reached to boathouse and were in position.

Slowly, quietly, they moved out, leaving Carl, with a walkie-talkie, to take a short hike up the southern face of Lookout Rock. As the highest point on the peninsula, it offered a perfect view of the Brightside, the lake, and anyone approaching the Inn.

As the others slipped quietly down the slope to the grounded touring boat, Adam peered through the window of the bunkhouse. The only light was that of the moon which cast a ghostly pale silvery hue on the furniture and walls inside. All seemed to be quiet.

There was a faint shuffling sound from within and he thought he noticed movement off to one side of his peripheral vision, like a curtain wafting in the breeze. He had difficulty peering in through the window. His window and the windows to the front and side of the building appeared shut. He moved away off to one side and pressed himself against the clapboard siding of the building. Again he heard a faint shuffling sound. To his surprise, the window next to him started to open, making a barely audible sliding sound.

Adam clicked the safety switch of his weapon to "off". He had a suppressor on the end of his gun, but knew he should only use it as a last resort.

A young lady with flowing brown hair stuck her head out of the window and without hesitation turned her head and stared directly at him. She put her fingers to her lips, signaling silence. Adam was startled especially as she seemed to be expecting him.

"Quiet. I'm Anna, the caretaker of the Brightside. They know you're here. And they are expecting you. I can help you and your friends." She seemed to know that there were more of them than just Adam.

Confused by her direct comments, he stammered as he asked, "How do you know about us... I mean, me? What are you doing out here?"

"We don't have much time. You'll have to trust me. They sent me out here to get wood for the fireplace in the Great Room. I have to get back to the house now." She disappeared from the window and soon after walked through the front door of the bunkhouse, carrying a large bundle of firewood.

"Follow me over to there, in the shadows over to that side of the house where the fire escape is attached to the back wall."

Adam anxiously followed her until they came to a copse of trees that offered some cover. He pulled out his walkie-talkie and gently pressed the send button.

"What?" came a hushed, irritated reply from Sam.

Adam quickly described his meeting with the caretaker and his position. Anna had also told him that Eva Bielewski was on the third floor and could be reached via the fire escape where he now was. He also reported that, according to Anna, there were five men in the house, all armed. One was upstairs with Anna and the other four were somewhere downstairs, probably in the Great Room and the kitchen. She had said there was a hatch to a root cellar below the laundry room, off the kitchen, and a crawl space that led to another hatch on the far side of the fireplace of the Great Room. She had to return to the house and would try to distract them.

"OK. Adam, you go up the fire escape. We need you there. We'll see if we can get into the laundry room through the side door," Sam radioed. "Maybe we can get inside this place without being noticed and catch them on all sides by surprise without firing a shot."

"Anna said she would make sure that door is unlocked and she'll leave the hatch to the root cellar open. You'll see it right next to the large white refrigerator at the southern corner of the room, towards the lake side."

"Copy that. Over."

"Sam," Adam called in. "They know about what happened on the train. They're all on the alert. They figure that someone might try and come up here. Anna said they got a call a little while ago that some guys would be coming up here to take Mrs. Bielewski away."

Sam radioed Carl on Lookout Rock. "Keep an eye out for any movement on the lake, could be a boat with no light on coming up. Reinforcements. Just let me know by pressing the send button three times if you see something like that. Otherwise keep radio silence. Copy?"

"Copy," came a hushed reply. Carl released the "Talk" button as he mumbled, "We may be getting some very interesting fireworks shortly."

The three men walked gingerly along the grassy lawn on the west side of the main house to the laundry room. Janusz put his hand on the knob to the entry door and slowly turned it. It was unlocked. With Sam and Michal covering him he crouched down and practically slithered into the room. He turned and motioned for the others to follow him. Not a sound was made by any of them. They could hear a murmur of conversation in the kitchen on the other side of the wall where they were.

There was a faint sound of footsteps to their left, just outside the laundry room. They raised their weapons and quietly turned towards the outer door through which they had just come. There was the same, young beautiful woman that Adam had seen minutes earlier at the bunkhouse. She had flowing, auburn-colored, shoulder length hair and wore an ankle length sheer, cotton dress with a short apron tied at the waist. Seeing them, she put her fingers to her pursed lips, motioning calm as well as quiet, and walked to the refrigerator. As she opened the door, flooding the room with light, she motioned silently to Sam with her fingers that two of the men were in the kitchen. She seemed to signal that a third man was further away in another part of the house. She pointed upwards to the ceiling, as if to say that there were two more guards upstairs. Sam and the others understood. They nodded their heads.

The woman took two cans of beer from the refrigerator, closed the door and abruptly walked back into the kitchen. Janusz motioned for Sam to crawl down through the hatch and into the root cellar. He whispered for Michal to stay in the laundry room. If he heard any commotion or shooting, he was to storm into the kitchen and kill whoever was in there.

The root cellar was dark and damp with a low ceiling. Both men had to crouch as they walked. There was a faint light coming in through a narrow crawl space that led into the main cellar beneath the Great Room. As Janusz and Sam slithered along the dirt and crushed stone, sweeping years of cobwebs and dust away from their faces, the smell of cooked food wafted down from the kitchen overhead. Soon, when they had reached the main cellar they could smell the comforting aroma of wood burning in the large fireplace overhead. Groping about in the near dark with only slivers of light coming through a few narrow windows around the cellar, they soon found the stairs and entry hatch they were looking for.

Janusz carefully lifted the hatch up and peered into the Great Room. All of the lights were on in the large room. He could see sofas and chairs arranged in lines in the middle of the long room and along the wall facing the lake. Against the opposite wall he could see an old upright piano and a table with a guitar leaning against it. There were stuffed birds and raccoon and deer heads on the walls. In one corner stood a four-foot high stuffed black bear, arms raised and teeth showing, its face preserved in a growl for all eternity.

From his earlier study of a map of the floor plan of the Brightside, Janusz knew that to the left, beyond the fireplace, there was a hallway that led into the kitchen with one stairway leading to the upstairs bedrooms. In the far corner of this room to his right was another short hallway with a second staircase that also led to the upstairs rooms.

Janusz noiselessly climbed out of the crawl space. Sam followed him. They hid behind a large, worn leather covered sofa as they planned their next move. Sam felt a vibration in his pocket and a faint crackle of his walkie-talkie three times. It was the signal from Carl.

"We have new company arriving by boat," he whispered to Janusz.

"Fuck," replied Janusz in hushed tones. He turned to Sam, whispering. "Fuck. We've got to move and fast. Right now we have the advantage of surprise. We've got to take it. You go to the left and get those two guys in the kitchen and I'll go up the stairs to where the hostage is. Okay?"

Sam nodded. Simple plan. Those were always the best, the easiest to execute. He remembered that much from his military experience many, many years ago in Afghanistan when he was a doctor helping the mujahedeen fight the Russians. That was so many years ago. Complicated plans always led to disaster. Too many things could go wrong. Too rigid planning meant there was no room for changes in the situation. And the situation always changed. Like now.

Sam watched Janusz move quickly across the Great Room and into the hallway and disappear. Sam readied his weapon as he turned the corner to the left and peered into the kitchen. There in front of the wood stove stood one of the guards. The dark haired young woman was nowhere to be seen. The guard grabbed for his gun and Sam squeezed off a round, knocking the man backwards and onto the wood stove. The shot made a loud thud, muffled by the suppressor on the barrel. The man let out a loud scream as his back landed on the hot metal of the stove. He slumped to the floor letting out a long groan and abruptly stopped moving.

With his weapon at the ready Sam scanned the room and around and behind him. He dashed over to the laundry room to hook up with Michal. He crouched down at the doorway as he peered into the room. In the dim light coming from the kitchen and the moonlight he saw the second guard laying face down on the floor. A large pool of blood was growing from underneath him. Sam could see that a large portion of the back of his head was missing.

Michal shrugged his shoulders. "Just as you came into the kitchen, this guy came out here into the laundry room brandishing his pistol I heard you plug that other guy and I heard him scream. I knew that our surprise was just about over. So, I wasted him, just like you did the other guy."

Adam pulled down the extension of the fire escape. Slinging his rifle across his shoulder, he climbed upwards. He continued past the second story and went up to the end, to the third story. There was a light on in the room. Carefully he peered in through a corner of one glass pane. He saw a frail, elderly woman sitting up in the bed, fully clothed, reading a book. The caretaker, Anna, entered the bedroom as he watched. She seemed to notice Adam staring through the window but made no sign directly to him that she was aware of his presence.

She had brought a pot of tea and a cup on a tray for the woman. She set it on a nightstand. She bent forward and whispered into the lady's ear. The lady seemed to comprehend the situation immediately. She swung her feet around, off the bed, and slipped into her shoes at the side of the bed. From down the hall, Adam could hear voices and the sound of footsteps hurrying closer. One of the guards appeared at the door. He pushed Anna aside and started walking towards Mrs. Bielewski. He ordered her at gunpoint to lie back down on the bed. He was a large man with big hands. He rolled her up roughly in the comforter and effortlessly slung her over his shoulder as if she were a ten-pound sack of potatoes. She protested with a whimpering sound and started to kick her legs against the assailant.

Adam opened the window and fired into the man's hip. He fell to the floor screaming and dropped the woman. Adam was by her side in an instant. He unwrapped her from the comforter and helped her through the window and down the fire escape. He could hear the wounded man cursing and moaning. He heard loud footsteps stomping up the hallway and into the bedroom as he and Mrs. Bielewski made it to the bottom of the metal escape ladder.

Adam pulled the elderly woman along as they ran away from the house.

Four shots rang out from the open window of the third floor. Adam and the woman dropped to the ground. A searing pain in his face hurt more than the sting in his back as he fell to the ground. His head struck a large rock as he went down.

Sam heard the loud shots from the upstairs bedroom. A few seconds later he heard a fifth shot. He hoped it was from Janusz's gun. He carefully started towards the hallway just outside of the kitchen and slowly inched his way up the stairs. He held his gun at the ready. He felt very uncomfortable, knowing that he had no one to cover his back. Since he could only go up, he continued.

As he reached the second floor he saw shadows at the far end of the hallway. Someone was descending the stairs at the far end of the hall and down into the Great Room. He needed to go up to the third floor however and see if Mrs. Bielewski was there.

When he got to the bedroom on the third floor Sam could see the body of one of the guards, lying on his side motionless. His left hip was contorted and swollen, and the left leg lay in an awkward position. He looked out the open window and saw Adam writhing on the ground in the spotlight. He could see right away that the man was seriously wounded. He was holding his side, and blood was oozing out, soaking through his shirt.

"They got her, Sam," Adam yelled as he tried to speak clearly. There was no need to remain silent any more. "There had to have been some other guys we hadn't counted on. I don't know. They came out of nowhere. They kicked me and grabbed her, and dragged her away from me. They wrapped her up like in a big rug or bag. Each took an end and carried her away down to the boathouse. They're getting away. You've got to stop them!"

"OK, I will. But you need help. I can't just leave you here to bleed to death. Mirek and Rafel are down by the boathouse. They can hold them off until I get there."

"No time, no time. Others are coming. You've got to stop them from taking her away. Everything we've done for years depends on it. The world depends on it. There's no time. Hurry."

Sam clicked on his walkie-talkie and radioed Carl to have him come down and attend to Adam. He cautioned him to be careful just in case there were still any other unaccounted for bad guys in the area.

The two Alliance men hurried around the side of the Brightside and walked down towards the boathouse. Each carried one end of the limp body in the large comforter with which they had wrapped Mrs. Bielewski.

In the moonlight at the dock they could see a boat in the distance, with no lights, fast approaching the Brightside. A searchlight was suddenly turned on and the beam struck the men as they stood by a boat moored in the boathouse. The light veered off to their left along the water's edge catching sight of two other armed men partially hidden behind some trees.

Gunfire erupted from the approaching boat. The two armed men on shore, Mirek and Rafel, returned fire.

Realizing that they couldn't wait, the guards threw their bundle into the 17-foot aluminum hulled fishing boat, started up the engine, and cast off. The beam of the search light from the approaching boat found the two as they sped off, waving to their comrades to follow them.

The two guards were surprised as the comforter started to shake and move on the floor at their feet. The woman sprang up and jumped on the two, knocking one of them into the water. The motor stalled. She struck the remaining driver of the boat with an oar, knocking him senseless. She started the motor up again and headed straight for the second boat with their Alliance buddies in it.

Sam and the others had run onto the dock by this time and followed the two boats in the bright moonlight as the scene unfolded. They watched as the little fishing boat from the Brightside accelerated to top speed and crashed right into the side of the second boat. There was a sickening thud and a screech of metal against metal as the two vessels collided. Both boats capsized and everyone was thrown into the chilly water.

From the dock Sam could hear the screams. The silvery light from the moonshine ono the lake provided contrast, allowing him to see shapes, waves and the splashing of water.

There were cries of "Help!" and "Oh my God!" and "Don't pull me down!" While the thrashing and yelling and screaming may have lasted for some minutes, it seemed as if all was over in a flicker. Now there was only silence, and the lapping of waves on the shoreline.

Sam felt the horror of the moment. Not only for the violence and the bloodshed that he had been a part of and witnessed on the train and here at Brightside. He was sick with anger and felt defeat because Eva Bielewski had been ripped away from them, out of their reach. They had been unable to save her. And now she was gone.

From behind him he heard dull footsteps, coming towards him in the dark. Unsteady, slow footsteps that were followed by a familiar voice. "Sam! Are you all right?"

He turned to see Adam, with Carl and Michal offering support, struggling to walk up to him. He had a large gash in his left forehead and a small trickle of blood running down the side of his face and neck.

CHAPTER 25

Anna - Caretaker of the Brightside

Sam, Rafel, and Mirek stood on the moonlit dock shocked over their failure to save Mrs. Bielewski. They had planned and sacrificed. They had tried and failed. They almost lost Lisa. Adam was injured and would soon need medical attention.

Because of Lisa and her courage and willingness to go that final mile, the Zegota team had been able to destroy the most influential leaders and inner circle of the International Alliance. They had dealt a blow so devastating that this heinous organization might never recover. If it did, Zegota would be monitoring and watching and waiting.

The night was quiet now. In the solitude they could hear a gentle rhythmic lapping of waves off the lake as they rolled towards the pebble strewn beach. In the distance there came the occasional call of an owl. From the boathouse behind them came an unexpected cough and then a groan.

The three men turned around and lifted their weapons up. Rafel silently tiptoed to the left and Mirek to the right, towards the opening of the boathouse onto the lake. Sam carefully walked ahead to the corner of the building and waited. Rafel gingerly opened a side door, and then waited before stepping in. "Mirek. Sam. It's O.K. Come on in. Oh, my God. I can't believe it!"

There on the wooden floor of the boathouse at the feet of these three gawking men lay Eva Bielewski. She was barely conscious, moaning and coughing again. She soon opened her eyes and looked first with fear registering on her face until she caught a recognizing view of Sam. She broke out in the broadest smile. Her eyes lit up like those of a small child seeing presents under a Christmas tree.

"Oh, Sam! Oh, Sam! You're alive. Thank God you're alive. I thought for sure they were going to get you once they had me!"

"Don't talk now, save your breath. Let's get you out into the night air and some place where I can get a better look at you. Guys help me to lift her out to the big tree right outside here under the security lights.

She quickly told them how the two guards had brought her to the boathouse. They must have laid her to the side as they connected the gas tank and got the boat ready to launch. She felt herself being unwrapped by Anna, the caretaker, who motioned for her to remain silent. She covered Mrs. Bielewski with a canvas tarp in one corner of the building while she deftly wrapped herself in the comforter in the dark before the guards could come back.

"Anna was in the boat when it collided with the other boat that was coming to reinforce them!" Mirek said. The others nodded their heads, understanding.

"So it was Anna who attacked the guards on board and destroyed them all in both boats," added Rafel.

CHAPTER 26

The Death of Eva Bielewski

There on the lawn, propped up against a tree, was Eva Bielewski. She appeared to be resting, legs outstretched. Sam could see that the woman was having rapid shallow breathing. She was holding her left side. She had been shot in the chest and he knew that she was developing a tension pneumothorax.

"Quick, I need a large bore I.V needle," he shouted out, as if he were still in the emergency department, where he had decompressed so many of these types of wounds over the years. He quickly realized how silly that sounded now, here deep in the Adirondacks, on a peninsula, on a bay at Racquette Lake.

"I've got a long sharp knife that you could use, but no 'bore needles'," Rafel offered.

"That will have to do," Sam replied. He took the knife offered and knelt by the woman's side. "Mrs. Bielewski. You were shot in the chest."

She looked up at him, incredulous. "You think so?" She smiled. "I know. I know. You just gotta do what you gotta do. You're the doctor."

He explained to her that the only thing he could do would be to cut into her chest on the left side and let out air that had accumulated in her chest, compressing her lungs and making breathing difficult. They contemplated calling for an ambulance out of Old Forge. It would be almost half an hour or more before the team could get up to Racquette Lake Village. They could meet up with a helicopter and within an hour she could be at Upstate Medical Center in Syracuse.

She held up her hand and shook her head. "No, don't do that. No, you can't! Look at me. I'm an old lady. I should have been dead a long time ago. No, leave things as they are. I'm dying, I know I am. That bullet must have shot right through me and ripped up a lot of stuff on the inside."

"I'm sure it did," Sam answered. "But we still have to get you to the medical center."

She grabbed him by the arm. "Listen. Listen to me. I've got to tell you some things. Things you need to know and some things that you might not like."

Sam knelt by her, holding her frail little hands in his. He stopped talking.

"I know that Zofia told you a lot of things. She told you that she had adopted you.

Well, that's true, eventually. But actually, you had been thrust into her life at a time when the whole world was crazy. She was in Poland and in Warsaw during the German occupation during the war. She told you about Irena Sendler, yes?"

Sam nodded his head.

"She told you that you were a little Jewish baby taken out of the ghetto there in Warsaw. That was Irena Sendler and her people that did that. She was a saint. They saved your life and thousands of other little babies. You were allowed to live where others weren't so lucky."

"I know," Sam said. "I've had a chance over the years to learn a lot about the history of that time. Your husband, Saul, told me a lot of things too, explaining a lot of the incredible, often horrible things that went on during that time."

"And afterwards too," she added. She took a deep breath. "Go ahead and put a new hole into my side and let's get some of that air out. It might make it easier for me to talk with you before I die."

"Oh, don't give up so easily. You're not going to die."

"Oh, really? Don't give me that baloney."

Rafel had returned with some items that Sam had asked him to find or improvise. He had found a bottle of isopropyl alcohol and gauze pads and tape from a first aid kit from one of the bathrooms and some antibiotic ointment. He also had a rigid plastic drinking straw he had found in the kitchen. Eva winced as he made a stab wound over the fifth rib on her left side. They could all hear a faint whoosh of air as Sam stuck the plastic straw into that puncture site. He applied a stack of gauze smeared with antibiotic ointment over the entry wound in her back. He could feel the crunch of broken ribs below the skin and air bubbles underneath the skin there as well. He covered the gauze with plastic wrap and tape.

Eva was able to breath more easily now. She was very weak and getting more pale by the minute as they spoke.

"We need to get her into the boat and over on to the other side, to meet up with an ambulance and a medivac helicopter," Sam said.

"Don't bother," Eva said, mustering up what strength she could to counter him. "I'm not going to make it. Listen to me."

"I was that little young Jewish girl who gave you up to Sendler and her crew. I'm the one who bore you and hoped to raise you, until everything went to hell with the Nazis."

Sam straightened up. "You? How can that be? You're my real mother?"

"Yes, Sam...er, Samuel. I am."

He started to stammer and tried to make sense of it all. "But you came to the U.S. years ago. You were always friends of my family. You are Mr. Bielewski's wife."

"Yes, that's all true. I came to the U.S. to hide from the people who wanted to find me and take me away because I have some special genetic attributes. They wanted to use me as a laboratory animal, just like they did with so many countless other people during the war and even afterwards. And I wanted to be as close to you as I possibly could without putting you in danger. That's why it was decided with the help of Zegota that I would move to America and be close to you. But not so close as to arouse any suspicion as to who I really was. Or who you really were.

"You see, I carry some special genes. I guess I'm the only living person left in this world who carries the actual genes of the original Aryans. Do you know who they were?"

"Somewhat, yes," Sam nodded. He thought back to his trip to Nepal and his stay at the monastery.

"Do you know about mitochondrial DNA?"

"Yes, I do. But I didn't think it had anything to do with passing on physical characteristics from one generation to another. I originally thought it was all about metabolism and how the mitochondria work. I've learned that there's a lot more to it than just that."

"Well, I need to continue," she said. She moved herself over a little to the right. She was visibly weaker now. She asked for a drink of water. Rafel went to the house to get a glass for her.

"I was in the Nazi concentration camp at Auschwitz. Birkenau actually. There I was forcefully impregnated by a young SS man. I had twins from that. They were strong and healthy twins. They were your half-brothers. When the Russians came and liberated the camp, the SS man took the two boys and fled, eventually surviving the war and bringing those two boys up.

"Had they lived, they would have been the foundation of a new Aryan race. They would have been brought up in a New Order based on the ideals of fascism and the cruelty of the Nazis. They were stronger, healthier, and smarter than any children anyone had seen before. They truly would have been what the Germans liked to call *ubermensch*."

"Supermen," Sam muttered.

"Yes, but not in the comic book sense. They would have been the start of a race of devils, sadistic, horrible devils. We couldn't take the chance. Zegota, which officially stopped functioning shortly after the war, actually continued, and as you can see with your new friends here, continue to work to keep the old Nazis in their sights and to prevent the rise of a new order of Nazis."

"So, what happened to those to boys, to my half-brothers?"

"They are no more. They were destroyed, killed along with their father, my Nazi-sanctioned rapist, in 1954. I am the only living human vessel or container, if you will, who has the mitochondrial DNA that could be passed on to another generation, to make a new generation of Aryans, the real Aryans. But of course, I'm too old to have any more children but my tissues have the mitochondrial DNA in them. My blood, my skin, my bones, all of it."

"But what about me? Don't I have the mitochondrial DNA in my body as well?" he asked.

"Yes, you do. But that's our little secret. Only you and a few select people in Zegota know that to be true. No one else in the world knows that."

"And I can't pass any of that genetic material on to my children because it gets passed only from mother to daughter, who can become a mother in her own right, who then passes it on to her daughter, and so on."

"That's right. So you can't pass the DNA on, and your children don't have it. So, they aren't in any danger. But you could be if anyone learned that I was your mother."

"I guess I'm a dead end street with a price on my head," he said wryly.

She reached up and stoked his hair. "No, my son. You are the best son a mother could ever have. Over the years, I watched you grow up to become this wonderful man that you are now. I remember from when you were a teenager, when I came here to America. I remember you driving your first car. The girlfriends you would bring home. Zofia would gossip to me about them all of the time. She would tell me about your school work, your sports, and your friends."

"Did Zofia know that you were...that you are, my mother?"

"No, she didn't, but I think that she might have suspected. Especially at times when I got really upset or emotional when some things didn't work out right for you."

"Like what?" Sam asked.

"Like when you didn't get accepted to medical school that first time around. You were so devastated. I cried when Zofia told me about it. I think she kind of knew. But it was too dangerous to tell her. It would be one more person knowing, and that we couldn't chance. And then how happy I was when you did get accepted to medical school at the osteopathic college. I was full of joy!"

Eva gripped his arm even tighter now. She asked him to lean forward as she was getting weaker by the moment. "I'm an old lady. I've lived my life. And I'm so happy that you and I are able to finally talk openly like this. I never thought it would have to be this way but, well, it is what it is, as they say.

"You've got to promise me something. You've got to promise me. My genes, that genetic code as they call it, it can't fall into the wrong hands. You've got to help me. Promise me."

She looked at him, the pallor easily evident now, under the backyard lights, with pleading eyes. "I've got to tell you everything because I don't have much time left. I can feel the life slipping away from me with every breath, and every beat of my heart."

She stroked his hair with a weak, trembling hand. Her voice wavered as she carefully chose her words so as not to waste energy. She was noticeably pale and getting more so by the minute.

"My dear, dear Sam. You are so brave! I watched you over the years grow up to be even more than I could have imagined. Your father would have been very proud of you."

Gently, affectionately, he squeezed her hand. "Tell me about my father."

"Ah yes. Your father. Witold. He was a true Polish patriot. Your father was a wonderful man. He was so charming, so kind, and so handsome. When I look at you I see many of his features. He too stood tall and straight. He had piercing blue eyes as you have. He was strong, but he could be so gentle, so caring and thoughtful. And very intelligent. He loved music, and loved to sing. He played piano and violin. If only he could have survived to see you today."

She paused to get her breath. A faint moan escaped her tightened lips. With renewed energy she reopened her eyes and gazed firmly at her son. "Have you ever heard of the Battle of Wizna, during the war?"

"A little. It was called the Polish Thermopylae. Like the three hundred Spartans who held off thousands of Persians to give time for the rest of Greece to assemble an army to fight off the invaders. Zofia told me a little about it years ago. I later found out that there was a heavy metal group from Sweden, Sabaton I think, that had a song, 'Forty to One'. The song was about the Polish Army during World War Two, holding off thousands of Germans to give the Polish Army time to regroup after the initial surprise invasion in 1939."

"Your father was there, at Wizna. The only reason he survived was because, as a courier, he was ordered to report to their generals that the Army was taking a stand there. There was no thought of a retreat. They knew they would all die there. And they all did. Except him. He was so angry, that he was allowed to live while his unit all was killed.

"I later was reunited with your father, in the capitol, before the Warsaw Uprising, the *powstanie*. We were in love. It was a common-law, wartime marriage of passion. I was Jewish, he was not. These things happened more often than most people knew. Soon I found that I was pregnant. One day, while walking back from a friend's house, I was rounded up on the street with others and thrown into the Jewish ghetto. I was carrying you. Your father didn't know what happened to me for the longest time.

"Sadly, your father was killed a year later during the Uprising against the occupying Germans. You were born there, as I just told you, in the ghetto. I swaddled you there in old, dirty rags, all I could find. Often there was little to eat but I was at least, somehow, able to produce enough breast milk for you.

"I feared for your safety and your future every day. All around me, every day, people were dying of starvation and disease. Every day little wagons carrying the dead were rolled through the streets, pushed and pulled by survivors who realized that, soon, they too might be leaving the district in similar fashion.

"One day, like a miracle, this young Polish health worker, Irena Sendler, came to me and offered to help keep you alive, and to take you away from this hell, to safety. I knew it was the only chance. There were rumors that the Germans would either slowly starve us to death, or we would be sent off to work camps, to die there. There were even rumors that the Germans had death camps or liquidation centers where we would all be shot or burned alive.

"With the help of her assistants, you were sedated and hidden in a tool box with a false top, and taken away in their truck. The guards never suspected what she was doing. They thought she was just coordinating delousing with DDT or culling out those with tuberculosis or meningitis or typhus that could infect the German occupiers. I found out years later that she and her people had saved almost 3,000 Jewish children. Later, in the Spring of 1943, when the Jews staged their own uprising, the survivors were transported by train to Auschwitz where most were immediately murdered in the gas chambers with Zyklon B."

"But you survived!"

"Yes, I did. I was like one of the Nazi's lab rats, forced to be part of an experiment that kept me alive. But it also brings me great shame." She shifted to her right to allow herself to breathe a little more easily.

"Rest, mother. No need to strain yourself. It's over now. We'll get you to the hospital and get you fixed up."

There was an insistent glare in her eyes. The color momentarily rushed back into her face as she leaned forward and gripped Sam's hand.

"No! No, I told you. It's not over until I am dead and every remaining cell of my body is destroyed! I am dying, Sam, you know that. I know that. I can feel the life slowly leaking out from me, and I don't have much time.

"I will be closing my eyes soon, never to be reopened. I will never see another sunrise, never hear another bird sing. And I will never see you again. Not in this world.

"You will have to cremate my body so no one of those awful murderers of the International Alliance can get the Aryan code that I carry within me. That is why Zegota and Saul Bielewski protected me over the years. So now, one chapter in this sordid affair will close and I can die in peace."

"What do you mean by 'one chapter' will close," Sam asked, suddenly confused. "I thought that the International Alliance was after you and you alone, because of the genetic material that you carry in your genes. While I too have it, I can't pass it on to my son or daughter. It only goes from mother to daughter."

Eva sighed. Her eyelids were slowly covering her eyes as if she were starting into a deep sleep. She roused up long enough and with enough energy to say, "There is another chapter."

"What do you mean?"

"When the Germans left the camp and Herr Weinberg, the recruited rapist took the two little boys we had, but I was already pregnant with a third child. The Russians came and liberated the camp shortly afterwards. About 7 months later I delivered a little baby girl."

"You had another child?"

"Your sister. She carries the genes I possess within her."

"So, she's still alive?"

"Yes."

"And what happened to her? Where is she?"

"She is near. She lives in Upstate New York. The Zegota know about her and watch over her."

"Does Saul know?"

After a short pause and a deep breath, Eva answered, "Yes."

With that she took her last breath, and died.

CHAPTER 27

The Funeral Pyre

The flames and sparks shot up to the sky as the funeral pyre burned a glowing red and orange. They had gathered as much firewood as they could and piled it up to about four feet, making sure that there were air spaces in between to allow the fire to burn as quickly and as hot as possible. Sam knew that Jewish custom and law forbid cremation, and Eva was well aware of this. She demanded nevertheless that this had to be done, to destroy the genetic code that she harbored in her body. Every last cell had to be destroyed.

"Believe me, God will understand, this time, "Eva had told Sam. "I'll make sure to ask him, just in case, when I get to heaven."

They had soaked the wood with kerosene and lamp lighter fluid that they found in a nearby shed. Sam had tenderly wrapped Eva's body in a bed sheet, kissing her on the forehead before covering her face. It would be the last time he would ever see her. He placed her shrouded body on top of the pyre, stepped back and bowed his head. The others took off hats and bowed their heads as well. One of the group, Janusz, recited the following blessing:

Barukh atah Adonai Eloheinu melekh ha'olam, dayan ha-emet.
Translation: *Blessed are You, Lord, our God,*
King of the universe, the True Judge.

The men lit the pyre on each end and in the middle. Soon the stack of wood and Eva's body were engulfed in flames. Sam tore the pocket on the left side of his shirt, over his heart, as he silently prayed for his mother.

CHAPTER 28

At the Columbia

It was a quiet Monday night at the Columbia. Not too many people were venturing out. It was raining again outside; one of those late October drizzles in Upstate New York that keeps reminding people to keep their heads warm and their feet dry or hazard getting bronchitis or pneumonia. There were some regulars at the bar sipping on their favorite Saranac brew on tap. Barbecued chicken wings and pizza from O'scugnizzo's Pizzeria were the specialty of the day, laid out in bite-sized pieces during Happy Hour on the hors d'oeuvres table off to one side of the room.

Over in one corner, with a Mejda Ilona Inverted Pendant chandelier hanging over the round table sat seven people, quietly nursing their beers or soda. Sam and Helen. Lisa and Carl. Saul Bielewski. Adam and Mirek.

They had been through a stressful two weeks since the events on the train and at The Brightside. Now they all sat together, mulling over the events. Mr. Bielewski sat quietly, absorbed in his own, private thoughts. Sam and Helen Petrie were sharing a plate of Utica Greens. Sam sipped on a Seagram's and Perrier, while his wife stirred her Kettle One Vodka with tonic and a slice of lime. Lisa and Carl held hands as she leaned her head onto his broad shoulder. Ever since her resuscitation and their eventual reunion they had been inseparable.

They reviewed the events of the past week. So, where do we go from here, they had asked? Eva was gone. The International Alliance had been decapitated, stopped in its tracks towards world domination and the reestablishment of the Aryan Race, at least for now. Sam was finally at peace. In a short time he had learned much about himself, about his legacy and about his mother. He could finally lay his obsession over her to rest.

He looked around the Columbia, his eyes surveying Steve Valone's collection of memorabilia from around the world, displayed on shelves behind the bar, around the room or hanging from the walls or the ceiling. There were mounted taxidermy fish, a brass telescope, a large ceremonial kabuki doll in a square glass display case, a Viking drinking horn, a cricket bat from South Africa, an 1863 Civil War Springfield rifle with attached bayonet, and an interesting variety of other items collected over the years by the owner.

He took a sip from his Seagram's and turned to Helen. It was apparent from her demeanor that she too had been deep in thought. Were there any pressing concerns that they all had to attend to? Could they now finally let their guard down? Sam knew they all had been asking themselves similar questions.

They had ventured into territory where few people survive to return intact and bloodless.

Someone in the Alliance had known of Eva Bielewski, and possibly about Saul as well. Were there any dangerous, lose ends?

In the aftermath of Eva's rescue there was public shock and an FBI investigation into the mass murder on the Adirondacks Railway Train at Old Forge. The newspapers and television and radio reported what little they knew of the affair over the following week.

Canisters of Zyklon B, an insecticide still made by a Czech company and sold under a different name, had been used in the murders on the train. This was the same poison used by the Germans in the gas chambers in Auschwitz and other Nazi death camps.

Most of the victims in the rail car were easily identified. It soon became apparent that many, or most of them, were either known or strongly suspected of being involved in an organization tied to various drug cartels and international terrorist organizations. The group was known to intelligence agencies around the world as the "International Alliance".

On the back pages of the Observer-Dispatch in Utica and the Syracuse Post Standard was a brief article about a boating incident on Racquette Lake the same day as the carnage on the Adirondacks train. A small aluminum fishing boat had lost control that evening and crashed into the side of another, larger pontoon boat carrying some passengers. There were four bodies found in the tangle of the two boats. They were apparently all adult males. None of the four victims could be readily identified by the police. The bodies were mangled, some mutilated by the crash of the blades of the boat motors. There were no identifying documents found on any of them.

And what about Anna, the young caretaker of The Brightside? She had helped save Eva Bielewski. She had hidden herself, in Eva's place, in the rolled blanket and was carried like a bundle away that night by the Alliance guards and into the little fishing boat at the dock. It was she who had overcome the Alliance henchmen and run the boat into the oncoming boat with more guards. She had sacrificed herself in order to save Eva, Sam, and Carl, and the entire Zegota crew.

Mr. Bielewski put down the newspaper and looked up at the others, seated around the table at the Columbia.

"Yesterday I spoke with the owner of the Brightside, Pat Carlotto. He's a good friend of mine who lets me and some other friends go up and stay over or go hunting. He hadn't been up there in a long time. I told him that, while scouting there for hunting season, we came across some vandalism to the property. I told him that some idiots shot up some of the buildings. With all the damage and the shootings, there would have to be repairs, and he wanted to go through the insurance company to get the job done. But that would mean photos and a story and possibly some investigation as to why there were shots up there around the same time that those people were killed in the boating accident.

"He agreed to keep it all hush-hush, all quiet, especially when I told him we would come up with the money to fix it all up and clean up the mess there."

"No problem," replied Mirek. "Adam. Get Jadwiga on the cell, and let them know what's going on here, that we need some money transferred to the Bank of Utica here to cover the costs of a cleanup."

Adam nodded his head, grabbed his cell phone and quickly stood up and left the group.

"Who is this Jadwiga?" Carl asked.

"That's the code name for our section chief here in the U.S. for Zegota. Adam is calling them now to get clearance for the money."

"So what happened to the two guys that stayed behind? The one guy shot in the hip and the other guy shot downstairs?"

Mirek shrugged his shoulders. "Things happen. Mr. Carlotto doesn't need to know every detail of how we cleaned up the trash there or, respectfully Dr. Petrie, the ashes of the funeral pyre."

Sam moved around uneasily in his chair, cleared his throat and, after a pause, spoke up. "I do have one other little housekeeping problem. Something that hasn't been accounted for."

Everyone around the table looked up at him now.

"Mrs. Bielewski, Eva, my mother, was saved by that gallant young lady, Anna."

A few nodded their heads in agreement.

Saul leaned forward and, in hushed tones, said, "I spoke with Mr. Carlotto about that too. I asked him about her. We hadn't heard anything more after that night at the Brightside and nothing about her body having been found or washed up after the boating accident that night.

"He was quiet at first, like trying to prepare me for some shocking news. It turns out that Mr. Carlotto never had a caretaker up there, and definitely no young lady named Anna. He did tell me though that there was this story of a young woman who, with her husband, used to spend long summers at the Brightside. That was in the 1920's. While staying at the Brightside one summer, he took off in a boat back to the Village of Racquette Lake. He said he was going on some business trip. Well, he never came back for her. The story goes that he jilted her, ran off with another woman and never returned to his wife. Legend has it that after Anna died; her ghost started appearing at The Brightside. Some guests swore they would see her walking down the third floor hallway, or walking along the waters edge at sunset. Others saw a wispy white apparition floating along the sloping lawn behind the main house or out on the porch. It was like she was there waiting for him to return, like she wanted to make right from wrong, set it all back to good again."

They all sat in silence at this revelation.

"That she did there," said Carl.